CRITICAL ACCLAIM FOR LEIGH RUSSELL

'A million readers can't be wrong! Clear some time in
your day, sit back and enjoy a bloody good read'
– **Howard Linskey**

'Taut and compelling' – **Peter James**

'Leigh Russell is one to watch' – **Lee Child**

'Leigh Russell has become one of the most impressively
dependable purveyors of the English police procedural'
– **Marcel Berlins, *Times***

'A brilliant talent in the thriller field' – **Jeffery Deaver**

'Brilliant and chilling, Leigh Russell delivers a cracker
of a read!' – **Martina Cole**

'A great plot that keeps you guessing right until the very end,
some subtle subplots, brilliant characters both old and new
and as ever a completely gripping read' – ***Life of Crime***

'A fascinating gripping read. The many twists kept
me on my toes and second guessing myself'
– ***Over The Rainbow Book Blog***

'Well paced with marvellously well-rounded characters and
a clever plot that make this another thriller of a read from
Leigh Russell' – ***Orlando Books***

'A well-written, fast-paced a[...]
– ***The Book Lov[...]***

D0543715

'Another corker of a book from Leigh Russell... Russell's talent for writing top-quality crime fiction just keeps on growing...' – *Euro Crime*

'A definite must read for crime thriller fans everywhere' – *Newbooks Magazine*

'Russell's strength as a writer is her ability to portray believable characters' – *Crime Squad*

'A well-written, well-plotted crime novel with fantastic pace and lots of intrigue' – *Bookersatz*

'An encounter that will take readers into the darkest recesses of the human psyche' – *Crime Time*

'Well written and chock full of surprises, this hard-hitting, edge-of-the-seat instalment is yet another treat... Geraldine Steel looks set to become a household name. Highly recommended' – *Euro Crime*

'Good, old-fashioned, heart-hammering police thriller... a no-frills delivery of pure excitement' – *SAGA Magazine*

'A gritty and totally addictive novel' – *New York Journal of Books*

ALSO BY LEIGH RUSSELL

Geraldine Steel Mysteries
Cut Short
Road Closed
Dead End
Death Bed
Stop Dead
Fatal Act
Killer Plan
Murder Ring
Deadly Alibi
Class Murder
Death Rope
Rogue Killer
Deathly Affair
Deadly Revenge
Evil Impulse
Deep Cover

Ian Peterson Murder Investigations
Cold Sacrifice
Race to Death
Blood Axe

Lucy Hall Mysteries
Journey to Death
Girl in Danger
The Wrong Suspect

The Adulterer's Wife
Suspicion

LEIGH RUSSELL

GUILT EDGED

A GERALDINE STEEL MYSTERY

NO EXIT PRESS

First published in 2022 by No Exit Press,
an imprint of Oldcastle Books Ltd,
Harpenden, UK

noexit.co.uk
@noexitpress

ISBN
978-0-85730-477-3 (print)
978-0-85730-478-0 (epub)

2 4 6 8 10 9 7 5 3 1

Typeset in 11 on 13.75pt Times New Roman
by Avocet Typeset, Bideford, Devon, EX39 2BP
Printed in Great Britain by Clays Ltd, Elcograf S.p.A.

For more information about Crime Fiction go to crimetime.co.uk

To Michael, Jo, Phillipa, Phil, Rian, and Kezia
With my love

Glossary of Acronyms

DCI   – Detective Chief Inspector (senior officer on case)
DI   – Detective Inspector
DS   – Detective Sergeant
SOCO – scene of crime officer (collects forensic evidence at scene)
PM   – Post Mortem or Autopsy (examination of dead body to establish cause of death)
CCTV – Closed Circuit Television (security cameras)
VIIDO – Visual Images, Identifications and Detections Office
MIT   – Murder Investigation Team

Prologue

WHEN HE WAS A child, his mother used to take him for long walks along the towpath. She would cling to his hand, warning him to keep away from the water's edge.

'The river is very deep,' she told him. 'If you fall in, no one will be able to save you. The current will carry you away and you'll never see me again.'

When he asked her why people walked near the river if it was dangerous, she smiled.

'It's easy because the path is flat,' she replied, 'and what makes it even more perfect is that it follows the river, so you can't get lost.'

But there was more than one way to get lost. It was the week before his tenth birthday when they dragged his mother from the river. By the time she was discovered, it was too late to save her. She had been right. No one came to save her when she fell in the river. Forbidden to see her body, he became obsessed with reading about the effects of drowning. He wondered later whether it would have been less traumatic for him if they had allowed him to see her, but they never did. Instead, he was left to imagine her as she was pulled out of the river, grotesquely bloated and discoloured. Some of the pictures he found of people who had drowned gave him nightmares.

He never told anyone about his night terrors. He accepted that he was an orphan, and people were trying to look after him. But no one else seemed to worry that Death could come and take him at any time. His mother had understood that the end might arrive when he was least expecting it, with a squealing of brakes and voices yelling at him to 'Look out!', or sudden unexpected pain clamped across his chest as his heart ceased beating, or a misplaced step causing him to stumble and fall, cracking his head open and smashing his skull. But unlike his mother, he was a coward. Gradually he learned to suppress his memories, until the day his crippling fear returned, reminding him of his fragile grasp on life. Once again fear became his constant companion.

It took him a long time to realise that by taking control over life and death he could free himself from fear. One misty afternoon, he witnessed a woman plunging into the river. It could easily have been a tree root that had caused her to fall, or a tough weed growing on the uneven grass verge. There was no one else around to see the woman pitch into the fast-flowing water with barely time to shriek before she sank from view. Her head surfaced a few times, while her arms thrashed wildly, sending up sprays of water, until she disappeared from view. He watched the tragedy from a distance, curious to see how long the woman would continue floundering. He wondered whether his mother had struggled as vigorously to survive, or if she had simply surrendered to the current pulling her under. For a long time after that he slept well, but then memories of his mother returned to haunt him, and his nightmares returned.

1

STROLLING ALONG THE RIVER bank on a mild spring evening, he considered his options. It was less than an hour after the end of the working day, when many people would be on their way home, and the towpath was almost deserted. He didn't mind the solitude. On the contrary, it suited him. The grass beside the path was overgrown and speckled with weeds dotted with flowers of purple and white, some so tiny they could only be seen close up in the fading light of evening. It was a peaceful scene, movement discernible only in the fluttering of leaves high overhead, and the flowing water. A middle-aged couple strolled along the path in the opposite direction, a young woman jogged by, her blonde ponytail swinging behind her, and few moments later a bell shrilled as a man whizzed past, sturdy Lycra-clad legs cycling vigorously. After that, no one else appeared on the path as he made his way towards the old railway bridge. Perhaps it had something to do with the darkly flowing water, but by the time he reached the far side of the bridge, his mind was made up. He was going to kill George Gardner.

Having settled on a victim, he felt curiously calm. It was such a necessary step to take he wondered why it had taken him so long to come up with the idea. As far as he knew, George was an inoffensive character. But the Bible was wrong. Meekness never saved anyone. His mind racing, he turned and strode purposefully back along the towpath. The murder had to be meticulously planned, down to the very last detail, because the slightest mistake could betray him. It was common knowledge that murderers were usually apprehended straightaway. That was because most killers overlooked one vital consideration, making it almost inevitable the police would track them down. The killer's motive was always an obvious clue to their identity. There was a case for thinking that people who were that stupid deserved to be caught. He, on the other hand, would remain anonymous, and so he would be able to carry out his plan without being caught. No one would even suspect him, because there would be nothing to connect him to his victim.

Once he had realised where other killers blundered, and, confident he could go ahead without risk of discovery, he resolved to study his unsuspecting victim for a few weeks. The more he knew about George, the easier it would be to catch him off guard. There was no reason for George to suspect he was being watched, but it was as well to be careful. One phone call to the police to say he thought he was being stalked and the whole plan would founder.

George went to work in town at the same time every weekday, before spending the evening at home with his wife. Every Friday, after work, he drove his wife to the supermarket, for their one excursion during the week. It seemed an excruciatingly dull existence, but it made watching him easy, at least in the short term. The longer he was watched, the greater the risk he would notice he was being spied on, which meant the surveillance couldn't continue for long. On Saturday morning, George went for a bicycle ride. After about ten minutes, he turned off into wooded parkland near a football ground. Deep in thought, his unseen follower turned round and drove home. George was a creature of habit, so it was no surprise when he repeated his bicycle ride the next Saturday morning. Again, he rode through the woods, but this time he was not alone. Blithely he pedalled on, oblivious of his stalker silently following on a bicycle of his own.

It was early in the day, and there were few cars around. As

they cycled into the woods, the noise of traffic faded, until all that could be heard was the quiet whirring of bicycle wheels, and hushed rustling in the trees and bushes surrounding them. Apart from the two cyclists, nothing stirred but leaves fluttering in the breeze. George's stalker had not expected to despatch his victim so soon, but the opportunity presented itself and he seized it. There was no benefit to be gained from hesitation, and he had come prepared. He was always ready for such an eventuality. After all the planning and speculation, it was ridiculously simple to leap from his bicycle and steal up behind George, who had paused in his pedalling. If the victim had intended to offer himself up as a sacrifice, he could hardly have made it easier for his killer. Caught off guard, George wobbled precariously on his bicycle before crashing to the ground, hitting his head as he fell. Stunned from the blow, he allowed himself to be pulled along, groaning but otherwise unresisting. It was the work of a few seconds to drag him into the bushes.

Reaching a small clearing out of sight of the path, hidden among the trees, the killer pressed one knee on his victim's chest to prevent him clambering to his feet. Whipping a scarf from his pocket, he held it over George's face, covering his nose and mouth completely and pushing down with all his strength. If he had been able to prevent George from thrashing around with his arms and scrabbling at his sleeves, it would have been relatively easy. Above the scarf, George's eyes rolled wildly as he writhed and struggled to free himself.

'Keep still, damn you,' his attacker muttered under his breath.

Resisting his victim's pinching and grasping fingers, he refused to release the pressure on him for an instant. Hours seemed to elapse before George finally lay still. Even then his attacker did not release the pressure on George's face until he was absolutely sure he was dead. At last he dropped the scarf and fell back on his haunches, his arms trembling from his exertion. Just to make absolutely sure, he pinched the inert figure sharply on the cheek. There was no response. Leaning forward he listened for any sound of breathing. All he could hear were the creaks and rustling of the trees. It was difficult to feel for a pulse through his glove, but George gave no sign that he was alive.

With an effort, he rolled the body over onto its front and pushed George's head down so that his nose and mouth were pressed into the earth. No one could breathe with a face buried in mud. Just to make sure, he scraped the earth on either side of his victim's head, patting it against the sides of his face to create a seal. If George moved his head, the mud casing would crumble, but he did not stir.

It was over. Sooner or later someone would stumble on the corpse, but no one would ever find his killer. Trembling with excitement, he slipped away unseen through the bushes. Reaching the road, he cycled home and waited to see how events unfolded. Whatever happened, he was safe. No one would suspect him of being responsible for George's death. Why would they, when he had left no trace of his own presence behind? He had committed the perfect murder. It had been physically arduous, but other than that the task had presented no difficulties. On the contrary, it had been surprisingly easy. He wondered why he had waited so long before he had taken the initiative, when killing was so easy and afforded him such glorious relief because, for now, he had proved a match for Death. Not only that, his revenge was complete.

That night there were no nightmares.

2

THE SUN BEAT DOWN on them as they sat on Geraldine's balcony on an unseasonably balmy morning towards the end of March. A few wisps of white cloud drifted across the blue sky, and the breeze from the river was mild, heralding warmer days to come.

'We seem to be skipping spring and moving straight to summer,' Ian remarked. 'Not that I'm complaining. I could sit here like this all day.'

Geraldine smiled. 'The summer can't come soon enough for me.'

Ian returned her smile. 'Don't wish your life away.'

'Have you forgotten we're off on our first holiday together, as soon as we can organise something?' she asked.

She raised her arm and ran her fingers through his cropped hair. The white on his temples barely showed up against his fair hair.

'I haven't forgotten,' he said. 'I haven't forgotten anything.'

'We're not getting any younger,' she added, suddenly serious. 'And we've wasted enough time.'

Although they had been colleagues working on murder investigations together for years, they had only recently started living together, some time after Ian's divorce. Geraldine's flat in the centre of York, overlooking the river, was large enough to accommodate both of them so Ian had moved in with her.

'Come on,' Ian said, 'let's have a look online and get something booked. We've been talking about it for long enough.'

'Last night was the first time you mentioned it,' she said, laughing.

'Exactly,' Ian replied with mock earnestness. 'And we still haven't reached a decision about where to go.'

'We knew each other for sixteen years before you moved in here and now all of a sudden you're impatient?'

'Like you said, we have a lot of lost time to make up for,' he replied. 'I want to make the most of every moment.'

Still smiling, he stood up and pulled her towards him, but their embrace was interrupted by the shrilling of a phone.

'Looks like booking that holiday may have to wait,' Geraldine said after she had listened to the call. 'Come on, no time to waste. We'll have to grab something in the canteen later.'

'What is it?'

Geraldine was already going indoors. 'I'll tell you about it on the way,' she called over her shoulder. 'Leave the cups. I'll clear up later.'

Ian followed her. As experienced detective inspectors working on serious crime, they knew that vital clues could be lost if they failed to respond promptly when summoned to a crime scene. They hurried inside to dress and drove together to the location they had been given. On the way, Geraldine told Ian what little she knew. The body of a man had been discovered in the woods, lying face down in the mud. It was possible he had collapsed and died of natural causes, but the team at the site suspected it was an unlawful killing.

'What makes them suspect foul play?' Ian demanded. 'I'm not too happy about being dragged away from our holiday plans without good reason, not to mention my breakfast,' he added ruefully.

'You know as much as I do. We're nearly there,' Geraldine added, turning off the road into Rowntree Park.

The branches of trees that surrounded them were covered in thick foliage, casting dark shadows over the road. Shielded from the bright warmth of the sun, Geraldine shivered. A forensic tent had not yet been erected, and they pulled on their protective gear and followed a constable through the trees to where the corpse lay, as yet barely disturbed. Only the first constable on the scene had approached the body to check for vital signs and after him the duty medical examiner, who had inspected the man to confirm that he was dead.

'He died this morning, by all accounts,' a young scene of crime officer told them breathlessly, as they picked their way along the common approach path. 'We think he was suffocated. That's why it's being treated as suspicious. He's hardly likely to have dragged himself through the bushes and suffocated himself.'

'I don't suppose you'd like to become a detective?' Ian asked him.

Geraldine glared at Ian. The scene of crime officer was trying to be helpful. There was no call to rebuff his youthful enthusiasm.

'His bicycle was found a few yards away, on the path,' the scene of crime officer continued, seemingly oblivious to Ian's sarcasm. 'At least, we think it was his. It's been taken away for examination. If the bike hadn't been spotted by a passing pedestrian, the body might not have been discovered for a while. We've questioned the man who found him, but he didn't know anything. Here he is,' he added, gesturing at a narrow gap in the trees through which they could see a man lying on his back, apparently staring up at the sky.

'He's been turned over,' the scene of crime officer resumed. 'He was found lying on his front, face down in the dirt.' He paused, before adding, 'It looked as though the earth was built up around his face, to make sure he couldn't breathe.'

'Who turned him over?' Geraldine asked sharply.

'We did that,' the scene of crime officer replied. 'The man who found him had enough sense not to touch the body. He told us he could see the man must be dead because his face was buried in mud, so he thought it was best not to go anywhere near him.'

Geraldine suspected this was the scene of crime officer's first murder scene. A more experienced officer was unlikely to sound so exuberant about a dead body. She sighed. At forty she was older than many of her colleagues, and experienced enough in dealing with death to treat it with detachment. Not that she had ever been emotionally disturbed at the sight of a corpse. The dead had so many clues to offer up about the circumstances of their death, if the living could only interpret the signs accurately.

'What do we know about him?' Ian asked.

'Only that he's dead and he hasn't been here very long, and he probably cycled here, left his bike on the path and crashed through the trees to get here.'

'Crashed?' Geraldine asked.

'He might have been dragged,' the scene of crime officer corrected himself. 'The trees have been damaged and the undergrowth is flattened in places, more than if he'd just pushed his way through by himself.'

'So it doesn't look as though he came here to take a look around, or relieve himself. It's possible he met his killer before he was attacked, and they made their way here together,' Ian said.

The scene of crime officer nodded. 'That's a possibility,' he agreed.

Geraldine glanced at Ian. Often squeamish around corpses, he looked merely solemn at the sight of this particular body. To be fair, it was less shocking than many murder victims they had seen. The dead man was not lying naked on a table with his guts spilling out, or a section of his brain exposed, nor was he covered in blood as a result of violent assault. On the contrary, he bore no obvious outward sign of physical trauma. His eyes were closed, and his lips were fixed in a rictus of death that strangely resembled a grin. Apart from a coating of earth clinging to his face, he could have been asleep. Taking care to avoid touching the bushes, Geraldine edged closer. Hopefully forensic examination of the scene would confirm whether the dead man had crashed or been dragged through the trees. The distinction was significant, and she was impatient to know exactly what had happened in the trees while the man was still alive.

It was difficult to judge the dead man's age, with earth obscuring most of his features and soiling his hair. A small patch of mud had been brushed from around one side of his nose and mouth to reveal bruising which could have been caused by someone pressing against his face to suffocate him.

Correctly interpreting Geraldine's expression, the young scene of crime officer pointed to a grey woollen scarf lying to one side of his head.

'Do you think that was the murder weapon?' she asked, staring at it.

The scene of crime officer shrugged and the shoulders of his protective suit stirred.

'We think it probably was.'

Ian grunted. 'Probably,' he repeated. 'Let's wait until the post mortem. We don't even know if he was suffocated yet. So far all we have is reasonable supposition.'

Leaving the forensic team to their work, Geraldine and Ian returned to the police station where the detective chief inspector had summoned them to a briefing. They drove there in silence, each of them lost in thought.

'I wonder if he went to the woods alone.' Geraldine broke the silence as they reached Fulford Road and turned in to the police car park.

'We might be able to track his journey there, once we know where he lived,' Ian replied, following her train of thought.

'If he went there by himself, it could have been a chance attack,' Geraldine said grimly.

'If it was a mugging that went too far, we might never find his killer.'

'The killer could have followed him there,' Geraldine said.

They went inside, and made their way straight to the major incident room at York Police Station where the murder investigation team, headed up by Detective Chief Inspector Eileen Duncan, were gathering for their first briefing.

'The dead man's name is George Gardner,' the square-faced detective chief inspector announced.

She looked around the room, fixing her eyes on each of the officers in turn, as though challenging them to contradict her. Accustomed to her senior officer's prickly persona at work, Geraldine met Eileen's gaze with equanimity. Not for the first time, she wondered whether she herself would have been more even-tempered with colleagues, had she been responsible for a serious investigation. Behind Eileen's brusque facade Geraldine suspected the DCI was nervous. Glancing around, Geraldine noticed a young constable, Naomi Arnold, appeared cowed by Eileen's air of belligerence and made a mental note to encourage her colleague. Naomi was a smart and ambitious young officer, who deserved to do well.

'He was forty-one, Caucasian, living out towards Driffield,' Eileen added. 'You have his address. We are awaiting the results of the post mortem as we speak.'

Until they had more information, there was not much else to say and the officers dispersed to their separate tasks.

3

GERALDINE ALWAYS FOUND IT difficult to tell people their loved ones were dead. However sympathetically she shared the news, there was no way of mitigating the pain of such loss. In most cases, she felt as though she was witnessing mental anguish made palpable. On this occasion, she was conscious of the need to be particularly vague when speaking to the widow. Michelle Gardner's husband was dead, but they did not know for certain that he had been murdered. It was just possible he had accidentally fallen off his bicycle, crawled through the undergrowth, and suffocated with his head buried in the earth.

'Give me a corpse any day,' she said to Ian, when she went to his office before she left to speak to Michelle. 'At least they can't suffer any more. What I find hard is having to tell people someone they love is dead.'

Ian merely shrugged when she said that. He had heard her mention her views on the matter many times. They both knew how he struggled to look at cadavers. Even after years of working in serious crime, viewing a post mortem made him nauseous. However many times Geraldine tried to encourage him to feel less disturbed by cadavers, it made no difference.

'I prefer the living to the dead. I can't help it,' he told her. 'It's not a rational response.'

'It seems quite rational to me,' she replied. 'None of us like coming face to face with the reality of our own mortality, and murder victims are not always a pretty sight. But the fact is, we're all going to die one day, and there's no getting away from it. At least we can try to do something useful with our lives, while we are still here.'

'Well, thank you very much. Now you've really cheered me up,' he said. 'You know how the sight of a dead body upsets me. In fact, the only thing that will make me feel better right now is a live body.'

He pulled her towards him and tried to kiss her, but she wriggled determinedly out of his embrace.

'Stop it, will you?' she scolded him, smiling. 'We're at work. Someone might see.'

Leaving Ian's office, Geraldine mentally prepared herself for the approaching ordeal. George Gardner had lived in a small red brick semi-detached property in Montague Street, not far from the River Ouse. The house had a neatly trimmed hedge in front of it, shielding it from the road. The front door was opened by a dainty little woman in an old-fashioned flared skirt, and matching green blouse. She stared enquiringly up at Geraldine, her expression barely altering at the sight of Geraldine's identity card.

'Can I come in?' Geraldine asked.

Without a word, Michelle led the way into a tidy front room, which looked as though every surface had recently been dusted and polished. A pile of cookery books were stacked neatly on a gleaming wooden coffee table, beside an equally tidy pile of women's magazines. When they were both seated, Michelle gazed incuriously at Geraldine without enquiring the reason for her visit. Perched on the edge of an upholstered armchair, Geraldine launched into a well-rehearsed speech, sharing the tragic news as gently as she could.

'Dead?' Michelle repeated, looking faintly baffled. 'What are you talking about? He went for a bike ride. He'll be back soon. Although he has been gone for rather a long time.' She glanced at a carriage clock on the mantelpiece and shook her head. 'He must have popped to the shops on his way home. He does that sometimes.' She smiled contentedly. 'He likes to surprise me with flowers or chocolate.'

Geraldine leaned forward and spoke very softly. 'Listen to me, Michelle. I'm afraid your husband met with an accident while he was out.'

'An accident? What do you mean? What sort of accident? No, don't tell me, he wasn't wearing his helmet, was he?'

'No, you're right, he wasn't wearing a helmet,' Geraldine sighed.

'I warned him he'd fall off and bang his head one of these days, but he never listens to me,' Michelle grumbled, her complacency momentarily disturbed. 'Where is he now? Perhaps he'll be more careful from now on. I warned him, you know. So where is he?'

Geraldine knew that by now George would be lying naked on a slab in the morgue, awaiting a post mortem. Perhaps his skull had already been sawn open, and the foul-smelling contents of his stomach inspected.

'I'm afraid your husband suffered a fatal accident,' she said, speaking as gently as possible. 'George is dead.'

'No, he can't be. There must be some mistake. He was always so careful,' Michelle replied, contradicting her previous statement. 'I think you must be mistaken, Inspector.'

Geraldine explained the procedure for formally identifying the body, making it clear there was no doubt the dead man was George. He had been carrying a driving licence with his photograph in the wallet in his pocket. She did not add that the police were looking into the death. Although at first sight his death appeared to have been an accident, closer examination of the scene suggested that George might have been deliberately killed by a person or persons unknown. While Geraldine was expressing sympathy, she was conscious that as the dead man's spouse, Michelle herself was the most likely suspect.

'We argued about his wearing his helmet,' Michelle was

saying, as though she was angry with her husband for his recklessness, rather than shocked at hearing that he was dead. 'He swore he would wear it, but he used to hide it. I bet if you look in the shed, you'll find it there right now.'

She jumped to her feet and Geraldine followed her outside to a small garden. Michelle opened the door of a dilapidated wooden shed and began rummaging around inside among cardboard boxes, sets of tools, and several piles of old sheets and sacking. Shifting a large cardboard box to one side, she let out a triumphant cry.

'Here it is,' she said. 'What did I tell you? Hidden away where he thought I wouldn't notice it. If he's hurt, he has only himself to blame. What was he doing, going out on his bike without wearing his helmet? If I warned him once, I must have warned him a thousand times not to go out without his helmet. But would he listen? Well, he's going to have to listen to me after this. Getting the police involved, of all people. You tell him. He never listens to me.'

'Michelle, George is dead,' Geraldine said. 'You can't tell him anything any more. No one can.'

Michelle shook her head. 'No,' she said. 'He can't be. He was always so careful.'

There was nothing more to say to Michelle, who seemed too shocked and confused to take in what had happened. Having established that there was no one who could come and sit with Michelle, Geraldine took her back into the house and made her some tea.

'Are you going to be all right?' she asked.

'Oh yes. I'll just wait here for George to come home,' Michelle replied. 'And when he does, I'm going to give him a piece of my mind for going out on his bike without his helmet. I warned him this would happen.'

Thoughtfully, Geraldine returned to the police station. She barely had time to describe Michelle's odd behaviour to her friend and colleague, Ariadne, when they were summoned for a briefing.

'She certainly sounds like an oddball,' Ariadne said as they hurried along the corridor to the meeting room.

Geraldine nodded. 'It could have been shock, but there was definitely something strange about her.'

The detective chief inspector's square jaw was set in a solemn expression, her thin lips twisted as though she had a bad taste in her mouth, her small dark eyes glaring around the assembled team. On the wall behind her was an image of George Gardner, his face smeared with mud. There was something about the detective chief inspector's expression that made it clear they were investigating a murder before she spoke.

'Bruising around the mouth and nose indicate the victim was suffocated after falling off his bicycle.'

'He could have been deliberately pushed off his bike,' Ian pointed out.

'Or pulled from behind,' Naomi added, glancing at Ian.

'Yes, of course,' Eileen conceded. 'In which case there ought to be evidence of contact on George's clothes. Let's keep an open mind and see what the forensic team comes up with. Geraldine, you saw his wife. What was your impression of her? Do we need to bring her in for questioning?'

Geraldine hesitated. Michelle had seemed very confused. When Geraldine had explained that George was dead, his wife had not appeared to comprehend what had happened.

'But she knew where to look for her husband's helmet,' Geraldine concluded, describing how Michelle had found George's cycling helmet.

Eileen's eyes narrowed. 'Do you think she's as confused as she makes out?' she asked.

Geraldine hesitated again. 'It's impossible to say,' she said at last. 'Her reaction was certainly odd, but shock can make people behave strangely. Like you said, we need to keep an open mind for now. In the meantime, I think we should contact her GP and get someone to check on her.'

Eileen gave a brisk nod. 'Why don't you send an officer to have a word with her doctor?' she agreed. 'They can alert him to her current situation, and at the same time find out if she's been diagnosed with dementia. Or anything else for that matter,' she added thoughtfully. 'Let's bear in mind that she might have hidden George's helmet herself.'

'That seems an unlikely way to murder someone,' Naomi pointed out. 'I mean, what if he hadn't fallen off his bike?'

'Unless he didn't come off the bike accidentally,' Ian said, reiterating his earlier theory about what had happened to George.

'Plenty of people fall off bikes and come away with nothing worse than a few scrapes and bruises,' a sergeant said. 'It's hardly a sensible way to try and kill someone.'

'His wife doesn't sound like a sensible person,' Ariadne muttered, smiling at Geraldine.

'At this early stage of the investigation anything's possible,' Eileen said firmly. 'Now, let's start gathering evidence. If George was murdered, as looks likely, then we need to find his killer as soon as possible, and that means we don't overlook anything.'

4

NORMALLY GERALDINE WOULD HAVE asked a constable to question Michelle's doctor. It was the kind of task she would confidently pass on to a bright young officer like Naomi, who impressed her as sharp and thorough in carrying out her duties. But since the GP's surgery was on Geraldine's way to the mortuary, and she did not anticipate the visit taking long, she decided to speak to the doctor herself. When Geraldine explained the purpose of her visit, the middle-aged receptionist scowled and informed her that the doctor with whom Michelle was officially registered was not at work that day. Another GP was available.

'But I'm not sure why you insist on seeing a doctor,' the receptionist added acerbically. 'The doctors are very busy, and in any case medical records are strictly confidential, so there's nothing anyone here will be able to tell you.'

Geraldine sighed. She had never enjoyed throwing her weight around with aggressive members of the public, and as she grew older she found the exercise of her powers increasingly wearing. But she could be tough when necessary.

Holding up her warrant card again, she spoke firmly. 'I need to speak to a doctor now.'

'Yes, well, all of our patients would like to be seen immediately by a doctor,' the receptionist replied tartly, shaking her head so that her tight grey curls twitched.

A woman standing behind Geraldine muttered crossly that she was busy too.

'Now if you'd like to take a seat and wait, the doctor will

see you when she's free,' the receptionist added with an air of finality.

'I'm afraid I don't have time to wait,' Geraldine began.

'Then you'll have to phone for an appointment and come back another time, like all our other patients,' the receptionist snapped.

Geraldine leaned forward and spoke softly, hoping no one else would hear her. She had no wish to publicly browbeat the receptionist, however obnoxious she was.

'If you refuse to comply, you will be escorted to the police station and charged with obstructing a detective inspector in the course of an investigation into a serious crime.' She straightened up and raised her voice slightly. 'Step out from behind your desk now.'

As she spoke, she took out her phone, ostensibly to request back up.

'No, wait,' the receptionist bleated, her hostility giving way to alarm, just as Geraldine had anticipated. 'Dr Samuels will see you just as soon as she's free. Any minute now. Please, just wait right there.'

A moment later a patient emerged from a consulting room and, true to her word, the receptionist directed Geraldine to go straight in. Dr Samuels was a thin young woman who gestured at a chair with bony fingers.

'How can I help you, Inspector?' she enquired pleasantly. 'I understand you are requesting information about one of our patients?'

'You've been notified about the death of George Gardner?' Geraldine asked.

'Yes, although we've not yet been advised about the circumstances of his death. I take it you're here to discuss what happened to him?'

'Not exactly. I just passed the news on to his widow, Michelle, who is also registered here. She seemed unable to process news of her husband's death. Has she been diagnosed with any kind of mental condition that might cause her to struggle with understanding what has happened?'

The doctor shook her head. 'You want to know if she's suffering from some form of dementia?' She tapped at her keyboard and checked her screen. 'No, nothing like that. But shock can cause considerable confusion in the healthiest of minds.'

'Is there anything else you can tell me about her that we ought to be aware of? Any periods of depression, or injuries that could have been indications of domestic abuse?'

The doctor raised her eyebrows. 'Nothing that we are aware of.' She turned and scanned down her screen. 'Just the common reasons to contact us: flu jabs, an infected toe, shingles a couple of years ago. There is absolutely nothing out of the ordinary in our records, and no mention of any mental health issues.'

Geraldine nodded. 'Very well, we'll send an officer along to make sure she's all right. I just wanted to check there wasn't any history of abuse or mental problems, and that some kind of support wasn't already in place. Well, thank you very much for your time.'

The information Geraldine had gleaned could easily have been given over the phone, and the visit had proved a waste of everyone's time. Nevertheless, Geraldine had wanted to speak to the doctor in person, in case there was a scrap of information that had not been officially recorded. She did not regret the time she had spent at the surgery. Most detective work was thankless, because it just wasn't possible to identify which seemingly pointless line of enquiry might result in an unexpected breakthrough. But her visit to the GP's surgery had not thrown up a significant lead. Pointedly ignoring the receptionist, she strode across the waiting room and left. Reaching her car, she set off for her next stop: the mortuary.

The pathologist, Jonah Hetherington, greeted her with a smile and a cheery wave of a bloody hand.

'Geraldine, allow me to thank you for sending me the cleanest corpse I've seen in a long time. There was hardly a mark on him. It's a shame I had to make such a mess of him. Can you ever forgive me?' he demanded, heaving a melodramatic sigh. 'I've cleaned the mud off his face, but I don't think it's an improvement. What do you think?'

Geraldine looked down at the body, which was lying flat on its back. Apart from dark bruising around his mouth, he would have appeared uninjured, were it not for a neatly stitched gash on the side of his head.

'You've made him look very respectable, Jonah,' she replied, smiling. 'Now, what can you tell me about him?'

'Apart from the fact that he looked a lot more presentable when his face was covered in mud? Well, let's see, he was a healthy enough fellow, fortyish, with no underlying medical conditions that I can find. He was quite fit, with good muscle tone in his legs, perhaps from running or cycling. He was suffocated with a woollen scarf that was found lying nearby, half buried in the earth. SOCOs picked up microscopic threads of wool from around his mouth and nose, and we found more where he had breathed them in. After he was killed he was rolled over on to his front and someone, I'm guessing his killer, scrabbled at the earth around his face to form a kind of seal. It appears to have been done to make sure he couldn't recover and start breathing again. If that was intended to conceal the fact that he was suffocated, it failed miserably. The signs of suffocation arc clear to see.'

Jonah leaned forward and pointed at the dead man's mouth and nose, where the skin was discoloured.

'You can see where the scarf was pressed tightly against his face,' Jonah said. 'The funny thing is, he doesn't appear to have put up a fight.'

'He was probably caught off guard,' Geraldine replied. 'He fell or was pushed off his bike before he was killed. Perhaps he was injured, or at least shocked, in the fall.'

The pathologist nodded. 'Yes, there's a severe contusion on the back of his head consistent with a fall from a bicycle. Not enough to kill him, but enough to knock him out or at least leave him feeling dazed.'

Jonah raised the head of the dead man to expose a discoloured patch of skin where the hair had been shorn.

'That's a nasty bruise,' Geraldine said.

'He must have fallen backwards off his bike.'

'Do you think he was pulled off it from behind?'

'I've shown you his injuries,' Jonah said. 'Working out how he came by them is your job. But if you ask me, I'd say that's quite likely and would explain how he came to land on his head, without badly grazing his hands. If he was taken completely by surprise, he might not have had time to try and break his backwards fall.'

'You said the blow on his head was enough to knock him out?'

'It's difficult to say for sure. He might have lost consciousness, or at least been stunned for a few minutes, or he might have just been momentarily shocked by falling.'

'During which time the killer dragged him through the bushes, out of sight of the path, and suffocated him,' Geraldine said.

'That is certainly a plausible scenario. If the killer acted quickly enough, he might well have done all that before our chap here realised what was happening to him.'

'Can you think of an alternative sequence of events that is equally likely?'

Jonah sighed. 'It's not my place to speculate about what might or might not have happened,' he replied. 'Dealing with the dark workings of the human mind is your area of expertise. I can only report on what I can physically see.' He held up his bloody gloves.

Geraldine thanked the pathologist, who promised to let

her know straightaway if the toxicology report came up with any information that could be of particular interest to the investigating team.

'Let me know what you find, however trivial it seems,' she said. 'I want to know everything you find in there.'

'Even his last cup of tea?'

'Even his last cup of tea,' she confirmed.

'Your wish is my command.'

With a final smile and a wave, Jonah picked up a scalpel and turned back to his grisly work, whistling softly as he probed a bloody mess lying in a tray beside the body.

That evening, Ian flung himself down on the sofa while Geraldine brought in fish and chips, still in the paper from the takeaway restaurant. It had been a long day.

'Let's talk about a real holiday when this is over,' she said as she put a tray on his lap. 'Hopefully it won't take long to get the investigation sorted and then we can really focus on booking something fabulous.'

Ian smiled at her. Before leaving the police station that afternoon, they had learned that a sample of DNA had been found on the scarf used to suffocate George. They had no match for the anonymous DNA, and no clue to the identity of its owner, other than that it belonged to a Caucasian male with light brown hair and blue eyes. If they could trace all the victim's contacts and test them, there was a chance the case might be tied up quite quickly. Admittedly there was no proof that the DNA found on the body belonged to the killer, but it seemed likely. They both agreed that, with luck, the investigation would be over soon.

'It seems fairly straightforward,' Ian said. 'And then I'm going to whisk you away on the best holiday you've ever had.'

Geraldine smiled. 'Well, if that's not an incentive to solve this case quickly, I don't know what is.'

Murder investigations could drag on for months, but they were both hopeful that this one would be resolved quickly.

5

HE WAS DISAPPOINTED WHEN George's death failed to make the front page of the local paper. Inconsequential to the world at large, the event had been hugely significant for him. Watching his victim's struggle had been one of the most exhilarating moments of his life, irreversibly changing everything around him. The whole world suddenly became vivid and filled with exciting possibilities. The earth seemed to gleam more richly, and the green weeds poking up from the ground grew startling in their brightness as George's thrashing weakened and drew to an end. Whatever else happened, he had succeeded in taking a man's life with his own hands. In that moment, he had been Death's equal. Although no one else was ever going to connect him with George's murder, he himself would always glory in the truth. And even if he was somehow, impossibly, tracked down, after he had served his sentence, and his 'debt to society' was paid, he would be a murderer. Nothing could ever change that. The act of killing a man was not merely something he had done; it changed his relationship with Death.

Still, he was not worried that he would be caught. He had laid his plans too carefully for that. After all, the police were only human beings with limited powers, and they were fallible, in spite of their armies of officers, and their impressive technology. The most sophisticated computer in the world was no match for the cunning of a single man. He had expected to enjoy a transient notoriety, hugging his secret to himself in the safety of his own home. If anything, he had been afraid there might be too much publicity. He had certainly never predicted this freakish lack of reaction to what had happened. There was a short article in the paper, which he read and reread, searching for more information. He was reassured to see that the police didn't seem to know anything about the struggle that had taken place in the woods.

York resident, forty-year-old George Gardner, suffered a fatal injury as a result of a cycling accident in Rowntree Park on Saturday. He had lived in York all his life, and was well liked by his neighbours and associates. 'If the victim had been wearing a safety helmet, there is every chance he would still be alive today,' a police spokesman said. 'We urge all cyclists to remember to wear helmets when out on the road.'

That was it: a short paragraph on page two of the local paper, and a brief mention he managed to find online. He ought to have been pleased the police didn't suspect foul play. Far from investigating George's death, they seemed happy to dismiss it as an accident. He appreciated that he had been given a reprieve, yet he couldn't help feeling let down. He wanted to follow the case in the media, watching as the police cast around helplessly, before finally charging off in any number of wrong directions. The death might have attracted more attention if he hadn't covered his tracks so well. Starting with the local news channel, he had envisaged the story hitting the national news. But now, thanks to police incompetence, even the local paper would dismiss the story. He tossed the paper aside in a fit of pique. Whoever was looking into George's death must be blind as well as stupid. After a few moments, he calmed down. The so-called accident had only taken place on Saturday. There was still time for the police to become involved. He resolved to keep a close eye on the news, and look out for any further developments. He couldn't believe there would be no more reports about it. Death should be more important than that.

His patience was rewarded. By Monday, things had moved

on. The police had not actually stated they no longer believed George's death was an accident. There was no mention of the words 'murder' or 'unlawful killing' in the reports he read. Nevertheless, the story had not gone away. On the contrary, the reports continued, repeating what had previously been published. The only development was that the police were asking for witnesses to come forward. That suggested they suspected there was more to this death than they had thought at first. He wasn't surprised. It was unlikely the police would fail to realise something untoward had happened that day in the woods. Now all he had to do was sit at home, hidden and anonymous, watching as the investigation unfolded. But it was difficult to track down information. Most of what he was able to find in the media continued to reiterate what had already been published.

He wished he could follow the police activity in detail. Reading snippets in the papers was frustrating, but there was not much else he could do. There was no way he was going to return to the scene of the crime. He couldn't understand why anyone did that. It was what murderers were expected to do, and it had always struck him as singularly stupid. He guessed that guilt drove them to self-destructive impulses. Unlike stereotypical murderers, he understood the wisdom of keeping away. He never lost his ability to think clearly; the fear of being caught was nothing compared to the terrors he had experienced in his life.

Yet he yearned to know more. As a small boy he had been helpless, banished from witnessing the scene of his mother's death. Now, as an adult, he could at least watch someone else die. He was no longer shut out, and the experience felt like a cleansing, bringing him closer to the mother he had been unable to hold on to. But even that was not enough to satisfy his craving. He needed to know what happened next. He struggled to wait patiently, while they kept him in the dark. Somehow he had to find out what was happening to George, now he was dead. He wanted to know what he looked like now. He wondered if he could befriend a police officer, who might tell him how the investigation was progressing. The more he pondered the idea, the more it appealed to him. He thought a female police officer would be easiest to get round. If he could gain her trust, she might be indiscreet, especially if she believed he was romantically interested in her. He was confident he could manage that. He was not bad looking. Tall and slim, with blonde hair and blue eyes, he had never had much trouble attracting women. If they had interested him, he could have enjoyed a fling or two. But there had only ever been one woman in his life.

If he managed to befriend a policewoman, she would have to be an officer working on the team investigating George's murder. He could not afford to take any risks pursuing someone who would not actually serve his specific purpose, and it might be dangerous if she thought he was asking too many questions. Still, once he had thought of it, the idea was tempting. It would be really entertaining to hear how the police were stumbling around in the dark, with no idea who they were really looking for. He would be like the proverbial fly on the wall. But he had no idea how to attract a policewoman without arousing suspicion. On balance, he reluctantly decided it would be sensible to keep away from the police altogether. He had carried out his plan, and could not afford to ruin things now, when everything was going so well. The fact was, the police were never going to arrest him. They wouldn't even know where to look, unless he did something stupid. And he was too careful for that.

6

GEORGE HAD WORKED IN the head office of a railway company as a signalling document controller, responsible for checking electronic data records. According to the office manager, who spoke to Geraldine on the phone, it was an important job requiring a great deal of concentration. After arranging to be shown around, on her arrival Geraldine was taken to an open-plan office, where several staff were seated at computer terminals. Although George had spent his days staring at a screen, the office manager assured her that his colleagues all knew him well, and were devastated by the news of his sudden death.

'We're trying to build a picture of George: who he knew and how he spent his time here,' Geraldine explained to the manager, a middle-aged ginger-haired man with a thin face and a whiskery moustache.

The manager nodded and his moustache fluttered with the movement. 'George was steady and dependable. In all the seventeen years he was with us he never took a single day off. Can you believe that? He was dedicated to his job, and will be missed by everyone he worked with.'

It sounded like a rehearsed speech, probably one the manager had delivered when he had announced the news of George's death to his colleagues. Geraldine nodded, wondering if the manager was being a little too earnest in his protestations. But he was adamant he had never seen George outside of work, and had never had cause to be dissatisfied with him.

'On the contrary. To be honest, we're going to struggle to

replace him. Not everyone is as conscientious as George. Between you and me,' he lowered his voice, 'some of the youngsters we recruit these days are pretty useless. You wouldn't believe how often they call in sick on Mondays. Not George. Never. And he kept his nose to the grindstone when he was here. I'm telling you, he did the work of three men. They don't breed them like that any more. He was like a carthorse, you know, just plodding along doing what needed to be done without any fuss.'

It was a strange turn of phrase, but Geraldine said she understood what he meant.

'Did he fall out with anyone here?' she asked. 'Were you aware of him exchanging any cross words with anyone about anything, anything at all? Perhaps there was something you overheard, or were told about?'

The manager shook his head. 'To be honest, he barely spoke to anyone while he was here,' he replied. 'He just kept his head down and got on with his work. I don't think he had much to do with anyone else, unless he needed to ask something about the records. If he did get in a fight with anyone – which I find very hard to believe – it certainly had nothing to do with anyone here. We're a well-run outfit, and everyone is professional in their approach to their work.'

'Even the ones who regularly take Mondays off,' Geraldine thought, but she merely thanked the manager, and said she would like to speak to each of George's colleagues in turn. Sitting in the manager's office, she questioned his colleagues individually. Contrary to what the manager had told her, most of them did not seem to know much about George, beyond his name.

'George? You mean the little bald guy? The one who died suddenly?' they asked, or something similar.

'How well did you know him?' Geraldine asked each of them.

The first woman she questioned answered at length, but to little purpose. 'I can't really say I knew him,' she said. 'I knew who he was, of course, and what he did, but he was a quiet sort, you know. He liked to keep himself to himself. I mean, some of us, we go for a drink on a Friday after work, just a quick one. But he never joined us, not once. We invited him along. Everyone's welcome. We just go to the pub, you know. Nothing formal or anything. But he never came. Not even on birthdays. He did use to come to the Christmas party, though. He always brought his wife along. She was as nondescript as he was, but I expect you've seen her?'

'Did you speak to her?'

'No. They didn't socialise much.' She smiled at a private thought. 'They just sat together, side-by-side, not even looking at one another. We used to joke they were waiting for a train that George had forgotten to schedule. But they seemed happy enough,' she went on, serious again. 'Contented, you know, just sitting together. Some of the girls used to talk about them, you know, making up all kinds of unlikely stories. They weren't true.' She looked slightly shamefaced. 'I mean, it's not as if we knew her. It was just a bit of harmless fun.'

'What sort of stories?'

'Oh, you know, they were secretly Russian spies, or they were nudists, or they hosted wild orgies at the weekends, that sort of thing.' The woman lowered her voice and shifted her chair closer to Geraldine. 'Old Molly, who worked here forever, was the worst.'

'Worst at what?'

'At making up stories about them. She told us George's wife had an affair with a minor royal. Of course none of us believed it. Have you seen his wife?' She chuckled.

Despite her willingness to talk, that was as much as the woman knew about George. When Geraldine asked to speak to Molly, she learned that the old woman had retired over ten years ago and had died two years later. No one else admitted they had heard any unusual or entertaining rumours about George and his wife. Other than the accusation of spying, or being sexually liberated nudists, there was nothing remarkable in the descriptions Geraldine heard. George and Michelle sounded like a dull ordinary couple. All the staff who had known George came up with similar vague responses. No one admitted they had ever succeeded in engaging in conversation with him, although no one had actively disliked him.

'He was an inoffensive little man,' the first woman concluded.

'George was harmless,' another woman said.

'He was decent enough,' a man said. 'There was nothing about him anyone could object to, unless you object to people who have absolutely no personality whatsoever. He really was unbelievably boring.'

Geraldine wondered why anyone would want to murder a man who seemed to have spent every day for seventeen years in the company of people who had scarcely noticed him.

'Why would someone so innocuous be murdered?' Eileen asked at the briefing the following day, echoing Geraldine's bewilderment. 'There must have been more to him than we have uncovered.'

They had been unable to trace any friends of George and his wife, who had no children and no living siblings. They appeared to have lived very quietly, seeing no one socially. Yet someone had dragged George through the bushes in the woods and held a scarf over his face until he stopped breathing.

'It must have been his wife,' Naomi said. 'Apart from the fact that it almost always is the spouse in these cases, he doesn't seem to have known anyone else. How can people live like that?' she burst out, as though indignant at the Gardners' quiet lifestyle. 'They must have been so bored.'

'They had each other,' Geraldine replied. 'Perhaps that was enough for them.'

She felt, rather than saw, Ian glance at her, and she looked down, afraid of letting her guard down and revealing her emotions while she was at work.

7

A TEAM OF VISUAL images identifications and detections officers had been studying CCTV from around the area where George had been killed. On Tuesday afternoon, one of them called Geraldine to report seeing two cyclists arriving at the park at twenty past eight on Saturday morning. Geraldine went to see for herself what they had found. Sitting beside a young female officer, she watched grainy footage of two cyclists disappearing along the road into the wooded park. The first one appeared to have short dark hair, but the second one was wearing a hood, preventing them from seeing anything of his face or hair. The film did not yield a clear view, but either of them could have been George.

'Do you think the second cyclist is following the first one?' Geraldine asked.

The constable shrugged. 'Maybe. Could be. It's impossible to say, isn't it? Bicycles are the worst to trace because they don't display number plates and, unlike people's unique gait when they're walking, there's not a lot to distinguish one cyclist's pedalling from another, unless the bike is the wrong size for them or they have a particularly awkward posture. But take a look at this.'

The constable fast forwarded the film and they watched in silence. At eight forty-two a solitary hooded figure on a bicycle appeared, pedalling out of the woods and away in the opposite direction. It could have been the second of the cyclists from earlier on. The first one did not reappear. From what Geraldine had seen, it looked as though the first cyclist could have been George Gardner, followed by the killer who re-emerged twenty minutes later. She suggested this to the visual images identifications and detections officer who shrugged.

'It's possible,' she agreed. 'As far as we can tell from the model of the bike, and the estimated height of the cyclist, the hooded rider appears to be a man.'

'How far are you able to follow the hooded cyclist's journey after he left the woods?' Geraldine asked.

'We've been looking at that,' the constable replied.

Further study of CCTV footage showed the hooded cyclist hunched over his handlebars, riding very rapidly back into town. It was impossible to discern much about him. Even his hair was concealed beneath the hood of his jacket. They tracked him along Bishopthorpe Road, around Station Road, past the Minster and along Gillygate, where he disappeared from view. There was no further CCTV, and no way of telling where he had alighted. The last shot they had was of the bicycle turning into a side street.

'We fast tracked through the tape for hours, but he didn't reappear,' the constable said. 'He went to ground somewhere there, along Claremont Terrace.'

'The victim lived in Montague Street,' Geraldine said thoughtfully. 'Is that a coincidence?'

She thanked the visual images identifications and detections officer and went to speak to Eileen.

'The hooded cyclist appeared to be a man,' Geraldine concluded her account.

'Set up a team to do a door to door and let's find that cyclist,' Eileen said.

Geraldine nodded and left. Within an hour officers were calling at every house in Claremont Terrace. It was a cul-de-sac, although with a bicycle the man could easily have slipped along a passageway between two properties and disappeared.

By the evening, two adults living in Claremont Terrace had been identified as being in possession of bicycles. They were a tubby middle-aged woman and a tall thin man, neither of whom resembled the cyclist who had been spotted pedalling away from Rowntree Park on Saturday morning. Geraldine went to speak to them. Maisie Walters was a dental hygienist who worked at a practice close to the Minster.

'Yes,' she said in response to Geraldine's question. 'Yes, I have a bicycle at home.' She stepped to one side to reveal her bicycle leaning against the wall in her hallway.

'Did you go out on it on Saturday morning?'

'No, so if you're looking for someone who was involved in a road accident, or witnessed one, you've come to the wrong place,' she replied, sounding irritated.

'Does anyone else ever ride your bicycle?'

'No, I've never lent it to anyone, and I keep it in the hall so it's never left out on the street. These days, you can't leave anything outside. I learned that the hard way when I left my daughter's buggy out, just for five minutes, while I was taking my granddaughter into the house. By the time I went back out, it had gone. My daughter gave me a hard time, but it was hardly my fault. I only left it outside for a minute. I have to say, I was very disappointed with the way the police responded when I reported it, like they really couldn't have cared less. I mean, I know it's not exactly the crime of the century, but it was an expensive buggy and someone stole it. I don't suppose you could find it for us?'

Geraldine murmured her regrets and the woman continued, barely pausing for breath.

'I remember when we used to leave our front door unlocked when we went out, but these days, nothing's safe. So I never leave my bike outside.' She shook her head to emphasise her words. 'Can you tell me what this is about? Only we've never had any dealings with the police. We've never been involved in anything criminal until my daughter's buggy was stolen.'

Geraldine reassured her that she was not in any trouble. The woman was adamant that the bicycle had been safely locked inside her house on Saturday morning. There was nothing more to be learned so Geraldine moved on. The other bicycle owner in the street was less forthcoming, demanding to know why Geraldine was interested in his bicycle, and what she was doing on his doorstep.

'We've already had a policeman in uniform here asking about bicycles. What the hell's going on? If people are going around stealing bikes, that's nothing to do with me. I bought my bike, fair and square, and it's never been stolen, not since I bought it.'

He frowned and Geraldine guessed he had bought his bicycle second-hand, and had no paperwork as proof of his purchase.

'How long have you owned it?' she asked.

To her surprise, the man held up a bony hand and asked her to wait. He dashed away into the house and she heard raised voices, the thin man yelling to 'just find it', while a woman's voice screeched something incomprehensible in reply. A few moments later the man reappeared, clutching a slip of paper.

'There!' he cried out triumphantly, brandishing a receipt from a second-hand bicycle shop in Walmgate.

He also denied having lent his bicycle to anyone else, and said he had not been out on it on Saturday morning.

'That was a complete waste of time,' Geraldine grumbled when she returned to her desk and sat down opposite Ariadne. 'Still, at least we've eliminated those two bike owners in Claremont Terrace.'

'But the door-to-door team have spoken to every householder along there now, and we're still no closer to finding whoever rode to the woods and back again on Saturday,' Ariadne replied. 'If he even was the killer. We don't seem to be getting anywhere.'

'Oh well, it's early days, I suppose,' Geraldine said. 'We'll just have to keep looking.'

Very often a murderer was discovered almost immediately.

Sometimes a witness came forward, or more frequently the culprit was known to the victim and confessed straightaway. But around seventy-six hours had passed since George had fallen from his bicycle, and had crawled, or been dragged, into the bushes, and as yet they had no leads.

'It's as if George was never killed,' Ariadne said.

'He's like a man who never existed at all,' Geraldine murmured, remembering how little his colleagues at work had known about him.

'Even the cranks are ignoring his death,' Ariadne added.

After three days, in most unsolved cases numerous stray crackpots contacted the police station with spurious so-called information, psychics, people with telepathic powers, and so on.

'Just wait,' Geraldine replied with a grimace. 'Once Eileen puts out a request for information, we'll be inundated with useless information.'

8

ARIADNE HAD BEEN TASKED with organising a team of constables to contact local bicycle shops, in an attempt to find out who had bought a bicycle recently. She grumbled to Geraldine over lunch.

'We have to try and identify any men with brown hair and brown eyes who bought a bicycle in York some time over the past two years,' she told Geraldine. 'There are just so many reasons why this is a complete waste of time. For a start, the majority of men who bought a bike in York over that period probably had brown hair. Secondly, there's no way of knowing when the killer bought his bike. He could have owned it for twenty years, or borrowed it, or bought it second-hand from a private seller. Two years is a completely arbitrary time scale. Thirdly, no one who works in a shop selling bikes is going to remember the colour of a customer's hair. To think they will is just crazy. And then, once we have our incomplete list of brown-haired men who bought a bike from a bike shop recently, we're going to have to trace them all so we can ask them where they were last Saturday morning. We're really looking for a needle in a haystack in fields and fields of haystacks with no idea which is the right one. And to top it all off, the bike was probably bought somewhere else entirely, or it might have been borrowed or stolen. Oh well, I suppose we have to do something, and you never know, it might throw up a useful lead. But I'll be amazed if it does. It's all such a waste of time.' She sighed.

Geraldine was already regretting having agreed to go to the

canteen with Ariadne who had done nothing but complain since they had sat down. There was no sign of Ian, and Geraldine didn't want to call him in case he was busy. He often came by her desk on his way to lunch, but she hadn't seen him that morning. She was keen to discuss the case they were working on, although there was little to talk about. The killer had conveniently left traces of his DNA behind at the crime scene, but they had not come up with a match for it, so unless the killer committed another crime and was caught, having his DNA was not much help. Investigating the victim was proving equally unhelpful.

'He doesn't seem to have had any enemies,' Geraldine said. 'He had no money to speak of, so no one was going to kill him for his estate, his wife was devoted to him by all accounts, and his colleagues at work barely noticed his existence. No one seems to have even vaguely disliked him, let alone hated him enough to want to kill him. And he was found with cash in his wallet in his pocket, so he doesn't appear to have been mugged.'

With no leads, and no one with any reason for wanting George dead, the general consensus was that his death was the result of a random attack, and the killer had no connection to George at all. They had just happened to be in the woods at the same time. In the vain hope that they would find a clue to his killer, they were looking into George's past.

'There could be some information somewhere that will give us a lead, however tenuous,' Geraldine insisted as she stabbed at a flabby omelette with her fork.

Ariadne grunted and sat staring at her food without touching it.

'Is everything all right?' Geraldine asked, putting down her fork and frowning at Ariadne. 'You seem distracted. I know it's pretty dull talking about the case when there's nothing to go on.'

Geraldine waited, but Ariadne didn't reply. Taking another forkful of her omelette, Geraldine watched her friend.

'Come on,' Geraldine said at last. 'Spit it out. What's eating you?'

Ariadne smiled weakly. 'It's this blasted wedding. My mother's driving me crazy. For two pins I'd call the whole thing off.'

Geraldine leaned forward. 'Ariadne, it's your wedding. You can't let your mother dictate what you do. If you want, you and Nico can go to a registry office, get hitched, and then tell your family when it's a fait accompli and there'll be nothing they can do about it. You wouldn't be doing anything wrong. And there's no point in making yourself miserable over it. You should be happy about getting married.'

'I could just call the whole thing off,' Ariadne repeated, and pressed her lips together.

Geraldine hesitated, uncertain whether to take her friend's comment seriously or not.

'Would you like to call it off?' she enquired cautiously.

'I don't know. I'm just thinking, if I'm tempted to call it all off over something as petty as my mother's interference, then maybe I'm not as committed to this marriage as I should be. Perhaps it's not right and I should just walk away.'

Geraldine took her time over replying. 'I don't think your mother is unimportant to you. She's your mother. And marriage is a big deal.'

Ariadne shook her head. 'I know, I know. It's probably just the case getting to me. We're all feeling frustrated and helpless and I'm desperate to feel I have some sort of control over my own life, but with my mother around, that's impossible. Oh, I know I'm lucky to have a mother who cares so much about me that she wants my wedding to be perfect, but it's infuriating all the same. I'm forty, and a detective sergeant. I can run a team of constables, all professional men and women, without batting an eyelid. But when it comes to my mother, I revert to behaving like a child. Anyway, enough about me and my problems which aren't really problems at all. I just need to get my emotional responses under control in my personal life. So, how's it going with you and Ian?'

Geraldine felt her face growing hot and wished she could stop reacting every time Ian was mentioned. In her own way she was just as poor at suppressing her emotional reactions as Ariadne. She had always thought of herself as capable of remaining dispassionate whatever the circumstances. It turned out she had just never really cared about anyone else enough for them to affect her so strongly.

'Yes, it's all good,' she replied vaguely, nodding her head and smiling.

If she was truthful, 'good' was a mild way of expressing how happy she was with Ian. Before Ariadne could speak again, they were summoned to a briefing. Neither of them said anything, but they both knew there were only two things that could cause Eileen to summon the team together in the middle of the day: a serious lead, or another body.

9

NORMALLY FORBIDDING, EILEEN'S SQUARE face was positively beaming as she addressed the team.

'We have a match for the DNA found on the woollen scarf used to suffocate George. Don't ask me why it's taken them so long to get back to us,' she added, her face reverting to its customary scowl. 'We should have had this information two days ago.'

'There's always a delay when someone's killed at the weekend, and George was murdered on Saturday morning,' Ian replied.

'When we're investigating a murder, any delay is unacceptable,' Eileen snapped. 'But the important thing right now is that we have a match for the DNA found on the murder weapon.'

It sounded odd to hear a woollen scarf referred to as a weapon, but that was exactly what it was in this case.

'The DNA matches that of a man called Ben Foster, who lives here in York. We have his details because he was charged with dangerous driving four years ago, after he knocked someone down. The victim was rushed to hospital where she died the following day, without ever recovering consciousness. Ben was given a suspended sentence after his defence argued that the woman had stepped into the road between two parked cars, so Ben couldn't have seen her before the impact. They argued that the victim alone was responsible for the accident. Ben's sole crime had been driving slightly over the speed limit which, according to his defence counsel, did not warrant a custodial sentence. There was a witness,' Eileen went on. 'A householder happened to be in her front yard, putting out the rubbish. She confirmed Ben's statement that the victim just stepped out in the road right in front of him. Ben was apparently too shocked to remember much about what happened. In his initial statement he claimed he didn't see her at all, just heard a horrible thud. Realising he'd hit someone, he slammed on the brakes and skidded to a halt, smashing into a parked car.'

There was a brief pause after Eileen stopped speaking.

'The courts are far too lenient with speeding drivers.' A middle-aged constable broke the silence, shaking her greying head. 'They're a menace, and every once in a while something like this inevitably happens. Well, he may have got off once, but it's caught up with him now.'

'You can't say he got off, as though he was guilty,' Geraldine protested. 'This is a completely different situation. He wasn't found guilty of dangerous driving four years ago, just of driving over the speed limit. That's hardly a serious crime.'

'It is if you end up killing someone,' the constable retorted.

'The fatality was a matter of bad luck. It wasn't caused by dangerous driving. If he'd been culpable, he would have been found guilty,' Geraldine insisted. 'How many times have we all driven slightly above the speed limit?'

'Never, I trust,' Eileen snapped.

'The woman died,' Ariadne said.

'I know,' Geraldine conceded, 'but it was hardly the driver's fault if someone stepped out right in front of him. In any case, he's had to live with the knowledge that he accidentally killed a woman. Surely that's a punishment enough for something that wasn't really his fault. He just happened to be there.'

'Well, now he's going to be arrested for murder, and it's all thanks to that accident that we've found him,' Eileen said with grim satisfaction.

'If you ask me, it serves him right. He got away with it once–' the grey-haired constable began.

'He didn't get away with anything,' Geraldine insisted, vexed by her colleagues' attitude. 'It was an accident.'

'Well, he can't argue it was an accident this time,' Ariadne said.

'You're talking as though he's already been found guilty,' Geraldine replied.

'We have the evidence, Geraldine,' Eileen said. 'What more do you want? His DNA was found on that scarf, which almost certainly means he's guilty and the investigation is over.'

'You said he almost certainly killed George, but what happened to innocent until proven guilty? There could be other reasons for his DNA being on that scarf.'

'Really? Such as?' Ian asked, raising one eyebrow and looking at her quizzically.

'Oh, I don't know. Maybe he borrowed it.' Geraldine mumbled, aware that she was a lone voice trying to defend the suspect. 'He could have found it and been wearing gloves at the time, and then lost it again.'

'And someone else wearing gloves used it to commit a murder?' Ian asked.

'It's possible.'

Unwilling to appear argumentative, Geraldine shrugged and let the matter drop, although something about the case against Ben Foster didn't make sense. A killer who had been so careful to cover his tracks was hardly likely to use his own scarf to suffocate his victim, and then leave it behind at the scene. Before going to speak to Ben, Geraldine scanned through the case notes of the accident. Ben had knocked down a woman who was crossing the road one evening in October. He hadn't been drinking but had been driving above the speed limit, keen to get home after work. The accident had proved fatal. The victim had been carrying a bottle of wine which smashed when she hit the road. The shattered glass slashed her face. A shard of glass penetrated her chest, severing an artery and she bled to death. By the time the paramedics arrived on the scene, it was too late to save her. They tried to resuscitate her, but it was over.

Driving to Ben Foster's house with Ian soon after the briefing, she tried again to persuade him to keep an open mind about the suspect.

'We don't know for certain that he's guilty,' she began. 'It wasn't directly the impact with the car that killed her, it was glass from a broken bottle. If it hadn't been for that, she probably would have survived the impact. He wasn't driving fast enough to kill her. And we don't know that he killed George.'

'No, but it's the most likely explanation for his DNA being found on the scarf.'

'Listen to yourself,' Geraldine countered irritably. 'Most likely. That isn't conclusive.'

'How else do you explain the evidence?'

'Like I said before, Ben could have given the scarf to the killer. Maybe the killer bought it in a charity shop.'

'Yes, and pigs might fly.'

'So that's why you're so keen to get this case over and done with,' she said with a smile. 'You want to go on that holiday.'

'Don't you?'

'Yes, of course I do, but not at the expense of an innocent man being convicted of a crime he didn't commit.'

'Well, it's just as well it doesn't come down to one or the other,' Ian replied, laughing.

Irritated by Ian's flippant attitude to such a serious issue, Geraldine kept quiet. She had no wish to argue with him, but she knew she was right to give Ben Foster the benefit of the doubt until they were sure he was guilty. When an investigation seemed to be going nowhere, it was easy to grasp at the first suspect who came along and become convinced he was guilty. But the more she thought about the details of the case, the more convinced she became that she had been misguided in sticking her neck out and denying the evidence, especially when everyone else was convinced Ben was guilty. There was no getting away from the fact that his DNA had been found on the murder weapon.

'You're not the only one who believes in the principle of innocent until proven guilty beyond any reasonable doubt,' Ian said quietly as they drew up outside Ben's house.

'I know,' she replied. 'And we do have enough evidence to put him away.'

'You can't argue with the evidence,' Ian said.

His smug response irritated her almost as much as his earlier teasing. She wondered if it was sensible for them to continue working as a team. But then he smiled at her, and all her reservations faded away. Life was good, and she felt even more determined to protect it and apprehend those who thought they could destroy it with impunity.

10

BEN FOSTER LIVED FIVE minutes' walk away from Rowntree Park, where George had been murdered. It was early evening by the time Geraldine and Ian pulled up outside a period red brick terraced house with large bay windows at the front. The sun had not yet set and, in the wake of a brief shower in the morning, the gardens looked fresh and alive in the still air. The property had been carefully maintained, with neat paintwork and a well-tended front garden. A forsythia bush beside the front door displayed a multitude of yellow flowers, and brightly coloured anemones lined the path. As Geraldine and Ian approached the house, somewhere inside a dog began a deep-throated bark. Ian rang the bell and the door was opened by a tall, willowy woman.

'Down, Roxy,' she commanded, with a faint air of desperation.

She was clutching the collar of a lively brown and white terrier which was much smaller than its bark suggested.

'Sorry, sorry,' the woman said, sounding flustered. 'He gets over excited when we have visitors. Can I help you?'

'Are you Christine Foster?'

'Yes. I'm sorry, do I know you?'

Geraldine held up her warrant card.

'I'm Detective Inspector Steel and this is Detective Inspector Peterson,' she said. 'We'd like to speak to Ben Foster.'

The woman's expression darkened into a scowl and she took an involuntary step back. The dog growled.

'Not again,' Christine protested. 'Haven't you people hounded him enough? The case is over, finished. Please, just go away and leave us alone. I can't take much more of this. Why do you have to go digging up the past all the time? He stood trial and he was found not guilty. That's it. You've already tried to ruin our lives once. I won't let you do it to us again. Leave us alone.'

'We'd like a word with your husband,' Geraldine said gently.

'He can come with us quietly, or we can summon backup,' Ian added roughly.

'Oh, very well,' Christine snapped. 'Wait there and I'll call him.'

She must have been attractive when she smiled, but right now her expression was peevish. Geraldine wondered whether Ben's wife knew more than she chose to admit, but before she could question her, Christine turned and called to her husband. Almost immediately, he appeared in the hall behind her. They had a brief muttered conversation before Ben came to the door. Tall, with rounded shoulders and a slight stoop, he glared defiantly at the two police officers standing on his doorstep. Straw-coloured hair hung over his forehead, nearly reaching his pale blue eyes.

'We'd like to ask you a few questions,' Ian said.

'There's no point,' Ben replied, crossing his arms and meeting Ian's stare. 'I've said everything there is to say, and I'm getting sick of you people pestering me. Listen, it was four years ago. It was an accident. I was tried and given a suspended sentence and now, as far as I'm concerned, it's over. History. I'm sorry it happened, but it did. If I could turn the clock back, believe me I would, and I'm going to be far more careful in future. I wish it had never happened, but it did. There's nothing more to say.'

'We'd like you to accompany us to the police station to answer a few questions,' Ian replied stolidly.

'You can ask whatever you want to ask right here and now, and then you can piss off.' His voice rose, and he appeared to be on the point of losing his temper.

'Ben, you'd better do what they want,' his wife interrupted him. 'There's no point trying to fight them. You'll have to go with them, but it won't be for long. And don't say anything without a lawyer.'

'We'd like you to come with us too,' Geraldine said to Christine.

'Me? What for?'

Grumbling, Ben and his wife followed Geraldine and Ian to the waiting patrol cars.

'Is this really necessary?' Christine asked as she climbed into the back of a police car. 'I don't understand what you want with us.'

No one answered her and Geraldine watched as the patrol car pulled away from the kerb, before she followed Ian back to their own vehicle.

Facing Christine across a table in a small interview room an hour later, Geraldine smiled reassuringly at her. Christine scowled.

'You're not in any trouble,' Geraldine began. 'We'd just like to ask you a couple of questions.'

'I'd like to go home please.'

'Does your husband own a bicycle?'

'What?' Christine's eyes widened in surprise.

Geraldine repeated the question.

'Since I'm not obliged to answer your questions, I can only say that's none of your business,' Christine replied.

'Is there a reason why you are reluctant to co-operate with us?'

'Is there any reason why I should answer more questions?'

'I would say so, yes, if you want to help eliminate your husband from an enquiry into a serious crime.'

'What? What serious crime are you talking about? Ben stood trial–'

'We're not interested in what happened four years ago,'

Geraldine interrupted her. 'We're investigating a recent crime.'

'Which Ben had nothing to do with.'

'How do you know?'

'Because my husband is not a criminal. I don't know why you're pursuing him like this, but you have no right to keep harassing him.'

'We have every right. Christine, we are investigating a serious crime. There is evidence which suggests your husband might be involved, and the best thing you can do for him now is co-operate and help us to eliminate him from our enquiries. Unless you believe he is guilty?'

'What serious crime are you talking about?' Christine muttered sullenly.

Ignoring the question, Geraldine asked again whether Ben owned a bicycle.

Scowling, Christine told them that her husband kept an old bicycle in the garage, which he never used.

'Has your husband lost anything recently?'

Christine said that she wasn't aware that he had lost anything. That in itself proved nothing, and Geraldine proceeded to enquire where Ben had been on Saturday morning.

Christine shrugged. 'Where he always is, taking the dog for a walk.'

'How long was he gone?'

Christine shook her head stubbornly, but she was beginning to look concerned. 'I don't know. I don't time his walks. But not long. He's never out for long. I would have noticed if he was gone for a long time. How many times do I have to co-operate with you? When is this constant harassment going to stop? Ben stood trial, it's over. Why do you keep coming back? What are you trying to pin on him with your constant questions? Is this going to start up all over again, with you questioning us all the time? Can't you leave us alone? How many more times are you going to come to the house and insist on coming in? We deserve our privacy.'

Geraldine and Ian compared notes. Neither Ben nor his wife had been particularly forthcoming, but their stories matched. According to them both, Ben had gone out for a short walk with the dog on Saturday morning. When Ian had asked whether anyone else could corroborate the story, Ben had grown irritable, insisting that it wasn't a 'story', but the truth. His account was perfectly plausible, but he couldn't prove where he had been, or how long he had been out of the house. He remained the obvious suspect in the case. His wife was allowed to go home as it seemed that even if she knew anything about her husband's movements on Saturday, she wasn't going to reveal anything to the police. She just kept complaining about police harassment.

A scene of crime officer was sent to examine Ben's bicycle and the team waited anxiously to read his report, hoping to learn that it had recently been ridden through mud. His findings turned out to be unhelpful but inconclusive. The bicycle was very rusty, the saddle was missing, and it did not appear to have been ridden for a long time.

'It would require a lot of oil to get it moving, as well as a saddle,' was the conclusion of the report.

'He could have removed the saddle after he killed George,' Ariadne suggested.

'So we can't entirely rule out the possibility that Ben was the cyclist who followed George into the woods,' Eileen said, but she didn't sound confident.

'It seems unlikely,' Geraldine responded. 'Rust takes time to develop.' No one disagreed with her.

After dinner, Geraldine and Ian were sitting side-by-side in the living room, gazing out at the lights on the opposite side of the river.

'If you knew I'd broken the law, would you report me?' Ian asked.

Geraldine hesitated, aware that there was no right answer to the question.

'I suppose it depends on what you did,' she replied at length.

'Not a blanket expression of unconditional support, then?' he asked.

Having stood by Ian when he had suffered from his ex-wife's lies and trickery, Geraldine was miffed that he wanted to test her loyalty with a ridiculous hypothetical challenge. At the same time, it was true that Ian had risked his own life to protect her from a criminal gang, proving he would not hesitate to support her, whatever the circumstances. She wondered if she was being unfair in refusing to give him the answer he clearly wanted. Her reluctance to commit herself to him unreservedly had kept them apart in the past.

'There's no need to look so serious,' he chided her, grinning.

She laughed, but she felt uncomfortable and looked away. It was hardly a fair question. She had spent all her adult life working to uphold the law, as he had done, and now he had put her on the spot. But there was no time to worry about theoretical crimes, when they had a real killer to put behind bars. The case against Ben Foster seemed to be watertight, but they had to make sure their paperwork was in order, and the suspect was given no room to evade conviction, if he was guilty.

11

'TELL US AGAIN WHERE you walked,' Ian said.

Ben sighed. After a night in a cell, his pale face seemed to have taken on a greyish tinge; he was unshaven, and there were bags under his eyes, making him look ten years older than he had the previous day. Were he not a suspected murderer, Geraldine would have felt sorry for him.

'How many times do I have to tell you?' he asked. 'Do you think I'm going to slip up and change my statement, so you can leap on me, like they do in the films, and catch me out in a lie?' He shook his head and turned to the duty brief sitting at his side. 'Do I really have to go through this all over again? I barely slept last night and I'm exhausted. I want to go home.'

The young solicitor wore her dark hair pulled back into a tight bun, perhaps in an attempt to make herself look older than she was. She sat very upright, nodding her head whenever she spoke.

'I think you might answer the question,' she said, her head bobbing. 'You've already given the police an account of your movements on Saturday morning, so there seems little point in withholding the information now.'

'How is it withholding information if I've already told them everything?' Ben grumbled. 'How can that be withholding information? Like I've already said, more than once, I took the dog for a walk. We went along Butchers Terrace, cut across Rowntree Park by the football pitch, where Roxy can run around off the leash, and down as far as the river bank. The river's only five minutes' walk from the house. I keep her on a lead there. We walked for maybe fifteen minutes, and then we turned round and walked back to the park and went home. It's nice and peaceful by the river, and we often go along there at the weekend. Lots of people do.'

'And you went out alone?' Ian asked.

'Alone with Roxy, yes. So my only witness is a dumb dog. Sometimes Christine comes with us, and sometimes she doesn't. It just depends on how she's feeling. Sometimes she takes Roxy out and I stay at home. It's not a crime to share the responsibility of taking the dog for a walk. Last Saturday, I took Roxy out. It was only five days ago so I'm quite certain that's what happened.'

'And you didn't see anyone else on your walk?' Geraldine asked.

Ben frowned. 'Well, we passed a few people along the path by the river, but I've no idea who they were. I didn't see anyone I knew, apart from my dog,' he added with a rueful grimace. 'There were just a few people out for a walk. It was a typical Saturday morning. The sun was shining and it was a nice day.'

Geraldine and Ian exchanged a quick glance.

'We have evidence that suggests you were cycling, not walking,' Ian said.

Ben looked up in surprise. 'I don't even own a bicycle,' he replied. 'Not one that works anyway. You're confusing me with someone else.'

'My client has told you all he can,' the solicitor said with an air of finality, nodding her head in what was evidently a nervous tic. 'Unless you are going to charge him, it's time my client went home.'

Ben looked up, fleetingly hopeful, but Ian shook his head.

'Ben Foster, I'm arresting you for the murder of George Gardner.'

'Who?' Ben blurted out. 'Who the hell is he? I don't know anyone called George.'

Ignoring the interruption, Ian continued to read Ben his rights, while the suspect protested and appealed to his lawyer to stop this ridiculous miscarriage of justice.

'You can't arrest me,' he insisted. 'I didn't kill that man. I don't even know who he is. Why won't you listen to me? I'm innocent.'

'That is for a jury to decide,' Ian replied quietly.

'I don't even know anyone called George. Why would I want to kill him? I don't believe this is happening. You're crazy if you think you can pin this murder on me, just because of what happened four years ago. No jury is going to take it seriously and you're going to look like complete idiots and I'll sue you for wrongful arrest and police harassment. I can do that, can't I?' He turned to his solicitor, who nodded without speaking. It wasn't clear if she was nodding in deliberate affirmation, or if it was an involuntary movement. 'Instead of trying to pin this on an innocent man, you need to go and find the killer.'

'We have evidence that places you at the scene of the murder,' Geraldine said.

'Evidence? What evidence? You can't have. That's not possible,' Ben cried out. 'I haven't killed anyone.'

He broke off, frowning, because they all knew he had knocked down and killed a woman four years earlier. Admittedly a jury had decided her death had been an accident, and Ben was innocent of murder, but she had died nonetheless.

'Who is this man George, anyway?' he cried out. 'And what makes you think I had anything to do with his murder? Jesus, I've worked so hard to get my life back on track after – after the accident. You have no idea how hard it's been. Do you really think I'd want to screw it all up again? I'm telling you, I don't even know anyone called George.'

Geraldine leaned forward. 'Ben, have you lost anything lately?'

He shrugged. 'Lost what? I feel like I might be losing my

mind right now. Either that, or everyone here is crazy because this makes no sense.'

'Answer the question,' Geraldine said. 'Have you lost anything lately? Any item of clothing?'

He shook his head, frowning. 'No, I haven't. Now can I please go home?'

'I know the evidence points to Ben but it's possible he's innocent,' Geraldine said when she discussed the case with Eileen that afternoon.

'Tell me how your theory works, exactly,' Eileen replied. 'With Ben's DNA on the scarf which was used to kill George, how do you propose to explain that, if he wasn't there when Ben was killed?'

'It's possible someone else used a scarf that had once belonged to Ben. I'm going to check on social media and ask Christine tomorrow to show me any photos of Ben to see if he's wearing a grey scarf in any of them, and I'll ask if she took any clothes to a charity shop recently.'

'Of course it's technically possible someone else held that scarf with Ben's DNA over George's mouth, without leaving any of his or her own DNA on it, and we certainly need to check that possibility, but you know it'll turn out to be a wild goose chase,' Eileen said. 'We have clear evidence that places Ben at the scene, and he has no alibi for Saturday morning.'

'He says he was walking, not cycling. He doesn't own a bicycle that works.'

'We can't be sure of that.'

'And he has no motive,' Geraldine replied.

'No motive that we know about,' Eileen pointed out. 'We need to look into his connection with George. There has to be one.'

'Can we put out an appeal for information and see if anyone spotted Ben out walking his dog on Saturday?' Geraldine enquired.

She was aware that the chance of finding anyone who

remembered seeing Ben and his dog walking on the towpath on Saturday morning was almost zero, even if he had been there, but Eileen agreed it was worth a try.

'No one wants to see a man convicted of a crime he didn't commit, but the evidence points to Ben, and he has no credible defence,' Eileen added, with an air of finality.

12

BEN SAT ON THE hard bunk, leaning forward, his hands dangling between his knees. It wasn't particularly cold in the cell, but he was shivering and it was an effort to gather his thoughts. He couldn't believe this was happening to him again. Having been arrested once, he had been really careful ever since, determined not to land in trouble again. He had kept well within the speed limit when driving, and had even given up drinking, just in case, because his solicitor had pointed out that it was fortunate he had not been drinking at the time of the accident. Had there been evidence of alcohol in his bloodstream, the outcome of his trial might have been different. But in spite of all his caution, he had been arrested again.

He gazed around at the sickeningly familiar sights: the small metal toilet stinking of shit and bleach, the faded whitewash on the walls, and a compass on the ceiling which he understood was painted on to enable Muslims to face the right direction when they prayed. As though prayers were going to help anyone in there. He stared miserably up at the barred window, too small to clamber through even if he could reach it. He had such a restricted view of the world outside his cell; he struggled against a wave of despair that threatened to engulf him. Gazing out at the distant sky, he wondered what his wife was doing.

Christine would know this was a horrible mistake. She would never believe he was capable of murder. But he had actually killed someone, and the police knew all about it. Of course Christine knew he was responsible for a woman's death, even if it had been an accident. And now he was here again, stuck behind bars, arrested for killing someone else. Anger welled up inside him at the injustice of it all. He didn't deserve this, not after he had been so careful to avoid trouble. He could feel anger building inside his head, like a volcano about to explode, and he had to struggle to control his temper.

He knew that banging on the door and yelling wouldn't help him. Last time he had been in this position, at first he had been too shocked to react. For days he had lain on the hard narrow bunk, too depressed to protest. Only once had he given in to a frenzy of rage and had ended up bruising his knuckles in sheer frustration. His fury had achieved nothing apart from hurting his hand. But what was the point in remaining calm? What was the point of anything? Once the police had got hold of you, they were bound to catch up with you again sooner or later.

He took a deep breath and tried to review his situation calmly. His lawyer looked hopelessly young. He needed someone older and more experienced if he was to have a chance of escaping a conviction this time. The last time he had been banged up, his lawyer, Jerome Carver, had been brilliant, working tirelessly to find character witnesses, and to establish the speed at which he had been travelling. He had even discovered how many cars had been parked along the road, and had found a witness who had identified the exact spot where the victim had stepped out into the road, proving that Ben could neither have seen her, nor stopped in time, even if he had been observing the speed limit.

'It is unreasonable to expect a driver to travel below the speed limit, on the off chance that someone might step out directly in front of his moving vehicle without bothering to look or listen for oncoming traffic,' the lawyer had argued, his black eyes seeming to burn with conviction.

Several members of the jury had nodded, and at that point Ben had begun to hope that, after so many months incarcerated, waiting for his trial, he might finally be released. By checking with different cameras, the lawyer had managed to prove that Ben could not have been driving much above the speed limit, and he challenged police at every turn, twisting their accusations until it really seemed as though Ben was a victim of false arrest. He had felt sorry for himself and, what was more important, the jury had judged him innocent of any serious misdemeanour.

'Who among us can say, hand on heart, that we have never driven less than ten miles over a speed limit?' Jerome had asked.

As he spoke, he had actually placed his hand on his own chest, in a dramatic gesture.

The prosecution had argued strenuously that in driving too fast, Ben had accepted the risks attached to dangerous driving, and must shoulder the responsibility. Otherwise, the lawyer pointed out, a precedent would be set that might cost more lives. But the expressions on the faces of the jury had progressed from impassive, through doubting, to sympathetic. Probably some of them had been fined for speeding themselves. Ben needed to find that same lawyer who had saved him from a custodial sentence once before, and beg him to represent him again. His fate lay in hands of his lawyer. He couldn't rely on the nervous young girl who had been appointed to defend him. He had to speak to his wife and tell her to contact Jerome Carver and persuade him to act for him again. His mind made up, he waited impatiently until he was able to call Christine and tell her what he had been thinking. Her voice sounded very far away, as though she was standing in a vast echoing chamber, although she assured him she was at home. He couldn't hear Roxy bark in the background.

'How are you managing?' she asked.

It was a stupid question, though kindly meant. All he could do was sit on his hard bunk and wait. There was nothing for him to manage.

'Fine, fine,' he lied, doing his best to sound cheerful. 'I'll be back home in no time.'

He enquired how she was coping, and she confessed that she

hadn't yet told her family that he had been arrested again.

'If it comes up, just tell them I'm helping the police with their enquiries,' he said. 'But hopefully I'll be home before anyone even notices I've gone.'

Aware that their time was limited, he instructed her to contact Jerome and secure his services.

'But you're innocent, aren't you? So surely it makes no difference who speaks for you in court?' she asked when he raised the question of the lawyer.

'Don't you want me to get out of here?' he replied, unable to conceal his exasperation.

'Ben, if you're innocent it won't matter who the lawyer is.'

'Surely you can't be that stupid? You must realise that whatever lawyer we have is going to make all the difference?'

'Your innocence will protect you,' she replied doggedly. 'We have to hold on to that. We have to.' She was nearly crying.

'Oh, don't start on one of your bloody religious rants,' he snapped. 'I'm in the hands of the police and I don't trust any of them, not for one minute. They would have had me locked up for knocking down that woman, even though all the evidence pointed to it being an accident, and the courts do whatever the police say.'

'If judges are in the pocket of the police, how come they didn't lock you up last time?'

'Listen,' he said urgently, aware that time was running out, 'I can't talk for much longer. Just do what I ask, will you? Get in touch with Jerome and tell him I need him to defend me. Tell him I'm innocent.'

Before Christine could give him any assurance, he had to ring off.

'I love you,' she said hurriedly.

'Just do it,' he replied, but they had already been cut off.

Furious with Christine for not agreeing with him straightaway, and with himself for failing to raise the question of his lawyer earlier in the call, he followed a uniformed officer back to his cell where he lay down on his bunk, shivering. Christine wanted him to trust in the justice system, but he was not even sure he could trust her to follow his instructions. He had determined not to give in to despair, but as the light outside his window faded, alone in his cell he began to sob. The first time he had stood trial he had been exonerated of anything worse than careless driving. Even so, some people had shunned him, not blatantly, but effectively. After an absence of several months while he had been awaiting trial, he had lost his job, and some of his friends had regarded him with suspicion, even as they voiced sympathy for his ordeal. He understood their reservations. He might have felt the same way himself. He had managed to find another job as a car mechanic at a garage in York where the boss had been understanding.

'I don't give a toss about your accident,' he had said. 'As long as you turn up on time and work like the clappers, we'll get along just fine. I won't stand for any nonsense with calling in sick, or knocking off early, mind. You try any stunts like that and you're history as far as I'm concerned. A day's pay for a day's work.'

He had no choice but to agree to a lower rate of pay than he was used to, and became resigned to having a smaller circle of friends. But how many people were going to give him a second chance in life now that he had been arrested for a second time? Even if he was found not guilty, it was unlikely he could ever return to the life he had worked so hard to rebuild.

13

THE FOLLOWING MORNING, AFTER attending an early briefing, Geraldine returned to Ben's red brick house in Bishopthorpe Road. She hoped Christine might be more inclined to confide in a woman visiting her on her own. The forsythia bush was smothered in even more little yellow flowers than Geraldine remembered seeing two days earlier, and the anemones that lined the path made a colourful display in the bright sunlight. Once again, Roxy let out a series of deep-throated barks as Geraldine reached the front door and rang the bell. She waited for a while before ringing a second time, and at last Christine called out from inside the house.

'Who is it? Who's there? What do you want?'

As soon as Geraldine introduced herself, the door opened a fraction and Christine peered out through the crack. Seeing Geraldine, she pulled the door open with a frown.

'I had to check,' she explained with a miserable grimace. 'Reporters have been pestering me on the phone, day and night. They won't bloody let up. One of them even turned up on the doorstep demanding an interview. I just can't take any more of their questions.' She sounded on the point of tears.

'They can be very intrusive. You'd be wise not to say anything at all to them,' Geraldine advised her. 'Whatever you tell them, it's never going to be enough. It just encourages them to keep at it, and then they'll twist your words into something you never said, but far more sensational, just so they can make a story out of it.'

'Like you'll twist Ben's words in court,' Christine replied, 'to get a conviction.'

Geraldine shook her head, hiding her indignation. 'That's not fair,' she chided the other woman gently. 'Christine, I understand you're under a lot of pressure with Ben being in custody, but the fact remains that someone murdered George Gardner. If it wasn't Ben, the last thing we would want is for a jury to find him guilty. We're not in the business of locking up innocent people, and if the wrong person were to be convicted, that would signal the end of the investigation, meaning a murderer would have got away with a serious crime. That's not what I signed up for when I joined the police force, and I know my colleagues would all say exactly the same thing. If Ben is innocent, you and I are on the same side, and we both want to prove he wasn't involved. If he's guilty, then he has to be put behind bars. I'm working to establish the truth. Nothing else will do.'

'Yeah, yeah,' Christine answered, her voice heavy with sarcasm. 'Sure we're on the same side. We're in this together, aren't we?'

Muttering under her breath, she went to close the door, but Geraldine put out her foot to prevent it closing.

'Christine, you have to believe me, I'm not trying to convict an innocent man. But I came here to speak to you, which means I'm afraid I can't leave until you've answered a few questions.'

'Questions, questions,' Christine grumbled. 'Everyone wants to ask questions. You're here every week with your questions. Do you think you can wear me down until I confess to something my husband didn't do?'

Her words were hardly fair but Geraldine let that go. Antagonising Christine would only make her less likely to co-operate, if that was possible.

'Can I come in?' she asked.

With a resentful glare, Christine opened the door again so that

Geraldine could go inside. Roxy wagged her tail and jumped up excitedly.

'Down, Roxy,' Christine said dully. 'Sure, come on in. You've only arrested my husband on a trumped-up charge. Why wouldn't you be welcome in my house?'

Her shoulders were drooping and her expression was anything but welcoming, but she stepped aside to allow Geraldine to enter. As the front door closed, the phone rang. They both ignored it. Geraldine tried to imagine what it must be like for Christine, being hounded by reporters while knowing that her husband was locked in a police cell from where he might go to prison for many years. It was a miserable situation for anyone to endure.

'Christine,' she began, and hesitated.

There was nothing she could say to lessen the other woman's distress. Geraldine's own discomfort was fleeting and superficial by comparison. She would leave the house in a few minutes and return to her own life, where she wouldn't need to give Christine or Ben another thought once she had written up her report. She would go home to the man she loved and enjoy her evening.

'I'd like to take a look at any photographs you have of Ben,' she said briskly, determined to focus on practicalities.

She followed Christine into a narrow living room furnished with a comfortable leather settee and two matching armchairs. A large television screen stood on a wooden chest beside an ornate wooden fireplace in front of which was an old-fashioned embroidered fire screen in a wooden frame. A few photographs on display on the mantelpiece looked like wedding pictures. Ben was wearing a suit and tie in them, and grinning. He looked very young and optimistic, as though he trusted the world to be wonderful and full of glorious opportunities. Christine's phone was more productive. She had hundreds of images of her husband in a variety of poses, most of which had been taken outside with the dog at his side. Geraldine downloaded them all on to her own phone, scanning quickly through them as she did so. She didn't spot any pictures of Ben wearing a grey scarf, or riding a bicycle, but she would set a constable to study the images carefully to check. In the meantime, she was careful not to mention what she was looking for. Christine was capable of passing key information on to a skilful lawyer who could convince a jury that Ben could have lost the grey scarf shortly before George was murdered with it. That was possible, but it was also quite likely Ben was actually guilty, in which case there was no point in offering him an opportunity to construct a plausible defence in advance. Everyone involved in the police investigation had been strictly forbidden to mention the grey scarf to anyone, and there had been no mention of it in the media. Reporters had been told only that the victim had been suffocated.

'Has Ben lost anything recently?' Geraldine asked, as she handed Christine back her phone.

'His liberty,' Christine replied sourly.

'Have you thrown any of his old clothes out?'

Christine shook her head, frowning. 'I wouldn't throw his things out. What's this about?'

'It's just a routine line of enquiry,' Geraldine lied. 'Does Ben own a bicycle other than the one we've already seen?'

'No.'

Thanking Christine for her co-operation, Geraldine left. She had learned nothing that could help, either to exonerate or to convict Ben. But there was no evidence he had ever worn a grey scarf, nor that he owned a working bicycle, and she felt increasingly uneasy about his arrest.

'There's nothing to suggest he didn't own both,' Eileen pointed out, when Geraldine reported back to the detective chief inspector.

'That's true,' she agreed. 'We don't really know much about him at all.'

'We know he killed a woman four years ago,' Eileen reminded her.

'In a traffic accident that has nothing to do with the current murder investigation,' Geraldine replied.

'And he left his DNA with us when he walked free,' Eileen reminded her.

Geraldine nodded. She wasn't sure why she had wasted an entire afternoon checking through pictures of the suspect. Not finding any image of him wearing a grey scarf proved nothing. But she wished she had found just one picture of him playing in the snow with Roxy, with a grey scarf around his neck, just to put her mind at rest. Still, the evidence against Ben seemed irrefutable, even without any proof he had ever owned a grey scarf. No one could argue that traces of his DNA had been detected on the scarf used to suffocate George. Geraldine could not have explained why that bothered her.

14

'I ALWAYS THOUGHT THAT man was up to no good,' Christine's mother said, as she poured the tea.

She was using the best china, which was decorated with tiny pink roses. Putting the milk jug down, she raised her head and pursed her lips.

Christine's father nodded gravely. 'That's what we always said, isn't it, Hilary? Isn't that just what we always said?'

Her mother handed Christine a cup of tea. 'The first time you brought that man home, we said he was no good for you, didn't we, Derek? Well, maybe this will turn out to be a blessing in disguise.'

'A blessing in disguise?' Christine blurted out indignantly. 'What the hell is that supposed to mean?'

'We'll have no swearing in this house, thank you very much,' her mother snapped, reaching for the cake and offering it to her husband. 'And no taking of the Lord's name in vain. It's seed cake, Derek.'

'What did you mean, it's a blessing for my husband to be – where he is – helping the police?'

Her mother nodded primly and took a sip of her tea. 'I mean that you might finally come to your senses and see that man for what he is. An atheist.' She enunciated the word with a grimace of disgust. 'He never belonged in this family.'

'Your mother's right. He's a layabout,' her father said bluntly. 'There's no point in beating about the bush. We all know what he is. No one in our family has ever been in trouble with the police before. You were quite right to bring this up, Hilary.'

'And now that man has dragged your name through the mud,' her mother went on. 'And it's not as if this is the first time. Do I need to remind you that four years ago we stood by you? But now this. It's too much, Christine. This time it's not dangerous driving he's been accused of. It's murder. Murder! Now have a slice of cake. It's seed cake.'

'I don't want any cake, thank you.'

Scowling, her mother sipped her tea.

'What are you talking about?' Christine went on, without touching her cup. 'You all seem to be convinced Ben is guilty, when he's no such thing. Who are you, anyway? Are you his judge and jury?'

'The fact is, he's been arrested,' her sister pointed out, her pitying look more maddening than their parents' censure. 'Poor you. Poor poor you. This is absolutely the most terrible thing that has ever happened to our family. Honestly, Chrissie, I don't know how you've put up with him all this time. I can't bear to see you suffering like this.'

'Francesca's right. The man's a monster,' her mother added.

'There's nothing to put up with,' Christine replied, glaring at her sister. 'Ben is just helping the police, that's all. He'll be back home soon. So you can all stop being so judgemental. As for you,' she turned on her mother, 'who do you think you are to speak about an innocent man like that? Are you without sin, to start casting stones like you're God almighty?'

Her father sat forward in his armchair. 'Now, now,' he said, 'there's no need to take on like that. Your mother is only trying to help you. Don't take any notice, Hilary. She always had a mouth on her.'

Christine turned to her sister. 'And I can do without your fake pity.'

'Francesca is trying to be a friend to you as well as a good sister,' her brother-in-law protested, waving a pale hand ineffectually in the air.

'There's no need to pretend with us,' her mother added. 'We all love you, Christine. We're on your side. We're your family. That man was never any good, that's all we're saying. And now his crimes have found him out. Who knows how many other people he's killed? And it could be you next.'

'Oh for goodness sake,' Christine cried out. 'Just listen to yourselves. This is typical. Ben's helping the police with an investigation and you're all talking about him as though he's been arrested.'

She wasn't sure what prompted her to lie like that, but the words slipped out before she could stop herself.

'We've seen the news, and we can read the papers,' her sister said quietly. 'You can't hide the truth forever.'

'And do you really believe all the lies the media come up with?' Christine replied. 'Then you're even more stupid than I thought.'

'I don't think you should speak to your sister like that,' her brother-in-law said feebly.

They drank their tea in silence for a moment, while her father's face grew red with irritation, and she suspected he was struggling to control his temper. If she said one more word against her mother, he would probably erupt in rage and order her to leave the house shouting at her for daring to speak to her mother like that. They had been through it all before, when she had told them she was going to marry Ben, in spite of her family's objections to her godless fiancé. She was tempted to stand up and raise her voice, demanding to know by what right they felt entitled to pass judgement on her husband. But something held her back. If Ben was found guilty, she would have no one else to turn to for support. Without the backing of her own family, she would be utterly alone. In that moment, she realised that she no longer believed Ben was going to walk free, not this time. Whether or not he was really guilty, he might have to serve a prison sentence, and she had no idea what would happen to her.

'So, now that's out of the way, I don't think you should wait any longer,' her mother said.

'Mother, she has to leave a decent interval,' her sister protested gently. 'She can hardly turn her back on him as soon as he's in trouble. He is still her husband.'

'As soon as he's in trouble?' her mother repeated. 'What do you mean? Hasn't Christine stood by that unbeliever all these years?' She turned to Christine. 'You need to act, while you're still young enough to find another husband and have children, as the Good Lord commanded. We'll find you a decent man who will take good care of you. This time, you'll be more careful, I'm sure. And we're here to help you. We'll have a word with the vicar tomorrow. He'll be able to advise you. The sooner we set things in motion the better. No one is going to blame you. You're an innocent victim of that man's villainy. Thank the Lord he never raised his hand against you.'

Her father nodded. 'Hilary's right. What use is a man when he's behind bars? Who knows when he'll be released.'

'And even when he has served his sentence, how is he going to earn a living after all this?' her mother added. 'No, it's for the best, Christine.'

With a shock, Christine realised they were suggesting she start divorce proceedings against Ben. She slammed her cup down, careless that she was slopping tea on the tablecloth, and stormed out without another word. Not until she reached home did she break down in tears.

'You don't think Ben's a murderer, do you, Roxy?' she asked, through her sobs.

She ruffled the dog's ears. Roxy's low growls rose to a whimper when he heard Ben's name, as though even he suspected his master was bad. Christine leaned over and buried her face in his warm fur. As she gave way to a fit of weeping, her phone rang.

15

'PLEASE, GERALDINE. WE CAN'T get rid of her.'

Geraldine looked up and frowned at the young constable who had interrupted her in her re-examination of the photos Ben's wife had saved on her phone. Geraldine had gone through them several times, without finding any sign of a grey scarf on either the suspect or his wife, and she was looking at them again, even though she knew there was no point.

'Is she hysterical?' Geraldine asked.

'No, she seems perfectly calm. I mean, I don't know if the doctor has given her something to keep her quiet, but on a scale of robotic to overexcited I'd say she's right at the robotic end, and definitely not hysterical.'

'Just listen to what she has to say, and then send her home.'

'I would, but she insists on speaking to you. She asked for you by name, and says she won't leave until she's seen you. No one else will do.'

'Oh, very well.'

Heaving a sigh, Geraldine left her desk and went to the interview room where Michelle Gardner was waiting for her. She found the widow sitting very upright, waiting patiently.

'Ah, Inspector, thank you for seeing me,' Michelle said, smiling pleasantly, as though she was paying Geraldine a social call.

She was wearing an old-fashioned flared skirt similar to the one she had been wearing when Geraldine had first met her. Above her dull brown skirt she was wearing a short fitted black jacket over a white shirt. Perhaps she had chosen sober colours in view of her recent loss. Other than that, her husband's death did not appear to have disturbed her in any way. Her black leather shoes were polished, her hair was clean and neat, and she sat with her hands neatly folded in her lap. It was not quite a week since her husband had been murdered, making it difficult to believe she could have come to terms with her loss so soon after his violent death. On balance, Geraldine concluded that since her own visit to the doctor, the widow had been given a mild sedative to help her through the initial difficult period of grieving.

'How can I help you?' Geraldine enquired as she took a seat opposite Michelle.

Michelle's smile failed to mask her latent excitement, which made it even more probable that she had been given medication of some description.

'You've arrested someone,' Michelle said.

Geraldine did not answer immediately, preferring to wait and hear what the widow would say next.

'It's the killer, the man who murdered my poor George, isn't it? You've got him, haven't you?'

'A man is helping us with our enquiries,' Geraldine replied carefully.

'Don't give me that slop,' Michelle barked suddenly, her mask of composure slipping. 'Helping you with your enquiries indeed. We both know that means bugger all. Don't treat me like I'm some sort of imbecile. I can read the papers. I know it was another cyclist who killed George, and I know you've got him locked up.' She nodded. 'It didn't take you long, did it? Well, good for you. George didn't deserve what happened to him. He was a good man. The best. Speak to anyone who knew him, and you won't find a soul who will have a single bad word to say about him. I'm right, aren't I?'

Geraldine inclined her head. 'He was liked by everyone who knew him,' she said.

She didn't add that, by all accounts, Michelle's husband had been a harmless little man. Perhaps, after all, that was the best anyone could ever hope to attain, and by remaining inoffensive he had in fact been as good as it was possible for a man to be.

'He was a good man,' Michelle repeated fiercely.

'Yes, from everything we've been told, he was a good man.'

'He was the best,' Michelle replied.

There was something faintly manic in her insistence. Not for the first time, Geraldine wondered if she was crazy. Certainly her clothes were eccentric, and her demeanour was odd. Geraldine recalled how Michelle had gone straight to where her husband's helmet was tucked away out of sight in the garage. But if Michelle had hidden the cycling helmet from her husband, she would hardly have revealed that she knew exactly where it was concealed. Something about her simply didn't add up. Michelle began talking again, and Geraldine had to force herself to focus on her words.

'I have to see him. I have to face him across a table, just me and him, alone in a room together. You can't refuse to grant me this one request.'

'I'm sorry? I'm not sure what you mean.'

'I'm talking about George's killer. I need to see him.'

'I'm afraid that's not possible.'

'You don't understand,' Michelle became plaintive. 'I have to speak to him. Let me in his cell, just for a moment.'

'No, I'm sorry, I don't think we can allow that. Unless you're related to him?'

'Related to him? What do you mean? He killed my husband. How much closer could we be?'

Geraldine hid her perplexity as she repeated that such a meeting was out of the question.

'You don't understand,' Michelle repeated. She was pleading now, her voice raw with a desperate determination. 'I have to speak to him. I have to know why he did it. Unless I ask him,

I'll never know why this happened. Just let me into his cell so I can look him in the eye and tell him he killed the best man who ever lived. What possible reason could he have had for doing what he did?'

She was no longer attempting to control herself. Her eyes shone with unshed tears, and she reached out as though she was going to seize Geraldine by the hand.

'Michelle, I understand all this must be very painful for you.'

'No,' Michelle cried out in a sudden paroxysm of emotion. 'You don't understand. How can you possibly understand? George was more than my husband. He was my life. He was everything to me. Without him there is nothing for me. Nothing.'

'I'm truly sorry, but what you're asking is simply not possible.'

'Please. I've lost my husband. All I'm asking is for one moment alone with his killer. Is that so much to ask?'

Geraldine wondered what this grief-crazed woman might do to Ben, given one moment alone with him. Quite possibly she intended to kill him and then kill herself. But her intention would have to remain forever obscure, because she would not be allowed to enter Ben's cell at all, let alone by herself.

Geraldine stood up, to indicate the meeting was over. 'I'm very sorry, Michelle, but we don't yet know who killed your husband and I'm afraid we can't let you speak to the man who is helping us. It goes against all the rules that govern our conduct, and the detective chief inspector would never allow such a flagrant breach of protocol. So you see, it's out of my hands, and no one else is going to agree to your request. Like the rest of us, you'll have to wait until his killer is arrested and stands trial. In the meantime, you will just have to be patient. I'm sorry I can't help you.'

16

HE FINISHED THE HOUSEWORK and gazed around at his handiwork with a flicker of pride. Whatever the task, he liked to do a good job. All the crumbs and flecks of fluff on the carpet had gone, and the surfaces on his furniture gleamed in the soft light that fell on them through the net curtains. Rejecting his usual armchair, he sat on the floor, hugging his knees and grinning to himself. After a moment he heard a faint tune and realised with surprise that he was humming to himself. He would have to guard against doing that in public. He had to be careful not to draw attention to himself. For now, alone in his house, he could sing in triumph as loudly as he liked.

It was hard not to gloat. His outing had been an unqualified success. George was dead. There could be no doubt about that. His killer was alive, and George was most decidedly dead. No longer his dreaded foe, Death had become an accomplice in a dark game. The truth about George's death was their secret. There was no way Death was going to want to claim him now. Having taken the bold step of sacrificing the life of one insignificant man to remove any risk to his own survival, he was safe, at least for a while. Yes, he was entitled to gloat. More than that, he was going to celebrate. A week had passed since his outing, and no one else had the faintest idea that he was responsible for George's death. Only Death itself knew, and they were partners in what had become an impenetrable mystery to everyone else.

He knew from reports in the media that a man had been

arrested for the murder. Over the course of the week since George's death, local papers in particular seemed to have become obsessed with the story. Presumably there was not much else going on locally that equalled a murder for excitement, or perhaps the police had deliberately passed information on to journalists. After all, it was understandable they would want to make public the success of their investigation. 'A man is helping the police with their enquiries' had progressed to 'A suspect is being questioned'. A less reputable website which favoured click bait headlines had even announced 'York murderer arrest', although the brief article that followed made no mention of an arrest and merely repeated what was published elsewhere in less sensationalist reports. But it was clear the police were satisfied the case was closed, which meant that he was off the hook. It really was wonderful the way things had worked out so perfectly for him. It was no more than he deserved, after all his careful planning and his courage in carrying out the task. It was only a shame that he was unable to boast about his success to anyone else. But Death knew everything and Death was on his side, at least for now.

He knew the exhilaration of exercising power over Death wouldn't last. Sooner or later his fear would return and, in the end, Death would claim him. All he could do was postpone the dreadful moment of his own demise. But he shelved those thoughts for now, happy to enjoy the freedom he had won for himself by killing George Gardner. It was an apt punishment. Soon he would have to start planning his next project, but he knew that none would be as fitting, or as satisfying, as killing George Gardner. George's death had done so much more than merely stave off his own fears; it had been just retribution. The police, and the law they served, were useless, because they had missed the truth, but that wasn't his problem. On the contrary, their clumsiness in leaping to conclusions and grasping the easiest solution had served his purpose because he had killed

George and was free. No one even suspected he was guilty. Yes, it was time to celebrate.

He was not much of a drinker, but today he opened a bottle of Champagne. After a couple of glasses he felt his head spinning, but he persevered. He was not one to give up on anything before he finished. He had proved that to himself in his persistence in carrying out his plot to kill George. It hadn't been easy. It had been risky, but he had carried on, right to the end. He was heroic. Triumphant. It was not his head that was moving, but the walls. He realised he was sitting on his chair. He must have sat there automatically after going to fetch the bottle of Champagne. It was a pity he wasn't still on the floor where there would not be far to fall if he lost his balance. The prospect that he might slide off his chair on to the floor suddenly struck him as hilarious, and he heard himself laughing out loud. Just in time he put his glass on the table before he pitched forward on to the carpet where he lay, still laughing, and safe from harm. The carpet brushed his cheek like a caress as he turned his head. Its gentle touch brought tears to his eyes, and he was overwhelmed by a sudden rush of grief. For a while he lay there, weeping for the only woman who had ever truly loved him.

Tomorrow he would begin to think about his next outing, and it would be another brilliant success. Feeling slightly sick, he closed his eyes and drifted into an uneasy sleep; terror lapped in the shadows of his dreams where Death was waiting for him.

17

EILEEN STARED AT GERALDINE and tapped a pen irritably on her desk.

'It seems you are not prepared to be convinced by anything as paltry as evidence,' she said. 'Very well, Geraldine, what do you suggest we do?'

Geraldine hesitated. She was reluctant to annoy her senior officer with unnecessary fussing, but a man's liberty was at stake. Despite her determination to see Ben behind bars, Eileen would be the first to want him released should he turn out to be innocent after all. If there was even the slightest chance he had not killed George, they had to pursue every possible avenue to establish the truth. Quickly Geraldine outlined her proposal to the detective chief inspector.

'If anyone saw him while he was out walking by the river on Saturday morning, as he claims, it has to be better to find that out now, rather than in the course of a trial.'

Eileen nodded briskly. 'Very well. We'll have the appeal broadcast this afternoon. I doubt very much whether anyone will come forward but you are right, we have to make sure.'

Later that day, in a short item at the end of the local news, an appeal was made for anyone who had been walking along the towpath by the river near the Millennium Bridge on Saturday morning to contact the police station in Fulford Road. A team of constables were tasked with taking calls, and extra officers were drafted in to help answer the phones. Any appeal to the public inevitably provoked a spate of spurious responses. There were people who could not really help at all but were desperate to be useful, along with a host of crackpots and cranks, mediums who could commune with the dead, and people who listened to voices that they alone could hear. In among all the calls, there was a slim chance a genuine witness might come forward. Ben was described in the broadcast as a man wearing a grey jacket, accompanied by a brown and white terrier on a lead. The only distinguishing features of the pair were Roxy's bright red collar and lead, but even they were nothing remarkable.

Ariadne agreed with Eileen, as did almost everyone else on the investigating team.

'There will be gazillions of people who call in to say they've walked along there, maybe on Saturday, and they might have seen a man in a grey jacket,' Ariadne said to Geraldine when they went to the canteen together at lunchtime. 'We're on a hiding to nothing with looking for someone who noticed a man in a grey jacket. But it doesn't matter, because we've got Ben's DNA on the murder weapon, and that's enough for me. I know you're not a hundred per cent convinced and sure there's always a chance we've got it wrong, but in this case I honestly can't see how, given the evidence. I'm glad we picked up the killer so quickly. It's so hard to focus on wedding arrangements while working on a murder investigation. You are coming, aren't you?'

'Of course. How are the arrangements coming along?'

Ariadne sighed. 'Terribly.'

'Really? How so?'

'Oh, it's this family feud. I'm telling you, it's doing my head in. My uncles are really insane. It's so ridiculous. It goes back years and years.' She shook her head. 'I don't think anyone has the faintest idea how it started, but no one is prepared to end it.'

Geraldine put down her fork and gazed at her friend thoughtfully. As far as they had been able to ascertain, George had no enemies, but maybe there was something in his past, something going back years and years, that had caused the recent assault on him. 'And they won't forgive and forget?' she asked. 'They still want to kill each other?'

'What?' Ariadne asked, taken aback. 'No one's talking about killing anyone. They just refuse to sit at the same table together, but both of them expect to sit at the top table. What am I supposed to do? My mother's no help. She just rants on and on about her brothers ruining the wedding of her only daughter. I don't even want them there. It's not as if I ever see them. They haven't even met Nico.'

Ian shook his head when Geraldine shared her thoughts with him that evening. 'What's this all about? Are you off on one of your flights of fancy again?'

Geraldine was surprised by his response. She always thought of herself as calm and rational.

'It's not a flight of fancy,' she replied crossly. 'I just think we need to dig around into George's past a bit and see if he ever seriously upset anyone.'

Ian nodded. 'Makes sense,' he agreed. 'And while we're at it, we should take a look at his wife's past as well, see if there's anything there that could have a bearing on what happened to him.'

They spent several hours researching George and Michelle but found nothing to connect either of them with Ben.

'Take a look at this,' Ian said at last, holding up his iPad so Geraldine could see the screen. 'I found it in the archives of the local paper.'

'That is interesting,' Geraldine agreed, seeing the headline.

She leaned forward and read through a short article that related how Michelle had been engaged to another man before she met George.

'They were more than just engaged,' Ian said. 'She almost married him, but then she jilted him at the altar. That's why the story made it into the paper. It's the same name and it could be her face, although it's not a great picture.'

Geraldine peered over his shoulder at a grainy black and white photograph of George's wife standing beside another man.

'Same kind of skirt,' Geraldine added under her breath. 'That's her all right. Look at her wedding outfit.'

Geraldine and Ian stared at one another, considering the possible implications of his discovery.

'Is it really possible he still held a torch for her, after thirteen years?' Ian asked.

Geraldine smiled, thinking how long she and Ian had loved one another before he divorced his wife and they were finally able to live together.

'But why kill him all these years later?' Ian asked. 'Why wait until now?'

'Who knows? People can harbour grudges for a lifetime.'

'But to kill him? It seems a bit extreme after so long.'

'I know, but maybe something happened to rekindle his resentment.'

Michelle's first fiancé was a GP named Rodney Gilbert. After his engagement with Michelle, he had never married, and it was feasible he had been emotionally scarred by his failed love affair with a woman who liked to wear flared skirts.

'Let's have a look into Rodney and maybe see what he has to say for himself,' Geraldine suggested. 'Here's hoping he turns out to be a potential suspect.'

Ian grunted. 'And in the meantime, we have evidence to place Ben at the scene, so you can relax, which is all to the good, seeing as we have the rest of this evening to spend together.' Smiling, he pulled her towards him and kissed her.

18

THE NEXT DAY BEING Sunday, Ian dropped Geraldine at the railway station in York in time for the nine forty-five train to London, where she was meeting her twin sister, Helena, for lunch. Identical at birth, they could not have grown up into more contrasting women. They had only met as adults, by which time Geraldine was pursuing a successful career as a police detective. Meanwhile Helena had followed a very different path, which had led to her becoming addicted to heroin. Geraldine had never asked for any details of the crimes her sister had committed to support her habit before they met. Now Helena had gone through rehab, thanks to Geraldine's intervention, and had survived to live free of addiction. They had not seen each other for several months, but the time apart made no difference. Every day Helena resisted the lure of her former habit, Geraldine was relieved. But the fear never left her. She knew it must be worse for her sister.

Helena had moved to a bedsit in Finsbury Park, and they agreed to meet for lunch in Granary Square, round the corner from King's Cross Station. The train arrived on time, and Geraldine hurried out of the station and along King's Boulevard to Granary Square. It was a warm day, and a few small children were playing in the central fountains, screaming when the cold water splashed them, while all around the square people were seated outside at tables, or on steps beside the canal. It was a carefree scene with people out enjoying themselves, and Geraldine felt as though she had entered a different world, far away from the murder investigation. It made a welcome break from thinking about George and Michelle, and Ben and Christine, and Rodney who lived alone and had once been engaged to George's eccentric widow.

Looking around, she caught sight of Helena, waving at her from a table outside the most expensive restaurant on the square. Geraldine smiled. That was typical of her sister. Of course Geraldine would foot the bill, but she didn't begrudge Helena the treat. Geraldine had enjoyed a privileged life. Her father had been a successful man and, despite her parents' divorce, she had wanted for nothing while she was growing up. By contrast, Helena had lived in abject straits with their birth mother, scrounging for scraps and prey to drug pushers and pimps. Geraldine was aware that, had their upbringings been reversed, she herself might have ended up on the street, begging for money to support her drug habit, while Helena could have become an educated and successful career woman. Geraldine was lucky to have been given up for adoption by a biological mother who had not given her other daughter away, only because Helena had been a sickly child and not expected to live long.

Geraldine took a seat at the scrubbed wooden table opposite Helena, and smiled at her sister's uncharacteristically healthy appearance.

'You're looking well,' Geraldine said.

It was her customary greeting to her sister, but this time she meant it. Helena looked less washed out than usual, and although hardly plump, she appeared to have filled out a little.

'I suppose I am well,' Helena replied cagily.

'You look healthier than I've ever seen you,' Geraldine added encouragingly.

Helena didn't answer, but stared at Geraldine with a faintly smug expression. Geraldine was skilled in dealing with people in general yet, despite her training in handling members of the public, she found her twin baffling. She lowered her eyes.

When she glanced up she was surprised to see that Helena was grinning at her.

'Well, I only went and did it,' Helena announced, with an air of triumph.

'Went and did what?' Geraldine enquired cautiously, wary of putting her foot in it.

'I only went and got myself a job. A proper job, innit? Not shlepping gear around for some ponce. This is a real job. It's like, well, it's like a proper job, innit?'

Geraldine smiled. 'That's fantastic. What's the job?'

Helena's grin broadened. 'Not as what you'd think much of, I know, but still, I done it.' She paused and glanced at Geraldine through lowered lids, and a crafty expression flitted across her ravaged face. 'I knew you'd be chuffed. And what's more, I'm moving.'

'Moving?'

Helena nodded. 'Somewhere better, now I got proper work an' all.'

Geraldine paused. If Helena lost her job, Geraldine might still be committed to paying a higher rent than she was now covering. On the other hand, she was reluctant to do anything that might discourage Helena from wanting to become independent, psychologically if not financially. Working was a huge step forward for her.

'How much is the rent in your new place?' she asked.

The figure was higher than Geraldine expected, but she could afford it.

'Where is it?' she asked.

'It's in a nice road,' Helena beamed, suddenly excited. 'Nicer than anywhere I've ever lived. It won't look much to you, but it suits me fine. I can take you there after lunch if you like. Only we can't hang about because I got to sign for it this afternoon.'

Geraldine had hoped Helena had suggested meeting because they hadn't seen one another for a while, not because she wanted

Geraldine to help with her increased rent. But Helena looked happier than Geraldine had ever seen her, and she seemed to be trying to sort her life out.

'I'd love to see it,' Geraldine replied, swallowing her disappointment. 'So, tell me about your new job.'

As Helena began to talk about the independent arts and crafts shop where she would be working, Geraldine felt a dizzying rush of happiness. She had never thought she would see her sister looking and sounding so positive about anything.

19

AT THE BRIEFING THE following morning, Eileen was keen to focus on Ben, who had had both the means and the opportunity to murder George. All that was missing from the police case against him was a motive.

'Not that we really need to know why he did it,' Eileen added. 'Sometimes the reason is never clear. But it would help us tie things up if we understood what prompted the attack.'

Geraldine and Ian questioned Ben again. He shuffled into the interview room, his eyes red from lack of sleep, his shoulders bowed in resignation. When he had first been apprehended, after his car accident, the police reports said he had been shocked and angry. Now he seemed like a man beaten. This time he was accompanied by a fast-talking lawyer in his forties. Jerome Carver had piercing brown eyes and slicked-back hair, and he was wearing an expensive suit.

'We know you killed him, Ben,' Ian said. 'We just want to know why you did it.'

Ben shook his head. 'I never killed anyone,' he said. 'That woman I knocked down wasn't my fault, and since then I've had no brushes with death, accidental or otherwise.'

'My client stood trial for that fatality and was found not guilty,' Jerome cut in. 'His previous accident has no bearing on your current investigation.'

The lawyer cut off every further attempt to question Ben, with the words, 'My client has already answered that question'. Eventually, he complained the interview was becoming tiresome.

'Unless you have something new to ask my client, or any new evidence to present, I suggest we terminate this interview. He has told you he was not riding a bicycle on the morning of the murder, and he did not kill anyone. He has clearly been charged in error and we are pressing for his immediate release.'

'Press away,' Ian said. 'But we know he's guilty and the court will hear the evidence against him.'

'Flimsy evidence,' Jerome replied, waving his hand as though to dismiss Ian's words. 'You have nothing to prove my client was responsible for this murder, because he had nothing to do with it. My client never even met the victim. What possible reason could he have for wanting to kill him? It makes no sense. And we all know that juries are not swayed by trumped-up charges.'

'Why would we want to see Ben convicted if he's innocent?' Geraldine asked. 'That's what makes no sense.'

'You need a perpetrator, but you're not getting one like this,' Jerome replied promptly.

'Do you really think we'd try and frame an innocent man just to see someone convicted?' Geraldine asked.

Ian leaned forward and spoke very slowly, staring at Ben. Taking her cue from Ian, Geraldine kept her eyes fixed on Ben who didn't react when he heard that George had been suffocated with a grey scarf.

'You seem to think that has some significance,' Jerome began.

'The scarf had Ben's DNA on it,' Ian said with an air of finality.

'Well, I might have had a grey scarf once, but I don't any more,' Ben replied.

'No, because you left it at the scene after you suffocated George Gardner.'

'What? No. I never did that,' Ben protested.

Jerome requested a brief moment alone with his client, after which Ben refused to say another word, leaving it to his lawyer to insist that his client had not owned a scarf for a long time, and the evidence was purely circumstantial. It was quickly apparent they were wasting their time in pointless arguments, and Ben was returned to his cell, whining that he wanted to go home.

'That Jerome Carver is a tricky customer,' Ian said when they went to speak to Eileen.

'Yes, Carver's the one who got Ben off his previous charge,' the detective chief inspector replied.

'His argument is that Ben didn't know George and had no possible reason for wanting him dead, and to be fair, the scarf only proves that Ben wore it, not that he was wearing it at the time of the murder,' Geraldine said. 'He as good as said that the defence will have it dismissed as circumstantial evidence, and it's true that by itself it doesn't make a watertight case. And I still can't help questioning why he would have left it behind, if he really did kill George.'

'There could be any number of reasons for that,' Ian said. 'Panic, or carelessness.'

'That's just speculation,' Geraldine replied. 'It still doesn't prove anything.'

'Which is why we have to uncover his motive,' Eileen insisted. 'We have to look deeper into his past, and also look into his wife's past. There must be a clue in there somewhere. All we have to do is find it. And when we do, he'll know it's all over, and he'll start to co-operate.'

Meanwhile, Geraldine was keen to question Rodney Gilbert, the man who had been engaged to Michelle before she married George.

'Do you really think he might have harboured a grudge against George? After thirteen years?' Eileen asked, clearly as doubtful as Ian had been.

But, like Ian, she agreed he was worth investigating. That afternoon, Geraldine set to work. It was growing late by the time her eye was caught by an item of information she came across online.

'Look at this,' she cried out suddenly.

'That is interesting,' Ariadne agreed, staring at Geraldine's screen.

Geraldine went to see Ian.

He looked up wearily when she entered his office. 'What is it?'

'Rodney Gilbert is a GP,' she began.

'Yes, I know. So?'

'Can you guess who's registered as his patient? Ben Foster.'

Ian's eyes brightened with interest. 'So you're saying Rodney could have persuaded Ben to kill George?'

'Let's assume Ben is the killer, given the DNA we found at the scene. All that's been missing is a motive. Well, here we have a man who might well have had a motive for wanting George dead, and now we know he was in contact with the man we believe committed the murder.'

Ian's eyes narrowed. 'So you think it's possible Rodney paid Ben to kill George?'

'Perhaps Ben needed money.'

'Let's look into Ben's finances, and see if we can find any unusual activity.'

A team spent the rest of the afternoon searching but found no sign that Rodney had paid Ben anything. Both accounts were investigated without any significant sums being traced. Nevertheless, the connection was still there, linking Ben to Rodney. They went to see Eileen, armed with new information.

'We've established a connection between Ben and Rodney,' Geraldine said.

Eileen looked up.

'We know Michelle dumped Rodney to marry George,' Geraldine went on.

'Not only that,' Ian added. 'Michelle left Rodney at the altar, humiliating him in front of his whole family and all his friends. So he might well have harboured a grudge against George.'

'But after all these years?' Eileen murmured, screwing up her eyes in disbelief.

'The point is, he could have had a motive for wanting to kill George in revenge, punishing Michelle at the same time,' Ian said.

'Why wait so long?' Eileen asked.

'That we don't know,' Geraldine admitted, 'and there's no trace of any money changing hands, although Rodney did occasionally withdraw quite large sums which he appears to have spent on cars.'

'How many cars does he have?' Eileen asked.

'He kept changing his car,' Ian said.

'Let's check his medical records and find out when Ben last went to see Rodney,' Eileen said. 'Good work. This is definitely worth following up. All that was missing was a motive,' she added thoughtfully.

20

As soon as they had finished speaking to Eileen, Geraldine went to Rodney's surgery. It was near the police station in Fulford Road. Since it was a sunny day, she decided to walk there. She passed a small group of women standing at a bus stop, chatting, and wondered if they were on their way to work or going out shopping. She could have been invisible for all the notice they took of her as she passed by. Watching them wistfully, she thought that it was a long time since she had stood with a small group of women, idly chatting and joking. Virtually all of her social interaction was with colleagues, and more often than not they were discussing a murder investigation. Even her personal life was filled with work, now that she was living with a fellow detective inspector. Not for the first time, she questioned her decision to surrender her entire life to the pursuit of justice for the victims of murder. It was an important job, but there was more to life than obsessing over death.

The receptionist at the surgery informed her that Dr Gilbert was not in, but she was able to speak to his partner, a middle-aged woman who smiled easily at her as she took a seat.

'How can I help you?' the doctor asked.

'I'm not here about a sick person,' Geraldine told her, holding up her identity card. 'I'd like to enquire about a patient who's registered with Dr Gilbert.'

The doctor's demeanour grew distant. 'I'm afraid we can't divulge any confidential medical information, unless you have a warrant to seize our records.'

'No, no, it's nothing like that. I just want to ask when a certain patient last came to the surgery. The name is Ben Foster.'

The doctor looked faintly worried. 'I can't tell you anything about his condition, you understand.'

'Just a date would be really helpful,' Geraldine said. 'When was he last here?'

The doctor hesitated, frowning. Then she turned to her computer monitor with a sigh and typed in Ben's name. After a moment she looked back at Geraldine and told her Ben had seen Dr Gilbert three weeks ago. That was all Geraldine needed to know. Thanking the doctor, she left.

Back at the police station, Geraldine and Ian had to wait for Jerome Carver to arrive before they could question Ben again. At last they were all present.

'I hope this won't take long,' Jerome said pleasantly as they sat down. 'I have a dinner engagement and must be off shortly.'

'Why did you go and see Dr Gilbert three weeks ago?' Geraldine demanded, without any preamble.

'What?' Ben asked, seemingly startled by her directness as much as by the question.

Geraldine repeated the question.

'I don't see that's any business of yours,' Ben replied sullenly.

'We'll decide what is and what isn't relevant to our enquiries,' Geraldine said evenly.

'Just answer the question,' Ian snapped.

Ben glanced at his lawyer who requested a few moments alone with his client.

'Very well, but don't be long,' Ian said. 'We'd hate to keep you from your dinner.'

After a few moments muttering together, Jerome recalled them.

'Well, Ben, why did you go and see Dr Gilbert?' Ian demanded as soon as he and Geraldine had taken their seats.

'Well, all right. It's no big secret. I've had a cough since January that I can't seem to shake off. My wife thought it might be an allergy, but it's as well to be sure, so I made an appointment to get it checked out. But Dr Gilbert didn't do anything about it. He didn't refer me on to anyone, or send me for tests, or anything. He just told me to come back in six weeks if it was no better. But I'd already had it for more than six weeks. I mean, if I'd gone to see him as soon as it started, I'd be having tests already, wouldn't I?'

He seemed to feel genuinely aggrieved by his treatment.

'I take it that's all for now?' Jerome said, shifting in his chair and glancing pointedly at his watch. 'I'm sure you can verify what my client has told you by referring to his medical records. And now, is it time to terminate this ridiculous interview? I have to say, this kind of intrusive harassment is hardly likely to help your case, Inspector.'

Ian leaned forward. 'What else did you and Dr Gilbert discuss? We know what happened, so you might as well come clean.'

'It will be better for you if you tell us everything,' Geraldine added half-heartedly.

Ben shook his head, looking puzzled. 'My athlete's foot,' he replied. 'I asked him what to do about my athlete's foot. But I don't see what that's got to do with you. And I've asked for my athlete's foot cream that I keep by my bed, but no one's listening to me.' He turned to his lawyer. 'Can't you do something? Christine could bring it in if you ask her. She knows where it is. Seriously, it's so itchy, it's driving me nuts. It keeps me awake at night and it's getting worse in here.'

'Take no notice of their questions,' Jerome said to Ben. 'They obviously have nothing or they wouldn't be fishing so desperately for information.' He turned to Geraldine. 'You need to attend to my client's medical condition.' He sighed and glanced at his watch again. 'Now I really think we've heard enough of this nonsense. I shall be lodging a complaint against you for harassment, lack of care, and infringement of my client's privacy, if this happens again.'

Scowling at Jerome, Ian formally terminated the interview.

'Well done,' Jerome said as he made his way to the door. 'You've established that my client has athlete's foot. That is certainly a brilliant piece of detective work. I'm glad you don't believe in wasting time.'

'Not just athlete's foot. There's my cough as well,' Ben added. 'I need to see a doctor.'

'Oh put a sock in it,' Ian muttered under his breath so that only Geraldine could hear.

They returned to Ian's office to discuss what had transpired.

'You have to admit that seemed to be a waste of time,' Ian said. 'He struck me as genuine enough, although he could be lying, and we still have to check out the doctor.'

'Until we try something we don't know whether it's going to be useful or not.'

'True,' Ian admitted. 'It's just that it feels as though we're constantly floundering around in the dark with nothing to go on.'

Geraldine nodded. 'We may end up just having to accept that we'll never know why Ben did it.'

'If anyone had told you before you took the job how much time you would spend chasing around to no purpose, would you have looked for an alternative career?' Ian asked.

Geraldine shrugged. 'So what is the alternative? I mean, not for me, but someone who has to investigate serious crimes, which inevitably means spending hours and hours chasing up cul-de-sacs before we hit on the right path. Someone has to do it, and we have to keep going, or society would descend into chaos.'

'I'm not sure we're that far off it now,' Ian replied with a rueful smile.

That evening, while Ian was banging about in the kitchen cooking dinner, Geraldine phoned her adopted sister, Celia. As always, her sister was pleased to hear from her.

'Geraldine, it's been too long,' she cried out.

Geraldine wasn't irritated by Celia trotting out her customary complaint. Quite the opposite; for the first time she appreciated that her sister wanted to see her. Years had passed since Geraldine had moved away from Kent, where her sister still lived, but Celia had not given up her attempts to persuade Geraldine to return to the area where they had grown up together. Only now Geraldine suspected that Celia importuned her out of habit, rather than any genuine desire to spend more time with her.

'I have to go soon, I've got a casserole in the oven,' Celia said, when they had exchanged greetings and assured one another everyone was well.

'Ian's making dinner,' Geraldine said.

'Oh my God, Geraldine,' Celia gushed, 'you have the perfect life. A brilliant career and a man who cooks for you. Well, I've got to dash. Speak soon.'

With a sigh, Geraldine hung up. Celia was the one with a perfect life, satisfied with a husband and children, and domesticity, instead of being driven by a fierce passion for justice. But if Geraldine's life had followed an unsatisfactory path, she had taken a wrong turning so long ago it would be impossible to alter course now.

'Dinner's ready!' Ian called out.

Geraldine's mood shifted on hearing his voice. If Celia felt fulfilled by her family, Geraldine had her career and the knowledge that she was working to help keep people safe from a killer. Whether George had been targeted as a victim, or his death was the result of a random attack, she was going to track his killer down. That was the path she had chosen to follow, and she would have no regrets. She smiled at Ian. It was certainly easier to be satisfied with her life with a homemade curry on the table in front of her.

21

GERALDINE AND IAN WERE confident of finding Rodney at home. All the same, they set off very early in the morning, and arrived at their destination shortly after seven. Rodney lived in a large square white house in a tree-lined avenue on the outskirts of the city, near the Tadcaster Road. The front garden looked as though it had once been well stocked with bulbs and flowering bushes, although it was now overgrown with bindweed and completely wild, but the house itself had been well looked after. It was a while before the door was opened by a tall man in a navy blue dressing gown. Striped blue and white pyjama trousers showed beneath its folds, and his feet were bare. He had thin bony toes, in keeping with his gaunt face and long nose. In common with everything else about him, his pale blond hair and light blue eyes seemed pallid and somehow devoid of life.

'Yes? What do you want?' he asked in a thin voice, his delicate eyebrows slightly raised in enquiry.

'Rodney Gilbert?' Ian replied.

'Yes, that's my name,' the man said. 'Can I help you?'

Geraldine and Ian introduced themselves.

'I take it you wish to consult me about one of my patients,' Rodney said, taking a step back. 'Presumably you know where my surgery is?' he added frostily.

'Actually, we need to speak to you about something that pertains specifically to you,' Geraldine replied. 'May we come in? This can't really wait.'

The doctor frowned. He appeared vexed but he was also

clearly intrigued and after a fleeting hesitation he invited them to step inside.

'Please wait in here while I get dressed,' he said, ushering them into a small study and indicating two upright chairs facing a large wooden desk.

They sat down and waited in silence for him to reappear. The chairs were elaborately carved, but not very comfortable to sit on.

'Is it mahogany?' Geraldine asked, after a long pause.

Ian shrugged. 'Sorry, I couldn't say.'

Behind the desk, on either side of a long window, bookshelves stretched from floor to ceiling, packed with volumes of medical books. The floor was not carpeted but polished boards.

'I wonder why he doesn't get a carpet in here,' Geraldine said.

'He seems to like to surround himself with wood,' Ian agreed.

'It's like being in a coffin,' she muttered. 'Only with books.'

Ian didn't answer, and they sat waiting in silence until Rodney returned. He had not kept them waiting long. Although he was wearing dark jeans and a T-shirt, somehow he contrived to appear as if he was dressed for a formal occasion. His jeans looked brand new, and his T-shirt could have been starched, the collar lay so straight. He took a seat behind the desk and leaned forward, his elbows on the desk, his long white fingers forming a dome shape beneath his pointed chin.

'Now then,' he said pleasantly, 'what's this about?'

Geraldine leaned back in her chair as though she was completely relaxed, and tried to give the impression that she was scarcely paying attention. But she watched the doctor closely as she spoke.

'You had a girlfriend called Michelle Taylor,' she said.

Rodney's eyes flickered in a barely discernible blink. 'Michelle,' he repeated softly. 'Ah yes, I was once in a relationship with a girl called Michelle, but that was a long time ago. A long time ago.'

'She was more than just a casual girlfriend, wasn't she?' Geraldine said. 'You were together for two years, and you were about to get married, but she left you at the altar.'

'And this is of interest to you, because...?' he enquired.

He spoke diffidently, but his pale eyes remained fixed on her like distant points of light.

'When did you last see Michelle?' Geraldine asked.

Rodney shook his head, looking faintly puzzled. 'I really don't recall exactly. It was a long time ago.' He paused and made a show of thinking. 'Let me see... let me see... Oh yes, it must have been the day before she abandoned me in the church, on our wedding day. You can look up the date in the church records, if you want a precise answer. And I think there was some gossipy piece about it in a local paper at the time. She tried to contact me afterwards, said she wanted to explain what had happened, and why she had walked out on me like that. But in the end the explanation turned out to be very simple, because less than a month after she left me standing at the altar, she married someone else. All the time we were planning our wedding, she was seeing another man. Perhaps you can understand why I refused to see her again? It was over between us and that was that. And now,' he went on, with more animation than he had yet shown, 'if there's nothing else, perhaps you'd like to leave? Pleasant though it is to sit here chatting, I do have other matters that require my attention.'

Neither Geraldine nor Ian shifted in their seats.

'What can you tell us about the man Michelle Taylor married?' Geraldine asked.

Rodney shook his head. 'I never met him, so I'm afraid there's nothing I can tell you about him other than that he married Michelle. Why? Is she all right? Has something happened to her? Don't tell me he turned out to be a poor choice of husband?

You will forgive me if I am not in the slightest bit interested in her marital problems, after all this time. Although I hope he isn't violent.'

'He's dead,' Geraldine replied.

Rodney stared at her. 'Surely you don't think Michelle is responsible? I know she let me down badly, but I honestly don't believe she is aggressive. If she attacked her husband, it could only have been after extreme provocation.'

Rodney appeared genuinely concerned on hearing the news, but something in his manner made Geraldine uneasy.

'Can you tell us the reason you withdrew two thousand pounds from a savings account two weeks ago?' Ian asked abruptly.

'What?' He seemed genuinely surprised. 'Oh, I see, I see. You think I might have been nursing a broken heart for thirteen years, and finally snapped and paid a hitman to kill Michelle's husband. Is that it?' He shook his head with a faint sneer. 'That's a very ingenious notion, but I'm afraid you won't be able to pin this on me.'

'We're not trying to pin anything on anyone,' Geraldine assured him. 'We are simply concerned to find the truth. And to do that, we need to eliminate any possible suspects, which means anyone who knew the victim or his wife, Michelle. So, can you tell us why you needed that money?'

Rodney drew in a deep breath. 'It was for a car. You can check with the car showroom.'

Again Geraldine watched Rodney closely as she put her next question. 'You have a patient named Ben Foster.'

Rodney scowled. 'Possibly. The name rings a bell.'

'He came to see you three weeks ago,' Ian said. 'Why was that?'

'That information is confidential,' Rodney replied haughtily. His eyes narrowed in sudden understanding. 'It was you sniffing around at the surgery asking questions, wasn't it? You were trying to find out about me. Well, I'm sorry, but any information we have on this patient is strictly confidential. You'll have to ask him not me.'

'He seemed quite guarded in his responses,' Geraldine said when she and Ian were in the car and driving away.

He grunted. 'The woman jilted him at the altar. I thought he seemed quite restrained when he was talking about her. She must be a cold-hearted bitch.'

'Who can judge what someone else might do for love?' Geraldine said gently.

'She didn't only abandon him at the altar,' he replied. 'She must have had an inkling before the day of the wedding.'

'Or she thought she would go through with it and then realised at the very last minute that she couldn't face it. He didn't seem as though he still harboured a grudge, but who knows? Maybe the opportunity just presented itself and he couldn't resist it. Perhaps Ben confided he was in financial difficulties, and Rodney saw an opportunity to kill his rival and punish Michelle.'

22

GERALDINE WAS THINKING ABOUT going home, when Naomi came to see her to tell her a woman had turned up at the police station claiming to have important information regarding the recent murder.

'What sort of important information? Have you spoken to her?' Geraldine asked.

Naomi's blonde curls bobbed vigorously as she nodded her head. Briefly she outlined what she had just been told, that the woman claimed to have seen someone fitting Ben Foster's description the previous Saturday.

'The thing is,' Naomi concluded with an anxious smile, 'I'm not sure what to make of her story.'

Geraldine frowned. Other than what Ben had told them in his own statement, they had no information about his movements on the Saturday morning of George's murder. Scanning quickly through Naomi's report, she appreciated her colleague's reservations. The chances of a stray caller having anything useful to tell them were slim. Nevertheless, what the woman had told Naomi certainly sounded interesting. Geraldine went to speak to the potential witness herself, aware that it was as well to pursue every possible source of information with rigour. She found Sallyanne Hodgskin waiting for her in a small interview room.

'Hello,' Geraldine greeted her, introducing herself. 'Please, take a seat.'

Sallyanne was a middle-aged lady with short grey hair, kind

eyes and a warm smile. 'Oh, Inspector,' she burst out, as she sat down, 'thank you so much for seeing me. It's been weighing on my mind ever since I saw that appeal you put out for witnesses to come forward. I would have called you sooner, but I didn't see the appeal until late on Saturday and then I had all my family round yesterday, and honestly I didn't have a minute to myself, and I was at work yesterday and today. I came as soon as I could. Of course it's probably nothing and I dare say I'm stressing for no reason, not to mention wasting your time. My sister didn't think I should bother coming here at all. You must have hundreds of people calling you about this. I do hope I'm not just being a nuisance.' She smiled uncertainly.

'What is it you wanted to tell us?' Geraldine asked gently. 'I assure you this isn't a waste of time, not when a man's freedom hangs in the balance. Please, if you have any information at all, tell me what it is. We'll judge whether it's important or not.'

'Well, the appeal mentioned a man in a grey jacket with a brown and white terrier wearing a bright red collar and lead, didn't it?'

Geraldine nodded. 'That's right.'

'Yes, well, I saw them, that is, I think I did. I mean, it could have been them.'

'What did you see? What makes you think it was the man we are investigating?'

'Right, well, like I said to the constable, it was on Saturday morning, a week ago last Saturday, that is. I live in Butchers Terrace, and I went out for a walk by the river.'

Listening to Sallyanne mention details of the route Ben claimed to have followed on his walk that morning, Geraldine felt a prickling sensation.

'I went through Rowntree Park, you know, by the football pitch, and that's where I saw a man matching the description you gave. A man in a grey jacket. I know that's not exactly unusual, but the thing is, he had a brown and white terrier with him, and

I particularly noticed his bright red lead and collar, because the man had let the dog off the lead and was waving it above his head, and calling to the dog to come back to him. He shouted for a while, you know how it is with dogs once they're let off the lead, and I remember thinking I hope that dog doesn't run down as far as the river. It's not a good idea to let a dog run around by the water, is it? Although it could probably swim if it did fall in,' she added thoughtfully. 'Anyway, that's what I was thinking as I walked past them. Well, the dog ran back to its owner, and he put the lead on and took the dog down to the river. I was pleased to see he was on a lead down there. I walked behind them for a while, but I had to turn back before nine because my daughter was bringing my grandson over.'

'What time did you see the man and his dog?'

'I went out early, and I saw them in the park a few minutes later. It must have been a few minutes after eight thirty.'

Geraldine sat forward. 'Do you happen to remember what the man called his dog?'

'Oh yes, I couldn't miss that, because the man was shouting the name repeatedly, calling to the dog, which was ignoring him for ages, as they do. So I heard it clearly. I don't know if any of this helps you at all, but I thought I ought to come forward. That was what the appeal asked us to do, if we saw a man out with a dog with a red collar and lead.' She gave a hesitant smile.

'And what was the dog's name?' Geraldine asked quietly.

'Roxy.'

'Think carefully, please. Did the man have a bicycle with him?'

'A bicycle? No. He was walking his dog.'

'And you're sure he wasn't wheeling a bicycle?'

'Absolutely sure.'

'Are you sure it was eight thirty when you saw him?'

Sallyanne nodded. 'Yes, or a few minutes after. My daughter always brings my grandson round just after nine, so she can be at work for nine thirty, so I needed to be home in time. I remember thinking I had just half an hour to go out for a walk.'

'Did you see the man with the dog again?'

'Well, yes, I followed him down to the river and he walked ahead of me for about ten minutes. I don't think he noticed me.'

'Ten minutes takes us up to maybe eight forty?'

'Yes, that's right because I remember I turned back at eight forty-five. It's lovely down by the river when it's so quiet and I would have stayed longer, but like I said, I had to get back. That's why I can be so sure about the time, because I checked. I didn't want to be late for my daughter.'

'And what about the man and his dog? Where were they when you turned back?'

'They were still walking along the river path but I lost sight of them when I turned round.'

'Did you see any cyclists?'

'Yes, there was one. I think it was a man, cycling away back to Bishopthorpe when I was walking back. I didn't see where he went. That must have been around ten to nine, because I was home by nine.'

Geraldine thanked the witness and made a note of her contact details and assured her that her statement was very helpful. Eileen had gone home. Geraldine returned to her desk to write up her decision log before dealing with Ben.

23

MOST OF THE TEAM had gone home, including Ian and Eileen, so it fell to Geraldine to inform Ben that he was free to go home. A scarf with his DNA, and the fact that he owned a rusty bicycle, were not proof against a statement from an independent witness. Geraldine was not often called on to share good news. Although it was disappointing to lose the suspect in a murder investigation, she was pleased to be releasing an innocent man after he had spent six nights confined to a cell. She nodded a greeting at the custody sergeant, a stolid man with a large head, pale ginger hair, and a smile permanently creasing his fleshy face. Even the most objectionable prisoners did not seem to bother him in the slightest. He treated everyone, criminal or colleague, with the same placid equanimity.

'Evening, Bert,' she said.

He looked up and smiled at her. 'Evening, Ma'am. All quiet here. So, how can I help you? After a comfortable bed for the night, away from noisy neighbours, are you? If so, you've come to the right place. No one's going to disturb you in this luxurious accommodation.'

Just then, they heard a muffled caterwauling coming from one of the cells.

Bert grinned. 'That lad was brought in earlier, a bit the worse for wear, so we thought it best to let him sleep it off in here. He's harmless enough. I think he might be singing. Either that or his head's started to hurt and he's crying with pain. It's difficult to tell sometimes, the way they carry on.' He raised his voice suddenly and bellowed, 'Hey! Stop that racket in there!'

The noise continued unabated.

'So this is the peaceful bed for the night you offered me?' Geraldine said, laughing, before explaining the reason for her visit to the cells.

'Damn,' the custody sergeant said, 'I thought you'd come here to spend the night with me.'

She found Ben lying on his bunk, fully dressed and looking half asleep. He was unshaven, his eyes seemed sunken, and his face had an unhealthy sheen.

'What is it now?' he asked wearily, looking up and seeing her. 'I've got nothing more to say to you and, in any case, I'm not saying another word without my lawyer present. You shouldn't even be here. So go away and stop pestering me.'

Geraldine told him he was free to go.

Instead of leaping to his feet, Ben closed his eyes. 'This is a trick, isn't it? Jerome warned me you'd try to catch me out. Well, it's not going to work, so you can piss off and leave me alone. I'm trying to get some rest. Believe me, that's not easy in here.'

'Ben, did you hear what I said? You're free to leave. Go home to your wife.'

He sat up and glared at her warily. 'What the hell are you talking about?'

Quietly, Geraldine explained that the murder charge against him had been dropped, and he was free to go home.

'How so?'

'A witness has come forward whose testimony proves you couldn't have killed George Gardner. You're free to go.'

'A witness? What witness? What are you talking about?'

'A lady who doesn't know you saw you walking your dog in Rowntree Park at the time of the murder.'

'So you wouldn't take my word for it, but you're prepared to believe some random stranger?'

Geraldine didn't bother to explain that the case against Ben would collapse in court, once the defence brought in an independent witness to testify to his innocence. 'Listen, I want to go home now, so you can either do the same, or you can remain here for another night. It makes no difference to me. Stay locked up in here until they pick you up and throw you out, if that's what you want. I thought you would have been keen to get out of here, but it seems I was wrong.'

'What am I supposed to do now?' he asked, without moving from the bunk where he was still sitting, hunched over, his arms dangling between his legs.

Geraldine warned him against leaving the area, in case the police needed to speak to him again, but in the meantime, he was free to go home and return to work and generally get back to his life. Still Ben sat on the bunk, shaking his head in disbelief. Taking her leave, Geraldine instructed the custody sergeant to go through the process of sending Ben home.

Back home herself, she discussed the development with Ian.

'So you just sent him home?' he asked in some surprise. 'Shouldn't you have waited until the morning to speak to Eileen? Just for your own protection?'

'And keep an innocent man locked up for another night? You can imagine what his lawyer would have done with that.'

'Can we be sure he's innocent, when the evidence points so firmly in the other direction?'

'The only way he could be guilty is if he had been both walking his dog along the river path between eight thirty and nine, and cycling through the park there at the same time,' Geraldine replied. 'We have an independent witness who has signed a statement to say she saw Ben Foster walking his dog down by the river at the time of the murder.'

'We don't know it was a cyclist who committed the murder,' Ian pointed out, with a worried frown.

'But we do know a cyclist followed George into the trees, while Ben was down by the river walking his dog as George was being attacked.'

'Well, our friend Ben must have been over the moon at his release.'

'To be honest, he seemed more surprised than pleased,' Geraldine replied. 'I can't imagine what it would be like to be locked up like that, out of the blue, when you're innocent.'

'If he is innocent,' Ian replied.

Geraldine nodded, but she began to feel uneasy.

The next morning, Eileen strode into the incident room with an air of suppressed fury. 'So it's back to the drawing board,' she said, glaring at Geraldine, as though she was responsible for the witness who had come forward. 'You never believed Ben was guilty, did you?'

Geraldine shrugged. 'The evidence could have been misleading. We knew that all along.'

'But why?' Eileen asked.

Geraldine shook her head. The case which had once seemed so simple had become disturbingly complicated. She hoped they would get to the bottom of it, and she would be proved right in her decision to release Ben. At the time it had seemed to her that she had no other choice but to release an innocent man. But from the reaction of her colleagues, she had an uncomfortable feeling that they questioned whether she had done the right thing. Even Ariadne avoided meeting her eye and that concerned Geraldine more than the attitude of all her other colleagues, because she had considered Ariadne her friend. She could only hope that the killer would not turn out to have been Ben after all. If Sallyanne Hodgskin was discredited as a witness, they could always arrest Ben again and no harm would have been done. On the other hand, the alternative was to keep an innocent man behind bars, an idea that filled her with dismay.

Looking for an answer, she went to question Rodney again.

This time the receptionist at the surgery gave her a frosty greeting and kept her waiting for half an hour.

'I'm sorry, but Dr Gilbert is with a patient and cannot be disturbed,' she said when Geraldine arrived and asked to speak to Rodney. 'You could see another doctor sooner.'

Geraldine said she would wait. When the patient finally left, the receptionist said Rodney was on the phone and could not be interrupted. Since he was not officially a suspect, Geraldine had no choice but to continue to wait. At last she was told she could go in and see the doctor. Rodney gave an exaggerated sigh when she walked in.

'Perhaps you should register as a patient if you're going to be visiting so frequently,' he said.

Geraldine went over his statement with him, but he had nothing new to add, and kept glancing at his watch and insisting he was busy. After ten minutes, she left, feeling more dissatisfied than she had been when she had walked in. She had just wasted nearly an hour.

24

IT WAS ALMOST INCONCEIVABLE that they would let him go. It was hard to believe the police would be so stupid, but there could be no mistake. Rage swept through him, making him tremble with fury. This was not how it was supposed to end. Barely able to control his rage he picked up a cup and hurled it against the wall. Splinters of white china flew over the carpet and lay sparkling like ice on a thawing grey landscape, while dregs of cold coffee dribbled down the wall. Even though, on some level, he knew that he was being stupid, he couldn't control his anger. One cup was not enough to calm his inner turmoil. Seizing the edge of the coffee table, he tipped it up. Cups, glass, papers and plates went sliding to the floor, spilling dregs of coffee and wine and crumbs on the floor. Raising his foot, he stamped on a glass and it shattered with a loud crack.

Shaking, he slumped down in a chair, his burst of energy spent. Muttering a curse, he went to fetch a dustpan and brush. He picked up the larger shards of china and glass and dropped them in the bin, taking care not to cut himself on any of the sharp edges. After sweeping up most of the fragments he fetched his hoover and finished removing every trace of his frenzied outburst. Having cleared away the results of his fit of temper, he sat down with a bottle of beer and a glass. Destroying his room wouldn't help anything. He needed more information. Not knowing what had happened, or why, was driving him insane. Whatever the risk, he had to find a way of keeping up with the police activity. It was beyond his wildest dreams to find himself in a position to actually influence the police, but perhaps he might be able to do something, however slight, to worm his way in somehow. He was desperate.

It was not difficult to park in Fulford Road, near the entrance to the police station. A few cars went in and out but the street was generally quieter than he had expected. He knew from films that carrying out surveillance was dull work; he had not anticipated quite how tedious it would be. He was ready to give up and go home when there was a small flurry of movement as a group of people emerged, spilling out on to the pavement in an untidy group. Guessing they were police officers, he watched them walk up the road and disappear into a pub not far from the police station. Leaving his car, he strolled thoughtfully along as far as the pub, where he stood outside hesitating. Reaching a decision, he pushed the door and went in.

The pub was large and buzzing with several subdued conversations, the soporific hum of voices occasionally disturbed by a sudden burst of laughter, shrill and raucous. Ignoring the hush as he approached the bar, he fetched a pint and carried it over to a corner table where he sat in the shadows, studiously avoiding looking up. The other drinkers were probably all police officers who were almost bound to know, as if by instinct, when they were being watched. He sipped his pint very slowly, with no idea what he was waiting for. The buzz of conversation resumed, but he sensed the police officers were aware of him skulking in the corner. He had only a hazy recollection of the group of drinkers at the bar. A stocky man in a denim jacket had shifted slightly to move away from him when he went to the bar. As he sat, waiting, he tried to recall who else was standing in the group at the bar, and he struggled with an almost irresistible temptation to glance up at them. He couldn't afford to meet anyone's eye. The police were no doubt trained to remember faces and he didn't want to give any of them the opportunity to notice him.

Eventually he became aware of movement. Head bowed and eyes half closed, he watched several pairs of legs walk towards the door and vanish from his line of vision. He waited. They did not reappear. Cautiously glancing around, he saw just two women were left, seated at a table. He wasn't sure if they were members of the police or not. As he watched, the younger of the two women stood up and went to the bar. Knocking back the dregs of his pint, he made his way over to where she was standing, laughing with the landlord. She was in her twenties, slim and blonde, and just the kind of girl a man might find attractive. He had to be careful to give the right impression, friendly but casual and not in any way wanting to pressurise her.

'Can I get that for you?' he asked.

He smiled easily and took care not to move too close to her. Personal space was important to some women, and above all he had to avoid alienating her in any way.

'Thank you,' she replied, returning his smile. 'But I'm with a friend.'

'No worries,' he answered, already turning away. 'Perhaps another time.'

He went back to his table with another pint and waited. He hadn't actually achieved anything, yet the blonde woman was probably a police officer, and they had exchanged a few words. It was a start. The two women were sitting sideways on to him, so he was able to keep an eye on them surreptitiously. Engrossed in their conversation, they remained oblivious to his interest, and the landlord never once glanced in his direction. At last he saw the women were stirring, preparing to leave. Swiftly he rose to his feet. He was closer to the door and managed to time it so he was leaving just as they reached the exit.

'Maybe next time?' he murmured as he held the door for them.

The older woman looked surprised, but the young blonde woman smiled and thanked him. With a surge of adrenaline, he looked directly into her eyes.

'Unless you'd like to stay for one more?'

She laughed. 'One for the road? I shouldn't.'

'A coffee then?'

Her colleague had already gone. The blonde hesitated, obviously weighing him up. Clearly she decided that a coffee in the pub was hardly risky.

'Why not?' she replied, turning back.

She returned to the table where she had been sitting earlier. He would have preferred to sit at his former table in the corner. In the middle of the room he felt vulnerable. Another police officer might come into the pub at any time and see them sitting together. But she had not asked him where he would like to sit, and he had no choice but to follow her. She was certainly confident, but perhaps there had been some guile in her choice of table. Unlike him, she might prefer to be easily seen. He was, after all, a stranger. Suppressing his nerves as well as he could, he took his seat. She seemed happy to chat, and he learned that her name was Naomi.

'Naomi,' he repeated, smiling.

He was only interested in finding out what she did and, if she was a police officer, whether she knew anything about the investigation into George Gardner's murder. But he had to proceed carefully, and make it look as though he was interested in her for her own sake alone.

'I didn't drag you away from your friend did I?' he enquired, hoping to give the impression that he was sensitive to her feelings.

She was pretty when she laughed. 'She was a colleague,' she replied. 'We see each other every day. It's nice to have someone different to talk to.'

He inclined his head at the compliment. He decided not to mention that she was the first person he had engaged in conversation for months.

'What do you and your colleague do?' he asked.

It was a risk, but she had brought up the topic. His breath caught in his throat on hearing she was a police constable. Her eyes narrowed as she answered. She was gauging his reaction. Not everyone was a fan of the police. He supposed it was a good sign, implying that she cared what he thought of her. When she asked him what he did for a living, he blurted out that he was a financial adviser.

'I work with pensions, taking care of the elderly.'

He didn't want her to start asking him for advice about her work pension. In reality, he knew very little about such matters. But she just nodded and smiled, and asked him if he enjoyed his work.

'Not really,' he said. 'I like to think that I'm helping vulnerable people, but it's pretty dull work all the same. What you do must be far more exciting.'

He could not risk appearing too interested in her work until they knew one another better. He wondered whether to ask her if she was hungry, but decided against it. He didn't want to arouse her suspicion by being too eager. Instead he said he hoped he would see her again. It was not easy to restrain his impatience when she smiled at this, but he had to let matters take their course, and see what happened. He had formed a relationship of sorts with a police officer, which he had barely dared hope to achieve. Now he needed to plan his next move.

25

JAMIE GLANCED AROUND THE office and smiled to herself. Everything looked tidy. The loose paperwork had been filed away, and her pens and folders were all neatly lined up, ready for the morning. She liked this moment at the end of the day when everyone else had left and she was able to put everything in order before going home for the night. The boss had gone, leaving Jamie to lock up. After so many years working at the garage, it still gave her a frisson of excitement, knowing that the responsibility for closing up was hers alone. It gave her a sense of belonging – no, more than that, it made her feel important. Her boss might go home to his wife every evening, but he left his office in Jamie's care.

'I know I can rely on you,' the boss had said to her once, and he was right.

She was nothing if not conscientious, and knowing the trust he placed in her made her all the more determined to not let him down. Carefully she checked the windows and doors, and then checked them again to make sure they were all secure before she set the alarm. The street door shut behind her with a reassuring click. Even after so many years, she still worried that she might have left a window ajar or a door unlocked, and she had to force herself not to go back and check everything all over again. She was not like that at home, but the garage was not her property and she felt a heightened sense of responsibility when she locked up there. The last thing she ever wanted to do was upset her boss. He was worth far too much to her for that.

As she was walking to the bus stop, a fine drizzle began to fall from a heavy grey sky. She had not brought an umbrella, since the weather had promised to be fine when she had left home in the morning. Without checking the forecast, she had assumed it would continue sunny until the evening. Now she regretted not having worn her boots and her hooded raincoat. She shivered and pulled her jacket more tightly around her, fumbling with the zip as she hurried on her way. She didn't want to stop to do it up, and risk missing her bus. Even though her stop had a shelter of sorts, it was miserable hanging around there, waiting. In any case, the roof over the bus shelter was virtually useless because with the slightest breath of wind the rain blew in, while the spray from passing cars reached her legs however far back in the shelter she stood. The worse the weather, the longer the gap seemed to be between buses, as though the drivers conspired to keep people waiting in the rain for as long as possible.

She had nearly reached the bus stop, when a car drew into the kerb beside her and she heard someone call her name.

'Jamie!' He smiled at her, winding down his window. 'You're getting soaked. Can I give you a lift home?'

Normally, she would have declined politely, but it had begun to rain more heavily, and her legs were getting wet. She leaned down to speak to him through his open window.

'That's very kind of you, but I don't want to put you out.'

'Well,' he hesitated, 'do you live a long way out of town? Only I haven't got all night.'

'No, no, that's not it. My lodgings are in Bootham Row, off Gillygate.'

'Oh well,' he grinned, 'that's where I'm going.'

'If you're sure it's no trouble.'

'Nonsense. Don't be daft. It's no trouble at all and you're getting wet. Come on, jump in quickly.' He smiled at her again.

Thankful to escape the chilly rain, she scurried round to the passenger door and clambered into the car.

'I hope I don't get the seat wet,' she began, but her words were drowned out by the sudden roar of the engine.

The car swerved away from the kerb and accelerated up the road. There had not even been time for her to put her seat belt on, and she fell against the door with a violent jolt. She was reluctant to remonstrate, after he had been kind enough to offer her a lift, so she struggled to pull out the shoulder sash in silence, and finally managed to drag it far enough for the buckle to reach the anchor point. Only then did she look up and see that they were driving away from Bootham. For the first time, she began to feel alarmed.

'Where are we going?' she enquired in a voice that shook ever so slightly.

He did not answer.

'Please slow down,' she said, doing her best to sound calm, although her voice was tremulous.

Without a word, he suddenly turned off the road into a lane behind a row of houses where she saw a series of lock-up garages.

'Where are we going?' she repeated, clutching at the door handle.

The light outside was fading and the lane that led to the lock-ups was not lit. In the shadowy interior of the car she saw the man's face leaning towards her, his expression curiously intense. Desperately she fumbled with the door, but it was locked and she could not open it. Turning to face him, she tried to push him away, but he pressed something against her mouth and nose, preventing her from screaming or drawing breath.

'You're not going anywhere,' he murmured.

Fear thrilled through her as she realised he intended to kill her. But by the time she had grasped what was happening, it was already too late to stop him, he had turned on her so quickly. She struggled frantically, but something foul-tasting pushed right inside her mouth, making her gag. There was a sickening stench of stale sweat and rubber. She tried to scream but the sound came out as a muffled groan that rose in her chest and failed to reach her throat. Desperately she tried to push him away but he slapped his free arm around her, pressing both her arms against her sides and pinning her down against the seat while his other hand kept shoving something down her throat with the heel of his hand, making her choke, and his fingers clamped onto her nose, pinching it painfully, so she couldn't breathe. She was going to die unless she could stop him.

Her head felt as though it would explode into myriad points of dazzling light, and the pain in her chest expanded until her whole body was stiff with terror. She began to convulse, and then blackness overwhelmed her. Her last thought before she lost consciousness was that it was over. 'What is over?' a voice in her head enquired. 'Everything,' she replied. 'It's the end of everything. But why?' And the answer came, 'You know why.' And then nothing.

26

IT WAS DONE, AND he had succeeded. Even now he trembled when he remembered what he had done. Every time he thought about it he began to shake with excitement. He couldn't help it. Mentally he felt completely dissociated from the scene, as though it had happened to someone else. Even more unreal than that, he recalled it as a scene in a film, a fiction that had never taken place in real life at all. It was a story that would haunt his imagination, nothing more. But, all things considered, he was quietly pleased that he had found the strength to do what had to be done. He didn't need anyone's help. He had learned his lesson. Revealing secrets to other people was dangerous. As long as no one else knew about it, he was safe. And he wanted to feel safe. He had lived in fear of discovery for long enough. All she had needed to do was keep her stupid mouth shut but she had threatened to expose him, so he had shut her mouth for her. That was all. There had been no other choice.

He grinned, thinking of the time and effort the police would spend looking for her killer, all to no purpose. If the situation had not been so entertaining, it would have been tragic. All by himself he had succeeded in throwing the whole police force into disarray. Running after clues that led nowhere, they were going to be like kittens chasing their own tails. His victim had been relatively easy to follow, and once he had made up his mind, he had pounced at the first opportunity. It had been ridiculously easy.

He would have liked to track his victim to an out of the way place and leave her right where he had killed her, but it hadn't worked out like that. It didn't matter, because with a little quick thinking he had made sure he had covered his tracks. How could he not make this work, when he had thought of everything? He had agonised over how to do it, but in the end he had been lucky because the weather had been on his side, enabling him to lure her swiftly into his car without anyone seeing. Once he had her safely in the car, despatching her had been easy. He had been careful to wear gloves and had avoided breathing on her. Despite the rain, he had kept the car windows open. Having done everything he could to minimise the risk of discovery, he was fairly confident he was safe. Even with all their forensic wizardry, the police wouldn't be able to find him.

Life was so easily snuffed out. It took so long to create, nine months of gestation, and in less than five minutes it was over. He smiled, thinking how lucky he was that it was not the other way round, five minutes to create and nine months to destroy. That would have seriously interfered with his plans.

Disposing of the body was far more challenging than the simple act of killing had been. He had no trouble driving away with her in the car, and it was already growing dark. Anyone passing them in the street would see only a man and a woman seated in the front of a car, driving past. If they had peered closely, they would have assumed she was asleep. Even close up she barely looked as though she was dead. Only if he had an accident, or was stopped by the police, would the truth come out. He drove very carefully, conscious of his motionless passenger. Her presence at his side both terrified and thrilled him, but there was no need for him to have worried. He and his silent passenger reached the woods where George Gardner had been murdered, without any hindrance. Concealed among the trees, he switched his lights off and removed her seat belt before running round the car to open the passenger door and yank her out of the front seat. Among the trees seemed a fitting resting place for a dead body, as well as a discreet drop-off point. There were no CCTV cameras to spy on what he was doing, and no windows through which he could be spotted by some prying householder. Once the path through the trees was empty, he could have been alone in a deserted expanse of forest – unless a dead body could be considered company.

Her body was floppy, but to his relief she was not too difficult to pull from the car, her limbs obligingly bending and twisting as he tugged. He had been afraid she might become rigid, obliging him to break her bones to manoeuvre her out of the car. The more he had to handle her, the greater the risk of discovery might be. But her body slipped almost effortlessly from the car and fell to the path with a thump that seemed to reverberate through the trees. A faint panic shook him and he stood rooted to the spot, fleetingly transfixed with the fear of discovery. But there was no answering sound, and no one came speeding along the path to investigate what had made the noise. Shaking himself free of his debilitating terror, he returned to the car and drove away, leaving her lying on the ground, prey to scavengers and insects. Before long someone would come along and find her, but by then he would be far away, safe from discovery.

He drove home slowly, constantly on the lookout for police cars, and went indoors to wait for the news to hit the media. He was quite looking forward to seeing his macabre exploit reported on television. In a way it was a shame no one would ever know who he was, but of course that would defeat the whole purpose of his plan. He would just have to be discreet and stay hidden, gratified that he alone knew the identity of her killer. They could hardly continue talking about the Scarf Killer after this, but that was up to them. No doubt some clever dick reporter would come up with something equally banal. He would just sit back and watch as the police ran around helplessly. At least one of his problems was sorted.

27

At breakfast next morning, Geraldine felt unusually tense and Ian was quiet. Neither of them mentioned work. She was on her way to the police station when Ariadne called her. 'Where are you?' Ariadne asked. 'You need to come in at once. Haven't you checked your messages? The DCI is holding a briefing in the major incident room and she wants everyone here. No exceptions.'

'Has something happened?' Geraldine asked, suddenly apprehensive, aware that her friend's voice was strangely taut.

She listened, horrified, as Ariadne told her that the killer had struck again. Ariadne did not say that Ben was the suspect in this new murder, but Geraldine thought the implication was clear. Geraldine had let Ben go and now he had killed again. She accelerated, keen to reach the police station and find out exactly what was going on, and whether anyone there blamed her for releasing Ben. Despite her misgivings, and this second incident occurring just when Ben was at liberty again, she struggled to believe he was guilty. He had not struck her as stupid or reckless enough to commit a second murder on the night he was released from a police cell, but she could not be sure. And whether or not he was guilty, someone had been killed shortly after his release. Most of the team had already gathered by the time she arrived, and Eileen was about to begin.

'You all know by now that another body has been found,' Eileen announced tersely. 'This time a rubber glove was shoved into the victim's mouth, blocking her windpipe, while her nostrils were held closed. She was killed some time yesterday afternoon, we don't know where but possibly in a car, and her body was deposited in Rowntree Park, not far from the site of the first murder.'

She made no mention of the fact that Ben had been released from police custody the previous evening.

'How could we have let this happen?' a constable demanded angrily.

'Why was Ben released?' someone muttered pointedly.

A few other officers began whispering, and Geraldine noticed one or two of them scowling at her, although no one openly accused her of having misjudged the situation. Uncomfortable about her decision to release Ben, Geraldine cleared her throat.

'Ben was released because he was innocent of George Gardner's murder,' she said firmly. 'A witness came forward and gave a statement which proves that Ben couldn't possibly have murdered George Gardner. And there is no reason to suppose he had anything to do with this second murder either,' she added, with a flash of irritation.

'So we released him on a single eyewitness account?' a constable murmured.

'How do we know the witness was reliable?' someone else asked.

'Geraldine reached a decision based on the evidence available at the time,' Eileen snapped, 'in response to a statement given by an independent witness.'

'The case against Ben Foster was hardly robust even without that,' Ian added in a voice low with tension.

Geraldine had the uneasy feeling Ian was only saying that to support her. He didn't really believe it, and nor did anyone else. The muttering ceased, but Geraldine felt awkward and could not wait for the briefing to finish so that she could leave the room where she was feeling so uncomfortable.

'The media are going to love this,' Ariadne said miserably. 'I can just see the headlines. Hoodwinked police release psychopath.'

A few other officers began to murmur again.

'That's enough,' Eileen barked. 'We need to get to work and we can't afford to waste time grumbling about the media. There will be time to investigate everything that's happened once we've got a suspect behind bars. And this time the case against him has to be watertight.'

On her way back to her desk, Geraldine did her best to ignore her colleagues' whispering. She was certain they were talking about her, perhaps speculating about why she had been demoted before her arrival in York. Worse than the suspicion that they were gossiping about her was the thought that, if she had blundered, her mistake would be responsible for a woman's death.

Geraldine and Ian drove to Rowntree Park in silence. Access to the crime scene had been closed off by a police van, and a cordon had been placed across the road to prevent pedestrians from contaminating any evidence at the site. It was guarded by a young constable. Beyond the tape, a forensic tent would soon be erected over the cycle path. This time, the victim had not been dragged into the bushes to be despatched somewhere out of sight. Either the killer had been in a hurry, or he had become reckless, taunting the police with his ability to slip away undetected. As soon as she left the car, Geraldine was accosted by a small group of reporters who had gathered outside the cordon to sniff out crumbs of information for their news hungry editors.

'Who has been murdered this time?' a tall woman in a bright blue coat demanded, barring Geraldine's way. 'Is it a coincidence that this death has occurred so soon after George Gardner was killed? Are the two related? And what can you tell us about this second victim?'

Geraldine decided the best response to the barrage of questions was silence. She moved to one side with the intention of crossing the cordon, but the tall reporter anticipated her move. Dodging sideways to block her retreat, the reporter continued haranguing Geraldine in strident tones.

'The public have a right to know what the police are doing to protect them!'

'Members of the media have no right to obstruct the police in the course of a murder investigation,' Geraldine replied quietly.

She wondered what the reporter would say to her readers if she knew that she was speaking to the police officer who had authorised Ben Foster's release.

'Is this the work of the Scarf Killer?' the tall woman bellowed, still standing directly in front of Geraldine. 'Why did the police release him?' she went on, before Geraldine had a chance to respond.

Other voices joined in. 'Is he back in custody yet?'

'Why was he released?'

'Are the police responsible for allowing this second murder to take place?' the tall woman's voice rose above the rest. 'Who is going to be held accountable for this?'

For an instant, Geraldine lost the composure that had been so carefully drilled into her and lost her temper. Just in time, she regained her self-control and shook her head.

'I'm afraid I can't comment,' she replied. The reporter had no idea how brittle Geraldine's mask of self-assurance was. 'You will have to wait for the press release, along with your colleagues. We cannot make an exception for you, however loudly you shout at me. Now please step aside or I'll have you removed.'

She nodded at the uniformed constable who joined them. Grumbling under her breath, the reporter stood aside and Geraldine passed through the cordon. She could hardly blame a journalist for criticising the police for releasing Ben prematurely, when she suspected her own colleagues held her responsible for freeing him to claim a second victim.

28

WITH A SICKENING SENSE of déjà vu, Geraldine saw that the location was similar, although this time the body had been dumped on the path, not concealed in a small clearing in the trees. Nevertheless, there were obvious parallels between this crime and the murder of George Gardner just twelve days earlier. Both bodies had been abandoned in a woodland setting, where the killer could deposit them without being seen. The forensic tent had not yet been erected so police vehicles and uniformed constables were shielding the corpse from view, in case any members of the public chanced along. They were also keen to protect the scene from reporters and prevent them from catching sight of the body, even from a distance. Geraldine and Ian pulled on protective shoe coverings before making their way across the grass verge, avoiding stepping on the road, which scene of crime officers were examining for tyre marks.

A woman was crouching down by the body when they reached it. She straightened up at their approach, and introduced herself as the medical officer. She looked very young and very serious. Her blonde hair was scraped back off her face and secured in a bun, which was no doubt practical in the circumstances, but emphasised the severity of her appearance.

'It's all right, I'm done,' she said tersely, although they had not asked her how much longer she would be. 'Rigor is advanced, which means she must have been dead for more than twelve hours, so she was probably killed early yesterday evening.'

As she was speaking, she stepped aside so they could see

the corpse. The dead woman was lying on her back, looking somehow crumpled. Her legs were twisted awkwardly in an unnatural pose, as though she had been dropped on the ground and left lying in an untidy heap where she had fallen. She was plump, and wearing black trousers, a white shirt, and a navy jacket, and at first sight there was nothing to suggest the attack had been sexually motivated. Geraldine's gaze lingered for a moment on the dead woman's face. She was quite young, with fair hair, full cheeks, and plain features. Her lips and nose were badly bruised, and her blue eyes stared blindly up at the sky.

A young constable stepped forward. He looked pale, and bore himself with an air of poorly suppressed agitation.

'I tried to resuscitate her,' he said. 'But by the time we arrived it was too late to do anything for her.'

A scene of crime officer joined them, holding up an evidence bag that appeared to contain gigantic brown slugs. On closer examination, Geraldine realised that what she had mistaken for slugs turned out to be the fingers of a yellow rubber glove.

'It's a glove,' she blurted out in surprise.

The scene of crime officer nodded. 'The victim appears to have been suffocated by having that glove thrust down her throat, blocking her windpipe, while at the same time her nostrils were pinched together, just to make sure she couldn't possibly breathe. Whoever did this wanted to make sure she didn't survive the assault.'

'So there's no question in your mind that she was murdered?' Ian asked.

'None at all, unless she pushed a rubber glove down her own throat and held her own nose until she suffocated,' the scene of crime officer replied promptly.

'Was she killed here?' Geraldine asked.

The scene of crime officer shook his head. 'It doesn't look that way, although she's been lying here overnight so the evidence isn't completely clear cut. But there's very little evidence of any disturbance on the ground around her, so it's more likely she was already dead when she was brought here.'

'The post mortem will be able to tell you more,' the doctor added. She was suddenly brisk, as though she had just remembered somewhere else she needed to be.

'So the murder weapon was a rubber glove,' Geraldine muttered. 'That's odd.'

'We've had a scarf, and now a glove. Perhaps next time he'll use a hat,' Ian said, with an irritable smile.

'There won't be a next time,' Geraldine said firmly.

'So it's looking like Ben Foster belongs behind bars after all,' Ian agreed grimly.

Geraldine turned away without answering. She was reluctant to admit that she was still not convinced Ben was guilty. If she voiced her opinion aloud, it might sound as though she was trying to cover up for her error of judgement in releasing him. The doctor took her leave. With a stab of envy, Geraldine watched her walk quickly away from the scene.

'Come on, then,' Ian said. 'Let's go.'

'We still can't be sure Ben killed either of them,' Geraldine pointed out as they drove away.

'On the face of it, he does seem the most likely suspect,' Ian replied. 'We have evidence that implicates him in George's murder, and as soon as he was out of custody, there's another murder.'

'But doesn't that suggest he's innocent? If he was a killer, surely he wouldn't have struck again as soon as he was free, when doing so seems to confirm his guilt? He can't be such a fool, can he?'

But as she was speaking, she recalled Ben's reaction when she had told him he was free to leave his cell.

'You can't ignore the DNA evidence found on the scarf that was used to kill George,' Ian said.

'You know perfectly well that someone else could have used Ben's scarf.'

Ian sighed and Geraldine fell silent, wondering whether she had released a suspect who had taken advantage of his liberty to claim another victim.

'If he is guilty, I'll never forgive myself,' she muttered.

Ian glanced at her anxiously. 'You did what you had to do,' he said. 'Don't beat yourself up over it.'

'Most people's mistakes don't cost someone else their life.'

'It wasn't a mistake. You followed procedure. That's the nature of the job,' Ian said. 'And if Ben's killed someone else that's hardly your fault. We're the good guys, remember? We're the ones who are trying to preserve lives. No one could blame you for releasing a man you believed to be innocent.'

Geraldine wanted to explain that she wasn't only upset that Ben might have killed again because of her error. She was afraid she might never again be able to trust her own judgement. She had an enviable reputation at work, built on her seemingly unwavering instinct for the truth. Her colleagues joked that she was infallible. It wasn't merely that her reputation would be dented if it turned out she had blundered. Without an unswerving confidence in her own powers of deduction, she would struggle to do her job. Despite the quantities of evidence that were thrown up in any investigation, the police were often working in the dark, unable to piece the minutiae together into a coherent whole. Geraldine's ability to complete the puzzle and reach the truth was at times almost uncanny. She often surprised herself when her unsubstantiated impressions proved to be right. If she lost confidence in her instinct for the truth, she would be just another member of the team, waiting for some bright detective to crack the case, her past successes mere fluke.

29

GERALDINE FELT AS THOUGH she had stepped into a nightmare when Eileen announced that forensic investigators had confirmed Ben's DNA was on the glove that had been used to stifle the life out of a second victim. She stared at the floor, willing everyone to forget that she had released Ben to kill again. This time the victim was a woman, but she too had been suffocated with an item of clothing. Again, Ben Foster's DNA was detected on the unlikely murder weapon. Yet Geraldine still had reservations.

'Something doesn't add up,' she muttered to Ian.

'I understand why you might be reluctant to believe the evidence,' he replied. 'It's a tough situation for you, given how things have turned out, but you just have to deal with it. We all make mistakes. You're by no means the first police officer to release a killer. At least you had good reason for what you did. It wasn't incompetence.'

Geraldine shook her head. Remembering what the witness had told her about Ben's walk with his dog, it was simply not possible for him to have leapt on a bicycle at the same time.

'The second bicycle was clearly irrelevant,' Ian murmured with exaggerated patience. 'It had nothing to do with George's murder.'

'But Sallyanne Hodgskin's statement proves Ben didn't murder George.'

Geraldine had spoken more loudly than she had intended, and several colleagues turned to stare at her.

'You don't think your witness could have been mistaken about what she saw, or when she saw it?' Ariadne enquired gently.

'That is the most likely explanation,' Eileen agreed grimly.

Geraldine shook her head. 'The witness had no reason to lie. She didn't know Ben.'

'That's what she said,' Naomi pointed out.

'No one's suggesting your witness deliberately lied to mislead us,' Ian said.

Geraldine didn't remonstrate, although she noticed how Sallyanne Hodgskin had become 'her' witness, as though the other members of the team were keen to distance themselves from the witness statement.

'I just think there are too many questions,' she persisted. 'For a start, if Ben is the killer, why would he leave a scarf and then a glove with his DNA on it at the scene? It's plausible that he dropped the scarf, but the glove was stuffed in his latest victim's mouth. Why would he leave evidence of his guilt, which we were obviously going to find? We couldn't miss it, could we? He knows we have his DNA on the database. And next, why would he choose to deposit the bodies so close to where he lives? Rowntree Park is five minutes' walk from his house. The second victim wasn't even killed there, but was deliberately moved and deposited there. Can Ben really be that stupid?'

'Or that arrogant,' Eileen said.

'Yes,' Naomi agreed. 'Having found a secluded spot in the park, it seems perfectly reasonable that he would leave a second body there after it worked so well for him the first time.'

'But it didn't work for him, did it?' Geraldine objected. 'We arrested him straightaway.'

For someone convinced Ben was guilty of both murders, it was easy to come up with the argument that the glove was still in his latest victim's mouth because Ben had been unable to pull it out once the victim was dead.

'And he probably didn't want to hang around,' Eileen added.

Geraldine was relieved when the briefing drew to an end and

she could leave the police station. Avoiding her colleagues, she went straight to speak to the pathologist conducting the post mortem. If they were going to arrest Ben again, she had to do everything she could to discover the truth, whether it proved him guilty or exonerated him. If the former, she would have to live with the consequences of her own decision. In time she would come to terms with her mistake, but for his second victim there would be no moving on from the tragedy.

'Well, well, well, you just can't keep away,' Jonah greeted her with a broad grin. 'I always knew you would fall under my spell if I only waited long enough. It just goes to show that it pays to be patient. Yes, it must be my irresistible charm.'

Geraldine interrupted him with a smile. At least Jonah did not appear to be censoring her for releasing Ben.

'What can you tell me?' she asked.

She gazed down at the body of a young woman, her naked skin so pale it was almost translucent. Narrowing her eyes, Geraldine imagined she could see blood vessels and organs beneath the skin. But no blood now flowed through the dead woman's veins and arteries; her heart was still, her brain starved of oxygen.

'We've got the same DNA inside the glove as was found on the scarf used to suffocate George Gardner, so this was clearly the same killer, Ben Foster,' Jonah began.

'It's all a bit too clear', Geraldine muttered.

Jonah looked up at Geraldine with a puzzled frown. 'What do you mean?'

'Only that it all seems a bit too convenient.' She hesitated. 'Don't you think someone else could be using Ben's scarf and gloves?'

Jonah glanced quizzically at her. 'Well, it's possible, I suppose, but that kind of speculation isn't part of my remit. All I'm paid to do is report what I find. I leave the clever deductions to you. Do we know who she is yet?'

'No, but we'll find out soon enough. People don't just disappear without someone noticing.'

He nodded. 'Not unless they want to. She's clearly a young woman, who took reasonably good care of herself,' Jonah went on, without explaining his cryptic comment. 'She was healthy and sexually active.'

'Was this a sexual assault?'

'No. There's no evidence she was interfered with in any way. I concluded she was sexually active because she was on the pill, and she's not a virgin.'

Geraldine felt an unexpected wave of pity for the dead woman, who looked so young and vulnerable, lying naked on the table. She was chubby, and her round face gave her a childlike appearance. Her dyed blonde hair was dark at the roots and her nails were bitten to the quick, reminding Geraldine of her own twin sister. Reining in an unexpected rush of emotion, Geraldine turned to the pathologist.

'What else can you tell us about her?'

'I'd guess she was about thirty,' he replied. 'You'll be able to confirm her age when you know who she is. For now, let's go with thirty. She has good muscle tone and was well nourished, with a robust figure, and naturally dark hair dyed blonde. She was dressed in black trousers, with a white shirt and navy jacket and low heeled court shoes, a kind of nondescript outfit suitable for a workplace.'

Geraldine nodded. She had seen photographs from the crime scene. The victim's hair, which had been scraped back in a high ponytail when she was killed, now hung loose, nearly reaching her shoulders.

'She could have been on her way home from work when she encountered the killer.'

Jonah nodded. 'That looks quite likely.'

'Which means her killer could have been a stranger.'

'Yes, possibly,' Jonah agreed. 'Or he could have been waiting for her.' Geraldine frowned. 'He could have been waiting for someone to be his next victim, and it just happened to be her.'

The killer had probably known the dead woman, but it was possible she had died as a result of a chance encounter. Somehow a random waste of a life seemed more poignant than a planned murder. It would mean that if the woman had passed a certain spot five or ten minutes earlier, or later, she might still be alive. The survival of a human being could depend on such a fragile chance.

'I'll let you know the result of the tox report,' Jonah said. 'Although my guess is that she had a very healthy diet.'

'I thought you didn't speculate,' Geraldine teased him.

She hid her feelings, but she was decidedly disgruntled. Even Jonah's good humour failed to cheer her up. She had spent her whole adult life so far attempting to capture killers and protect innocent lives. The thought that she was in some way responsible for a young woman's death was hard to tolerate, even if her blunder had been inadvertent.

30

ON RETURNING TO THE police station, Geraldine found an atmosphere of dismay among her colleagues. She was startled to hear that Ben had gone missing.

'What do you mean, he's missing?' she asked Ariadne.

'Just that. He's disappeared,' her friend replied, with a grimace.

Ariadne told her that Ian had gone to Ben's house, accompanied by a sergeant, to arrest the suspect, but had found no one at home. Having set up surveillance on the house, he had gone straight to the garage where Ben worked, only to learn that Ben had been sent packing after his earlier arrest.

'So he's not at home, and he's not at work,' Ian told Geraldine grimly when she went to hear about it directly from him. 'As you can imagine, the manager of the garage was not exactly complimentary about our policing,' he added. 'Let's just hope he doesn't speak to the media before we find Ben.'

Geraldine swore. She had not been convinced that Ben was guilty, but his vanishing seemed to indicate that he had reason to hide from the police.

'Let's wait and see,' she said. 'It makes sense that he wouldn't have gone back to the garage. The manager there was hardly ready to welcome him back with open arms. He's probably just out somewhere and will go home this evening. Maybe he's out looking for another job,' she added hopefully.

Ian gave her a sceptical glance. She was grateful when he did not reply. She did not need him to tell her that she was grasping at straws. In the meantime, with Ben missing, they had work to do. Eileen already had a team in place contacting stations and airports in case he tried to leave the country, and a warrant had been requested to search his house.

'We could wait until Christine gets home,' Geraldine suggested.

But it seemed that Ben's wife was not prepared to co-operate, if she even knew where her husband was. She was not at home, and Ariadne had gone to the shop where she worked to enquire about Ben's whereabouts. Christine had insisted she had no idea where her husband was. Of course there was a chance she knew exactly where he was and was not prepared to disclose his location. Reluctantly, Geraldine had to admit that Eileen had been right to instigate a search for the missing suspect, whose guilt was looking increasingly likely.

That afternoon, a handbag was handed in at the police station. A young woman had come across it in Rowntree Park, not far from where the body of the unidentified victim was found. The desk sergeant called Eileen straightaway, and she sent Geraldine to fetch the bag.

'It may be nothing to do with the dead woman,' the sergeant said as he placed the bag on the desk between them, 'but no one's reported a bag missing, so chances are it belonged to the woman found in the park. I mean, I could be wrong, but it could be hers.'

Geraldine slipped the bag into an evidence pouch and took it straight to a member of the technical team. Pulling on gloves, he examined the contents of the bag, while Geraldine watched.

'Unlock the phone,' she instructed him.

Her colleague plugged the phone into a charger, unlocked it and opened up the photographs. The images bore enough resemblance to the corpse in the mortuary to convince Geraldine that she was looking at the dead woman's phone. She looked quite different, but she had the same dark roots in her hair and the same bitten nails.

'The killer wouldn't have wanted to hang on to it, so he might well have discarded it near the body,' she said to Eileen a few moments later.

'But if he killed her somewhere else and moved her to the park, why would he take her bag all that way as well? Surely he would have dumped it somewhere else, perhaps where he killed her. Did he want us to discover her identity?'

Geraldine frowned. 'Unless he killed her in a car, and drove straight to the park with the body, and her bag was still in the car. He pushed her out, noticed her bag, and chucked it into the trees.'

Eileen nodded. 'Yes, that would make sense. Anyway send the bag straight off for analysis and hopefully we'll find something useful.'

Geraldine agreed, although she secretly hoped they wouldn't find Ben's DNA on the bag, which had belonged to a woman called Jamie Benson. If the evidence proved that Ben had handled the bag, that would confirm his guilt beyond any real doubt, proving that, indirectly at least, Geraldine was responsible for Jamie's death. It was a horrible thought. In the meantime, they knew the identity of the dead woman and Geraldine had work to do tracking down her family. It always felt like prying, investigating the life of someone who was dead, but it was a necessary part of Geraldine's job. On this occasion, she made a discovery that shocked her so much that for a moment she stared at her screen in disbelief. Jamie Benson had worked as a receptionist at the garage where Ben was employed as a mechanic.

'What's up with you?' Ariadne asked.

'What?'

'You just gasped and well, you look like you've just seen a ghost. What's wrong?'

'Nothing.'

Geraldine hesitated. Everyone was going to find out the truth soon enough. With a shrug of resignation, she told Ariadne that she had just discovered Jamie and Ben had worked together.

'So? It doesn't necessarily mean Ben killed her,' Ariadne said gently.

'No, but it makes it seem more likely.'

'Look, even if Ben murdered Jamie, you didn't do anything wrong. You only did what anyone else would have done.'

'But no one else released him.'

'Seriously, Geraldine, no one can blame you for what happened.'

It was true the evidence that Ben would have known Jamie was circumstantial, but it seemed pretty conclusive nevertheless. Just the fact that they had worked together made Ben's innocence seem unlikely. Even if no one else considered Geraldine in any way responsible for Jamie's death, as Ariadne had generously suggested, how could she not blame herself?

Ian gazed solemnly at Geraldine as they sat down together that evening.

'Are you all right?'

She grunted.

'You don't seem like your normal self.'

'How can I be feeling like my normal self, when I released Ben and enabled him to kill again?' she blurted out.

'Don't be ridiculous. You weren't to know what would happen.'

'Everyone else thought he was guilty.'

'Everyone else could have been wrong.'

'But they weren't,' she cried out in a burst of passion. 'I was the one who was wrong, and a woman died for my mistake.'

'Are you more upset about the consequences of your mistake, or the fact that you were wrong?' he asked, frowning.

Geraldine didn't answer.

'Listen,' he went on more kindly, 'Ben might still turn out

to be innocent. And even if he's guilty, there's no point in your stressing about what you did. Your motive was sound. And if you think about it, if Ben is guilty, that slimy fish Jeremy would doubtless have got him acquitted if you hadn't released him, and then he would have killed someone else anyway, and possibly got away with it. As it is, he's not going to escape justice and that's thanks to you.'

'That's a specious argument, and you know it,' she snapped. 'And the lawyer's name is Jerome, not Jeremy.'

'Right as usual,' he replied promptly.

'You did that deliberately to make me feel better, didn't you? Do you really think it's so easy to humour me?'

But she was mollified by his attempt to calm her concern. And when he approached and put his arms around her and held her close, she felt comforted. Not for the first time, she was thankful that she was no longer living alone.

31

Pressure at the police station was mounting. Eileen was increasingly tetchy and it was evident that she was being pushed to get a result. More officers had been drafted in to help with the investigation and a massive door-to-door questioning had been set up in York. Geraldine went to the garage where Ben and Jamie had both worked. A workshop was situated behind a small forecourt which was packed with half-a-dozen cars. Only a couple of them looked roadworthy. She made her way through the cars to the small office beside the workshop and enquired about Ben.

'I'm done with him,' the manager said, scowling at Geraldine's identity card. 'As soon as he stepped in the door again I told him he could get lost. There's no way I'm having him back here. He's a bloody liability.'

Andy Compton was a small man, red-faced and clearly agitated. He was dressed in greasy blue overalls, and his fingernails were black with oil. He stood behind a narrow desk, glaring at her.

'I gave the guy a chance. I didn't have to do that. Out of the goodness of my heart, I gave him a chance. He begged me for a job, and insisted he was innocent of any wrongdoing and, like a mug, I believed him, didn't I? He gave me the whole sob story: it was an accident, could have happened to anyone, he was innocent, he's got a wife to support, and all that crap. And muggins here was taken in. And now look how he repays me. It's utter chaos here. Ben was arrested, carted off by your people without a by your leave. All well and good but there's never a thought for anyone else, is there? How was I supposed to manage with all the work I had booked in, while I was a man down? Were you going to help me out? Huh? Fat chance of that. And now here you are, back again, asking to speak to him. Well, as soon as he turned up yesterday I told him to sling his hook. So what now? You're just here to disrupt our work again, are you? Well? What do you want? Only I haven't got time for this.'

Geraldine was duly apologetic as she asked to speak to his staff, and enquired whether there was anyone Ben had been particularly friendly with.

'No. He wasn't here to make friends. He was here to work. That's why I hired him. Because there's work to be done. Only now he's not doing anything because he's gone. He came back with some cock and bull story about how it was all a mistake this time round, and he was ready to come back to work. I sent him packing, work or no work. I can't be doing with all this. It's doing my head in.'

The manager folded his arms and glared at her as though to indicate that it was somehow her fault that Ben had been arrested.

'We appreciate your co-operation,' she said, attempting and failing to placate him. 'Who else works here?'

'Apart from Ben, there are two mechanics besides me, and a girl who answers the phone and books cars in, but you can't speak to her because she's not turned up for work. Can you believe it? She didn't even call in, just didn't show up. Is she that ill that she can't even send a text or pick up the phone? She spends all day on the phone, for Christ's sake. It's not as if she doesn't know how to use one.'

Geraldine shook her head with an expression of regret as she told him Jamie was not coming back.

'What do you mean, not coming back? She can't just walk out. She needs to give notice. What the hell is going on around here? Ever since your colleague turned up, it's like the whole world has gone to pot. Well, I need time to hire a replacement so, like it or not, she's going to have to work out her notice.'

Geraldine sighed. 'I'm afraid that's not going to happen. Jamie is dead.'

The manager gaped, momentarily silenced by the news. 'Dead? Dead?' he stammered at last.

'I'm sorry.'

'Dead? Jamie? What? How?'

The manager sat down abruptly behind his small desk and shook his head. 'I don't understand,' he murmured. 'I don't understand.' He looked up sharply. 'What happened? Was it one of the men she was seeing?'

'What makes you say that?'

He shrugged, his face twisted in a scowl. 'She was easy, you know what I'm saying?'

Something in his veiled expression made Geraldine wonder whether he had slept with Jamie himself. Quietly, she explained that Jamie's body had been found in Rowntree Park, and the police were currently investigating the circumstances of her death.

'Investigating? Circumstances?' he repeated. 'You mean she was murdered? She was–' He broke off suddenly and banged his fist on his desk. 'Was it him?'

'Who are you talking about?'

'Ben, was it him? Did he kill her?' He half rose to his feet.

'What makes you say that?'

Geraldine held her breath, waiting to hear of some violent row that had broken out between Ben and Jamie, or a relationship that had turned sour, provoking a passionate jealousy in the suspect.

'Because you arrested him and then you let him go, didn't you?' the manager replied, glaring at her accusingly and resuming his seat.

'If there's any reason why you might suspect Ben of being in any way angry with Jamie, or somehow emotionally involved with her, you need to tell me.'

But the manager shook his head, suddenly tentative. 'I'm not sure they even spoke to each other. Not in my presence, anyway. Jamie worked in the office. She hardly ever went into the workshop and the boys didn't have much to do with her. She books the cars in, but I deal with the invoices and payments myself. Not that I don't trust her – didn't trust her – but it's just the way things work here. Jamie had very little call to go in the workshop and I'm not sure she ever did. To be honest, I don't think she was too happy with all the oil and grease.' He glanced involuntarily at his blackened hands. 'She was a bit fastidious, if you ask me. I mean, if you object to oily hands, don't work in a bloody garage.'

Something in his belligerent tone made Geraldine wonder if he had engaged in the same argument with Jamie himself, perhaps when he had been putting his own hands on her.

'Could she have had a relationship with Ben outside of work?' Geraldine asked.

The manager shrugged. 'Not that I know of. That's not to say they couldn't have known each other outside of work, but I wouldn't know anything about that. Wasn't he married? He told me he had a wife. Not that that makes any difference to some men.'

'You're married, aren't you? Did it make a difference to you?'

He was so indignant at the implied accusation that Geraldine was almost sure he had been having an affair with Jamie. She let that line of questioning drop. If he had ever had a fling with Jamie, he was not going to admit to it. Storing her suspicion away, she asked to speak to the other two mechanics.

'Can't this wait? They're working flat out as it is, and with Ben gone, and me having to man the phones until I find a replacement, as well as helping out with the work, I can't afford for them to ease up for a moment.'

Geraldine assured him her questions could not wait and he

went to summon his mechanics. The first one came into the office, wiping his oily hands on a filthy rag. He responded to most of Geraldine's questions with a surly grunt.

'How well did you know Ben?' she asked.

The mechanic grunted.

'I'm sorry, what was that?'

He stuffed the black rag in his pocket and wiped his filthy hands on his overalls, which were already stained with oil. Geraldine repeated her question.

'I saw him and we talked about the cars, that's all.'

'Did you ever see him speak to Jamie in the office?'

'No.' He shook his head. 'None of us had much to do with her. Leastways, not me. She was a slut.'

The second mechanic was more talkative, but also more guarded. He entered the office whistling. Unlike his colleague, he seemed surprised to see Geraldine.

'Hullo,' he greeted her cheerfully. 'Who's this then?'

He lost some of his ebullience when Geraldine introduced herself and explained the reason for her visit.

'You want to know if Ben was friendly with Jamie?' he asked, frowning.

'In a nutshell, yes.'

'Why don't you ask them, then? What do you think I could know about it? I just come in, keep my head down, do my job, and go home. I don't go around spying on other people and it's none of my business what they get up to.'

'What did Ben and Jamie get up to?'

The mechanic shook his head and refused to be drawn. Geraldine asked a few more questions, but she was unable to glean any new information from anyone who worked at the garage. Eventually she gave up and left. But her time had not been wasted. 'Did you get the impression they were hiding anything?' Ariadne asked her when she returned to the police station to log her findings.

Geraldine shrugged. 'I don't know,' she said. 'But I wonder whether Ben had a fling with Jamie, and I'm pretty sure the manager did too.'

'So we're looking at a crime of passion?' Ariadne asked. 'One woman, two men.'

'I suspect there were more than two,' Geraldine replied.

Ariadne smiled. 'Well, since when was it a crime to want to have a good time?'

32

THEY HAD ALL GATHERED together for a fish and chips supper to celebrate her father's birthday. Christine did her best to control herself as she watched her mother bringing in the plates, two at a time. It was difficult not to break down and cry. She was tempted to seize her plate and hurl it across the room, spraying fish and chips over the table and carpet. She could just imagine her mother's startled expression. Only Christine's pride prevented her from allowing her feelings to get the better of her in front of her family. Her sister and brother-in-law were grinning obsequiously as the plates were brought in.

'Are you sure I can't do anything, Mum?' Francesca called out.

'Sixty-three years young and I don't feel a day over twenty-one,' her father said, smiling at his wife as she brought in the last two plates. 'You look even lovelier than when we first met, Hilary. And what's even better, all my loved ones are here to celebrate my birthday.'

Christine despised his forced jollity almost as much as she hated his gruff temper.

'The family isn't quite all here,' Christine's mother replied sourly.

She scowled at Christine, as though she suspected Ben had deliberately chosen to stay away, just to slight his parents-in-law. As it happened, the truth was far worse than that, but Christine bit her tongue and said nothing.

'I'm surprised your husband let you come here without him,' her mother continued.

Christine merely shrugged. She could not trust herself to speak calmly.

'Yes, it's a pity Ben couldn't be here,' Francesca murmured, nodding at their mother. 'I hope he's feeling better soon.'

She cast a sympathetic glance at Christine, who bristled. Having phoned her parents and her sister only three days earlier to share the news that Ben had been released, she had not yet admitted to them that he had lost his job and stayed out all night, or that the police had been to see her at work that morning looking for him. She had not seen or heard from him for a good two days, and she had no idea where he was or what had happened to him. She had a horrible suspicion the police wanted to arrest him again. She could think of no other reason why they were so keen to find him. It was difficult enough to cope with his disappearance and the fear of his threatened re-arrest, without having to put up with her sister's exaggerated expressions of sympathy, and her mother's rampant censure. Even without knowing the truth, her mother could not hold back for long. They finished their supper and Christine's mother began gathering up the plates.

'Why you ever married that good-for-nothing is beyond me, Christine,' she muttered. 'We brought you up to be a good Christian woman, like everyone else in the family.'

'Now, now, Hilary,' her father interjected. 'It's my birthday.'

'The truth is the truth,' her mother said. 'And if that man has seen the inside of a church once in all the years he's been married to my daughter, I'd be surprised. It's not right, Derek, and you know it.' She pursed her lips in disapproval.

'Not everyone is as devout as you are, Hilary,' Christine's brother-in-law murmured. 'More's the pity,' he added quickly to prevent his comment being misconstrued.

'Are we going to spend all evening talking about Christine's husband?' Francesca demanded. 'You seem to be forgetting why we're here. It's dad's birthday. This evening should be about him, not about your husband, Christine.'

'It wasn't me who brought him up,' Christine reminded her.

Her mother sniffed and went off to the kitchen, muttering about 'lowlife'. She returned a moment later bearing a large iced cake with about a dozen candles, half of which flickered and went out with the movement of air as she entered the room.

'Wait, wait!' Francesca shrieked, jumping up from her chair. 'We have to relight the candles so daddy can blow them out.'

'Oh for goodness sake,' her father said. 'I'm not a child.' But he was beaming.

'There are a dozen candles,' his wife replied, responding to Francesca's excitement. 'And you can blow them all out. It's the best I could do,' she went on with a conciliatory smile. 'I could hardly put sixty-three candles on one cake.'

She relit the candles and insisted her husband blow them out, while he repeated that he was not a child. As they all sang Happy Birthday, Christine's father cut the cake and served himself a large slab.

'It's chocolate cake with chocolate butter cream,' Christine's mother said.

'It looks delicious, my dear,' her father replied.

'Shouldn't Christine take a piece of cake home for Ben?' her brother-in-law enquired.

Francesca turned to glare at him. Afraid that he had said something inappropriate, he began to chatter nervously.

'What I mean is, this cake is so good, I'm sure he'd enjoy it. Who wouldn't?' He looked at his mother-in-law with an ingratiating smile. 'It really is delicious, Hilary. I've never tasted a cake as chocolatey as this. I know I'd want Francesca to bring a slice home for me if I hadn't been able to come.'

'But you did come to celebrate Derek's birthday with us,' Christine's mother replied. 'I hope you tell that husband of yours what he missed today,' she added sharply. 'And no, Christine won't be taking a slice of cake home for him. If he can't be bothered to show us the courtesy of coming here to celebrate Derek's birthday with us, then he can't expect any favours in return.'

Christine's brother-in-law lowered his head and concentrated on his cake. For a few moments they all ate in silence but with the subject of Christine's husband reintroduced, it seemed her mother could not resist carping again.

'I dare say there are plenty of people who would enjoy a piece of this cake. I spent all morning making it.'

'And very good it is too, Hilary,' her husband said.

'But this cake is for those of us who took the trouble to come here to celebrate together.'

At this point it occurred to Christine that she probably should have told her family the reason for Ben's absence. They were going to find out at some point anyway, and when they did, they would realise she had been lying to them. But she kept silent. After all, once Ben came home and everything was cleared up, her family would never have to find out that the police had been sniffing around again. Gazing at her family, so complacent and judgemental, she was frightened. For the first time, she allowed herself to consider the notion that Ben might be guilty. It was almost impossible to imagine her laidback husband as a multiple murderer. He was such a gentle man. She had never known him to fly into a violent temper. The worst she could say of him was that he was occasionally irascible. Yet the police were after him again on suspicion of murder. It was incredible, yet it was almost as unlikely that the police would have suspected him twice without any evidence.

'Are you all right?' her sister asked suddenly, leaning forward and peering at her.

'I'm fine,' Christine replied. 'Why are you asking?'

'Francesca is just concerned about you,' her brother-in-law said. 'All that must have been very difficult for you.'

'All what?' she replied, belligerent in her resolve to defend her husband. 'I don't know what nonsense you've chosen to believe this time.'

Her family didn't even know that Ben had disappeared, or that the police were looking for him again, yet they were busy judging him.

'You know perfectly well what he means,' Francesca said, leaping to her husband's defence. 'There's no call to snap. We're on your side.'

'Well, God protect me from my enemies.'

'Christine, you will not take the name of the Lord in vain in this house,' her mother scolded her.

Christine stood up. 'Well, it was a lovely evening, but it's time to go. Happy birthday, Dad.'

No one remonstrated with her or asked her to stay, even though it was still early. No doubt they would bitch about her and her godless husband after she had gone. Well, they could all go to hell as far as she was concerned. Her parents had raised her to follow Jesus, but she had never seen much evidence of Christian love or compassion in their household.

33

FRAZZLED AFTER SPENDING A couple of hours with her family, and exhausted from worrying about Ben, who had not come home and had not been home for two nights, Christine climbed wearily into the car. She tried his mobile phone once again before setting off, and it went straight to voicemail. She shivered. It was raining lightly, and she nearly skidded on a bend, driving too fast in her agitation. Taking a deep shuddering breath, she forced herself to drive more slowly. Although she had lost her faith many years ago, she found herself praying that she would find Ben at home. Telling herself he was probably fast asleep in bed, she did her best to reassure herself that everything was going to be all right. Ben had suffered more than his fair share of misfortune and, by association, so had she. There was no way he deserved to have further problems thrown at him. It just would not be fair. A firm nonbeliever, she found herself striking a silent bargain with God. Let Ben be there when she reached home, and she vowed to believe in God for the rest of her life. She would even attend church regularly, despite the unmerited satisfaction it would give her mother.

Arriving home, she flung herself through the front door in her haste to find him. The house felt empty.

'Ben!' she called out. 'I'm home! Ben! Ben!'

There was no answer. Thinking he must be asleep, she ran upstairs. He wasn't in the bedroom. She searched the rest of the house with increasing desperation. Ben was not there. She went all around the house again, checking in every room, even though there was no sign of him. She was alone in the house. Alone in the world. She did not know whether Ben had met with an accident, or had left her. Perhaps he really was a murderer, and had gone on the run. On balance, the first scenario seemed the most likely, and was preferable to the other two possibilities, especially if he wasn't badly hurt. She could hardly go to the police, so instead she spent a miserable half-hour on the phone to the local hospital, trying to establish whether anyone matching Ben's description had been admitted unexpectedly.

If Ben was conscious, she was sure he would have contacted her by now. That suggested he might be seriously injured. He had been missing for nearly three days and must realise she would be worried about him. She tried his phone again but it went straight to voicemail, as it had done for the past two evenings when he had not come home. At first she had assumed he had gone out on a bender. He had left for work before her, as usual, on Wednesday morning. Before she had left for work herself, he had called, virtually incoherent with fury, to tell her he had lost his job.

'That bloody muppet. Who does he think he is? Well, he can take his job and shove it up his arse.'

It had taken him a while to vent his anger. When she had finally been able to speak, her attempt to calm him down had only provoked him further.

'We can work something out,' she had told him. 'You deserve better than that. You never liked working there anyway. You'll get another job.'

'Don't be stupid,' he interrupted her. 'Who's going to give me a job now? After this? My life is ruined!'

Appreciating it would not be easy to find employment with his record, she had not been able to think of a single helpful suggestion.

'You've still got me,' was all she could think of to say.

It should have been enough to calm him down, reminding

him how she had remained at his side through all his past difficulties. She had suffered through the whole wretched business with him, visiting him in custody, and keeping her job which had enabled her to pay the best lawyer she could find, a lawyer who had eventually got him off with little more than a slap on the wrist when everyone had expected him to serve a custodial sentence.

But he had merely snarled that her support was no good to him. It wasn't going to keep him out of prison.

'You think you can find anyone else mad enough to stand by you at a time like this?' she had fumed.

'Piss off then, if that's how you feel,' he had snapped at her.

That was the last time they had spoken before he disappeared. She had tried to call him at lunchtime, but he had not answered his phone, and he hadn't come home. When she saw him again, she intended to scold him for leaving her alone, not knowing where he was or what had happened to him. But she was not really angry. She could not really blame him. The next morning, she had called the garage in case they knew where he was, but the manager had sworn at her and told her Ben was not there and would not be coming back. Only then had the reality sunk in that he had disappeared and she had no idea where he had gone. She began to worry seriously. His wallet and phone had gone, but nothing else. In a pathetic attempt to fool herself that she was not really concerned about him, she had gone to her father's birthday tea, as arranged. That had been a mistake. But at least she was home again. Praying that Ben would come back soon, she made herself a cup of tea and sat down to wait. There was no way she was going to be able to sleep.

Shortly after ten, there was a knock at the door. She leapt up, unable to stop herself grinning. The idiot must have lost his key, but he was home and everything was going to be all right. She flung open the door, with a broad smile of welcome, and started back.

'Christine Foster, step aside please. We have a warrant to search the premises.'

'No. What? Search what?' Christine stammered.

She made an involuntary move to shut the door, but the large foot of a uniformed policeman prevented it from closing. Christine stared at his broad black shoe, wondering stupidly if it was personal preference on the part of the wearer or regulations that caused him to polish his shoes until they shone.

'We have a warrant to search the premises,' he repeated in a loud monotone.

It was pointless trying to remonstrate. There was nothing she could do to stop them entering the house. She could hardly call the police. Damn it, she couldn't even shut her own front door.

'Can someone please tell me what the hell is going on?' she demanded.

She was aware that tears of rage and frustration were coursing down her cheeks but she didn't care. As two uniformed police officers entered the house, a familiar dark haired detective in a black jacket stepped forward and introduced herself once again.

'Christine, we have a warrant to search your house,' she said quietly.

'Yes, yes, I know you have a search warrant. So everyone keeps telling me. Maybe if you tell me what you're looking for, I might be able to help you,' she added. 'And you wouldn't have to go traipsing all round the house like this. If they break anything—'

Behind her Roxy began to bark frantically.

The inspector looked at her. 'The search team won't break anything. They're highly trained and are very careful when handling other people's belongings. We don't want to cause any trouble.'

'Why don't you all bugger off out of my house then?'

'We're looking for your husband,' the inspector said quietly. 'But you know that, don't you, Christine?'

'No,' she lied. There was no other reason why the police would be searching the house. 'I've no idea where he is, and if I did know I wouldn't tell you. But I can tell you he's sick of you hounding him like this when he's done nothing wrong.'

The police inspector smiled gently. 'If your husband's done nothing wrong, he has nothing to be afraid of.'

Christine waited for her to ask the obvious question: why would an innocent man run from the police? But the inspector didn't speak to her again.

34

On Saturday morning, Jamie's parents were expected at the mortuary, where they had been invited to identify the body. Geraldine arrived early to wait for them. At half past nine precisely, the anatomical pathology technician ushered a middle-aged couple into the visitors' room and introduced them to Geraldine as Mr and Mrs Benson. Although rain had not been forecast, they were both wearing raincoats and the woman was additionally holding an umbrella. Clearly they did not like to take risks. Somehow that made their daughter's untimely death seem even more pitiful than before. They had probably raised her with extreme care, yet for all their efforts, her life had ended in a sudden and violent manner. Danger threatened the cautious as well as deliberate risk takers.

'We've come–' the man began and faltered.

He raised his right hand and stroked his clean-shaven upper lip, while his pale grey eyes peered at Geraldine through rimless spectacles. She returned his gaze and he looked down and coughed. The woman at his side was short and slim, with dark hair and a round face that bore an unmistakable resemblance to the dead woman.

'We're Mr and Mrs Benson,' the woman muttered.

'We're Jamie's parents,' her husband added in a firmer voice.

Geraldine expressed her condolences and invited them to take a seat.

'When can we see her?' the woman asked, without sitting down. 'We want to see her.'

'To make sure,' her husband said. 'We don't know it's her, do we?'

The hope in his expression was hard to watch.

Geraldine sighed quietly. 'I'm afraid there is very little doubt about it, but we do need you to confirm her identity. You don't both have to come with me, if you'd rather not. One of you can wait here.'

Geraldine glanced from one to the other of them as she spoke. Mrs Benson reached out and grabbed hold of her husband's arm.

'We'll do this together,' she replied through gritted teeth.

Geraldine led them into the viewing room where the body lay, covered by a plain white sheet. Stepping forward, Geraldine carefully pulled the sheet back to expose the victim's face. Mrs Benson gasped and turned away, pressing her face against her husband's shoulder, while he stared as though mesmerised by the sight of his daughter's cold features.

'Yes,' he croaked in a voice that trembled with emotion. 'That's her. That's Jamie. That's our daughter. That's Jamie.' He broke off and lowered his head, unable to look any longer.

Without a word, Geraldine led them back to the visitors' room where they collapsed on to a sofa, side-by-side, and sat in silence for a few moments. Geraldine waited for them to speak.

'What happened to her?' Mrs Benson asked at last.

She spoke so softly, Geraldine had to strain to hear

'She was suffocated by a person as yet unidentified. We don't know why. Nothing was stolen from her bag as far as we can tell, and she suffered no other injuries. Your daughter would have known very little about the assault. She must have passed out almost immediately and she would have died without recovering consciousness.'

'How can you be so sure of that?' Mr Benson asked.

'There is no indication that she resisted the attack,' Geraldine replied. 'Normally we would expect to see defence wounds on the victim of an assault, but there were none.'

'She looked very peaceful,' Mrs Benson whispered, and burst into tears.

After a few moments, Geraldine said, 'When you are ready, I have a few questions.'

Mr Benson shook his head. 'We have nothing to say to you,' he replied in a flat voice.

'If you don't feel able to speak to me now, would you prefer to talk to me another time?'

Mr Benson frowned. 'What is there to talk about? She's dead, isn't she? There's nothing more to say. We'd just like to go home now.'

'She was a wonderful – a wonderful–' his wife stammered and broke off, unable to continue.

'Mr and Mrs Benson, we know someone attacked your daughter, and the attack was fatal. We suspect it was a mugging that went wrong. Apart from the suffocation, she was not interfered with at all.' She paused. It was a delicate subject to discuss, but she was doing her best to treat the tragedy sensitively. 'Mr and Mrs Benson, we need to do everything we can to track down whoever did this to your daughter and make sure he – or she – is locked up. We are determined to see justice done.'

'What difference does it make now?' Mrs Benson asked dully. 'She's dead. Nothing can bring her back.'

'No, we can't bring your daughter back,' Geraldine replied gently. 'But until we find whoever did this, it's possible that other young women may be at risk. So we very much hope you will be prepared to help us by answering a few questions.'

The bereaved mother stared stonily at the floor, but Mr Benson looked up and nodded. 'What do you want to know?'

'Did Jamie have any enemies?'

Mr Benson shook his head. 'Enemies? No, she wasn't like that.'

'Jamie's a gentle girl,' his wife said. 'A lovely girl.'

'Was she engaged in any arguments, or had she fallen out with anyone recently?'

'You think it was deliberate?' Mrs Benson asked, raising red-rimmed eyes to glare at Geraldine. 'Are you saying you think someone wanted her dead?'

'That's ridiculous,' her husband said. 'Jamie doesn't have any enemies, and she isn't one to fall out with people. Everyone likes her.'

His wife nodded her head slowly. 'She's a popular girl. She's got lots of friends. Everyone likes her. No one could want to hurt her.'

'Did she have a boyfriend?'

'No, there wasn't anyone,' Mrs Benson replied, unconsciously slipping into the past tense as the reality of her daughter's death began to sink in. 'Not that she would have told us if there was. We got on with her well enough, but we didn't talk about her personal life. It wasn't something we ever discussed.'

'She never brought it up,' her husband added. 'We figured if she had something to tell us, she would tell us. We didn't want to pry. Ask Lizzie, her flatmate. She'll know.'

There was nothing more to be learned from the parents of the murdered woman, and nothing Geraldine could do for them. Having made a note of Lizzie's details, and murmured her condolences again, she left Jamie's parents seated side-by-side on a sofa in the visitors' room at the mortuary. While the search for Ben continued, Geraldine went to question Jamie's former flatmate.

35

GERALDINE FOUND LIZZIE AT home in the flat she had shared with Jamie. They had lived above a gift shop in Gillygate that sold all kinds of kitsch china and pottery, crockery and ornaments. Lizzie came to the door straightaway and nodded when Geraldine introduced herself. It was clear she had been crying, and Geraldine guessed rightly that she had heard about the death of her flatmate. She was a slender young woman with straight mousy hair. She would have been attractive were it not for her extremely long teeth.

'It's so terrible, I just can't believe it,' she burst out when they were both seated in a small untidy living room. 'One of your colleagues told me what happened, but I just can't believe it. Jamie was such a great person, and such a good friend. I can't believe she's really gone.'

Geraldine glanced around. The room looked relatively clean, and smelled fresh, but clothes were strewn everywhere, as though the residents had used the living room as a dressing room. A large television screen dominated one wall but there were no shelves or ornaments. Perhaps the display in the shop they passed every day on their way to and from the flat had given them an aversion to bric-a-brac. Several fashion magazines lay on the floor, interspersed with shirts and jeans, and there were dirty plates and cups on a low coffee table. It was possible Lizzie had not cleared up because she was shocked about Jamie's death, but glancing around Geraldine spotted another dirty plate on the floor, and a bowl under a chair.

'Lizzie,' Geraldine said gently, 'I know this must be an extremely difficult time for you.'

'I've known Jamie since we were twelve,' Lizzie replied. 'We were at school together. I've seen her practically every day since then. She was my best friend, you know? I'll never have another friend like that for the rest of my life, will I? And now she's gone, just like that. Gone.'

Tears slid from her eyes and she wiped them away impatiently, apologising for crying.

'Not at all, it's only natural. I'm sorry to be disturbing you at a time like this, but we need to find out who did this as quickly as we can, and we're hoping you can answer a few questions that might help us.'

Lizzie nodded uncertainly.

'Had Jamie fallen out with anyone recently?'

Lizzie shook her head and repeated what Jamie's parents had said, that her flatmate did not fall out with people.

'She was easy to get along with.' Tears slid from her eyes again. 'She was just – she was so nice.'

'Did she have a boyfriend? Or was she seeing anyone?'

It crossed Geraldine's mind that Jamie and Lizzie might have been closer than platonic friends.

A faint frown crossed the girl's face. 'There was that man where she worked, but she said it wasn't going anywhere. I don't think it was serious, although I know she liked him.'

'What man was that?'

Lizzie shook her head. 'I don't know if I should tell you–'

'Lizzie, this is a murder investigation,' Geraldine interrupted her more severely than she had intended. 'Someone killed your friend. Surely you want to help us find out who did this terrible thing, robbing your friend of her life?'

The girl nodded nervously.

'So who is the man you mentioned?'

'I don't know. It's just that she mentioned a man she worked with. I mean, she talked about him a lot. She never told me his name. She talked about nothing else for a few weeks, and I could tell she was crazy about him, and then she stopped mentioning him, just like that, as though he had never existed. I asked her about him, and she didn't want to say anything at first, but in the end she told me what had happened. It turned out he was married, and he said he wasn't going to leave his wife, and so that was that. She didn't say much, but I think she was pretty cut up about it. I mean, like I said, I think she really liked him.'

'When did the affair take place?'

'It must have started about a month ago, maybe longer. The last time I saw her she told me he had dumped her. He told her he was married and he didn't want his wife to find out about her. He said she could carry on working with him, but nothing was going to happen again. I think she was pretty upset about it. She said she thought she'd been a mug to trust him and I told her to put it behind her and that was the last time we spoke. I don't know if she would have got over him because, well, she's dead now, isn't she?'

Tears rolled down her pale cheeks again, and she dropped her head in her hands and sobbed quietly. Geraldine waited a few moments before she continued.

'Lizzie, are you all right to carry on? Can I get you a drink of water?'

'No, no, I'm okay. But I've told you everything I know.'

'What about the man she was seeing?'

'He was her boss where she worked. That's all I know. I never met him. They used to see each other in his office, after work, after the mechanics had gone home.'

Geraldine thought about the cramped office at the garage where Ben and Jamie had worked, and the oily workshop, and sighed. It was a suitably squalid setting for a sordid love affair, with a middle-aged boss thoughtlessly screwing his young receptionist. She thought about the small red-faced man, and wondered what Jamie had seen in him. He could have been as much as twenty years older than her, but he was not bad-looking. At least his shock on hearing Jamie was dead had appeared to be genuine. But that could have been an act. Whatever the truth, Geraldine needed to question him.

Eileen listened, frowning.

'Talk to Andy Compton here,' she barked when Geraldine had finished, adding, with grim satisfaction, 'he won't be pleased at being dragged along to the police station, but I think it's time we put a little pressure on him.'

'I'll check what time the garage closes on a Saturday and pick him up when he knocks off for the night.'

'No, send a car to pick him up now,' Eileen said.

Geraldine nodded. Eileen was right. Disrupting Andy Compton's routine would rattle him. He was already struggling with a reduced work force, and could ill afford to take any time off himself. But whether that would encourage him to talk or not remained to be seen.

In the meantime, there was still no sign of Ben.

36

ANDY COMPTON WAS VISIBLY fuming when Geraldine and Ian entered the interview room where he was waiting.

'Right,' he snarled before they had even sat down. 'Would you mind telling me what the hell this is all about? Because much as I'd like to sit around jawing all day, my workshop isn't going to run itself.'

'We're looking for a mechanic, Ben Foster, who until recently worked at your garage.'

Andy scowled impatiently. 'Yes, yes, I know you're looking for him. You seem to have forgotten you've already been to see me to ask about him and I told you then that I fired him. Bloody waste of space he was. Nothing but trouble. He's nothing to do with me any more and, if you want the honest truth, I should never have hired him in the first place. Now,' he stood up, 'I'm going back to work and I'll thank you to leave me alone from now on.'

'Sit down,' Ian said. 'Please.'

Andy scowled. 'Jesus, don't you people ever give up?'

He glanced at a robust uniformed constable standing in the doorway.

'What the hell?' he spluttered, but he resumed his seat. 'What do you people want with me? Things are difficult right now, and you're not making it any easier. One of my mechanics has buggered off–'

'You sacked him,' Geraldine pointed out quietly.

'And you won't leave off pestering me about him. And now

my receptionist has been murdered, and I'm having to deal with all the bookings as well as doing the work of two men in the workshop. How am I supposed to manage? And now this. What the hell do you people want with me?'

'Tell us about Jamie,' Geraldine said, leaning forward.

'She worked for me,' Andy replied but he had lost his air of belligerence and his expression grew guarded.

'That's not all she was to you, is it?'

He was suddenly wary. His whole body tensed and his shoulders rose, but he spoke calmly. 'What's that supposed to mean?'

'Andy, we know about your relationship with Jamie.'

'What relationship?'

He was struggling to maintain his composure now. Ian and Geraldine waited, letting him speak.

'You make it sound as though there was something between us. What are you implying? Listen, she worked for me.'

'You were in a sexual relationship with her,' Geraldine said.

If he denied it, there was very little they could do. No one else could back up the claim now. Any accusation was already based on hearsay. To Geraldine's relief, Andy was too stupid, or too irritated, to deny it.

'Yes, yes, all right, all right, so we had a fling. That's not against the law, is it? Anyway,' he added sullenly, 'it didn't last long. I ended it. I told her she could keep her job and things went back to the way they were before. And that's all there is to it. You can try and make more of it if you want, but you're blatantly fishing.' He scowled. 'You can keep me here, or you can let me go, but I'm not saying another word without a lawyer here to defend me. I know how you people twist things.'

'You ended it because you didn't want your wife to find out, didn't you?' Geraldine asked. 'We know that's what happened,' she added after a long silence.

'If you know, why bother to ask me? Now, let me go or get me a lawyer, because I'm not answering one more question until you do.'

'Oh, we've got a lot more than one question for you,' Ian said, his pleasant tone belied by the menacing words.

Ian nodded at the constable who marched Andy from the room, protesting loudly that he needed to get back to work, and detaining him was unlawful as well as unjust. An hour later, they reconvened with a lawyer present, a tall thin man who nodded at them with a faint smile and put his head on one side enquiringly.

'You were having an affair with Jamie Benson,' Geraldine said. 'You didn't want your wife to find out about the affair, and now Jamie's been murdered.'

Andy glanced at his solicitor who shook his head.

'When did the affair begin?' Geraldine enquired.

'It was hardly an affair,' Andy replied, looking slightly embarrassed.

His face was red, but his shoulders were no longer raised and Geraldine had the impression he was relieved. That could have been because he was finally able to confess his infidelity, or it might have been that he thought the police were being distracted from something else he had done.

'You won't tell my wife, will you? It was a stupid little fling, a mistake. I never should have done it. But that's all it was, a stupid mistake.'

'My client does not wish to answer any more questions regarding his personal life,' the solicitor cut in, although it was too late for Andy to try and deny his adultery.

'What would you call your sexual intercourse with your employee, if not an affair?'

Andy shook his head. 'It was nothing. Just a fling, you know.'

'When did your fling begin?' Geraldine amended her question, and Andy frowned.

'It started last Christmas,' he replied. 'It only happened a few times. It was never really a relationship. It didn't mean anything.'

'Not to you perhaps,' Ian muttered.

Geraldine threw him a warning frown. They could not prove the affair had meant anything to Jamie either. It was only thanks to Andy's stupidity that they had established beyond doubt that the affair had taken place at all.

'Where did you meet?' Geraldine asked. 'We're just trying to build a picture of Jamie's life before she was killed,' she added, in what she hoped was an encouraging tone of voice.

'We never went anywhere,' he replied. 'We only ever saw each other at work.'

'But you just admitted to sexual relations with her,' Geraldine pointed out. 'You must have met somewhere.'

'In the office, after the others went home. Look,' he leaned forward suddenly. 'It was just a bit of fun. I never meant for it to happen. But when a young woman throws herself at you, after a day's work, well, I only did what any red-blooded man would do. I'm telling you, she was asking for it. I would hardly have noticed her if she hadn't been so up for it. I mean, it's not like she was that much to look at. And I'm a married man. I never asked for it. She came on to me.'

Geraldine stared coldly at him. 'And when did this fling end?'

Andy hesitated, thinking. He was sweating profusely, although the room was not warm. 'About a week ago last Saturday,' he replied at last.

'You finished it because she threatened to tell your wife, and three days later she was murdered,' Ian said.

'Yes, well, that had nothing to do with me. Look, am I being accused of something here? Because if not, I need to get back to work.' He turned to the man seated silently at his side. 'You're my lawyer. Aren't you supposed to be getting me out of here?'

The lawyer turned to Ian. 'Charge my client or release him,' he said quietly.

'You can go when we've finished questioning you,' Ian said.

'If you aren't willing to co-operate with us, you won't be helping yourself.'

Andy and his brief held a brief whispered conversation after which the lawyer informed them that in the interests of clearing himself of any suspicion as quickly as possible, Andy was prepared to answer their questions. At that, they agreed to take a short break.

Meanwhile, the search for Ben was continuing, with his image and details circulated to all airports, stations and ports. Wherever he was, they were determined to find him, but it wasn't proving easy. He seemed to have vanished without trace.

37

THREE DAYS HAD PASSED since Ben had disappeared, and Christine finally acknowledged the real reason for his leaving home. Depressing as the truth was, she had to face it. Ben was sick of her, and that was why he had walked out on their marriage. She had often suspected he was seeing other women, although she had never discovered any proof. It was just a feeling she had. She had tried to blame his desertion on the police, but it was only indirectly a consequence of their intervention. Christine had done everything she could to keep their marriage going. The saddest part of it all was that she knew Ben had done his best too. They had both tried so hard to create a life together, but it just hadn't worked. After that first run-in with the police, things had never returned to how they were before the accident and his arrest, which had led to him losing his job. Even after a jury had found him not guilty, he had never fully recovered from the experience. As if knowing he had accidentally killed a stranger wasn't difficult enough, he had been forced to endure months in a cell, awaiting a trial which had exonerated him too late. His confidence had gone, and he had never regained it. He was free, but he had come away from the trial a broken man.

She suspected that loss of confidence was what had led him to go chasing other women, as though he needed to prove to himself that he was still attractive. He had become a different person, and was never again the carefree man she had fallen in love with. She had turned away from her family and her church to be his wife, and now he had turned his back on her. If she hadn't abandoned her faith, she might have thought she was being justly punished. When they first met she would have followed Ben anywhere, as he laughed and whistled his way through life. But after his trial he had returned home a bitter and disappointed man. He had lost his place as foreman at a large workshop, and had struggled to find another job. Eventually he had been reduced to working as a junior mechanic in a small local garage. She hadn't minded the drop in their income. She was just happy to have him back home. But he had never regained his former cheerful outlook on life. Something inside him had broken, and she could not help him.

And now, after all they had endured together, he had finally deserted her. She still didn't really believe he had walked out on her. Every time the phone rang, or a delivery man knocked at the door, she stiffened, hardly daring to hope Ben had returned, and terrified of hearing that he had thrown himself under a train, or jumped off the roof of a tall building. As though she was living in a waking dream, she carried on with her life, going through the motions as though nothing unusual had happened. On Saturday she drove to Sainsbury's, as she always did. Climbing back into the car, she was surprised to see an envelope addressed to her lying on the passenger seat. She was sure it had not been there when she had arrived in the car park, and she was almost positive she had locked the car when she left it. Apart from her, only Ben had a key to the car. She shut her door and sat for a moment, staring at the envelope before she picked it up in a trembling hand. With a sudden determination, she ripped it open and drew out a sheet of paper that appeared to have been torn from an exercise book.

'Police hunting me and watching you,' she read. 'We have to meet. Don't be seen. Bring cash and passport.' He named a rendezvous point beneath the railway bridge over the river. The note concluded with a repetition of the instruction to avoid being seen. It was unsigned. Christine frowned. She should have been relieved to know Ben was alive, but it sounded as though he was planning to run away in earnest, and escape from the country before he could be caught. It wasn't clear whether he was expecting her to accompany him. He had told her to bring 'passport' in the singular which suggested he only wanted her to bring his but, in any case, the police had taken his passport, so that put paid to that. Meanwhile, she had to work out what to do. This was not a game, like the shows on television where people tried to avoid being captured by a professional team consisting of ex-policemen and ex-government agents. This was real. Her husband had been unjustly accused of a terrible crime and was hoping to evade capture. But he could not stay on the run indefinitely. Sooner or later, the police would catch up with him and, when they did, everything would be over. She wondered how other women might cope in her circumstances, and wished there was someone she could talk to. But of course confiding in anyone else was out of the question.

She was due to meet Ben in two hours and had to make sure no one saw her sneaking off. That was her priority right now, that and discovering if Ben was really intending to abandon her and disappear out of the country without her. Her immediate problem was to make her way to the bridge without being seen. Suddenly, inspiration struck. One of her colleagues at work had hosted a fancy dress party at Hallowe'en, and she and Ben had turned up dressed as characters from the Addams Family. She had worn a long black wig and no one had recognised her. She hurried home. Without stopping to unload her shopping, she cut the wig until it was shoulder length, and stuffed it into her largest handbag. She added a silk neck scarf and a pair of green trainers, an impulse buy that she had never worn. Wearing a nondescript khaki shirt over a grey T-shirt and jeans, she went out. There was no sign of anyone following her, but she guessed her phone could be tracked, and her car was probably also being registered on CCTV cameras using ANPR technology. Leaving her phone at home, she drove straight to the large shopping precinct on the outskirts of town, and parked her car.

Primark was busy, and there was a long queue at the changing room. She went to H & M where the fitting rooms were tucked away out of sight at the back of the store, and there was only a short queue. She noticed a surveillance camera and automatically looked away, but the store was packed with shoppers and she thought she was unlikely to be noticed there. She slipped into a changing room, and emerged a few moments later looking completely different. With her khaki shirt folded inside her bag, and her blonde hair concealed beneath a black wig, even the most sophisticated of CCTV would not reveal her identity. She could not use her car, but took the bus and paid for her ticket in cash. She reached York with only ten minutes to spare and hurried to the meeting point. Ben was not there. She hung around for a while, wondering how long to wait before returning to Monks Cross to reverse her disguise and pick up her car. A figure entered the tunnel and passed by, a middle-aged woman with a bulky shopping bag. A few moments after the woman had gone, a tramp entered the tunnel. Christine turned to walk away, but before she reached the end of the tunnel, she heard a hoarse voice whisper her name and stopped.

The tramp shuffled closer. There was no one else visible. As he drew near, he whispered her name again.

'Christine,' he muttered. 'Is that you?'

They stared at one another in bewilderment. He looked as though he had not slept for days, and as she drew near she noticed a foul animal stench, like a wet dog that had been rolling in compost. Ben's normally clean-shaven face was half hidden in thick stubble, his hands and forehead were ingrained with what appeared to be soot, and he was wearing an old stained raincoat with a torn pocket that looked several sizes too large for him. For a moment Christine forgot that she too was in disguise.

'I wasn't sure it was you,' he said, staring at her.

Other than his eyes, there was nothing about him she recognised. Even his voice was unfamiliar, hoarse and dry.

'It's the wig from Hallowe'en,' she explained, feeling awkward. 'I cut it to make it less noticeable. I didn't want to be recognised.'

'Are you sure no one followed you?'

'I'm sure.'

Quickly she told him how she had disguised herself and left the car at the shopping centre. She expected him to praise her for her foresight, but he scarcely seemed to be listening to her.

'Did you bring the money?'

She nodded and handed over an envelope. 'That's as much as I could get hold of so quickly,' she apologised. 'It's just over five hundred quid. I borrowed some from work,' she added, seeing his expression darken. 'It's all right, I didn't nick it. Mandy gave me an advance on next month's salary.'

'Five hundred? Is that all?'

'There wasn't time to try and get hold of more,' she replied, stung by his ingratitude.

'And my passport?'

He held out a grubby hand.

She shook her head. 'The police took it.'

'The police?' His outstretched hand began to shake. 'What the hell, Chrissy? What are the police doing with it? Why did you give it to the police, you stupid bitch?' He swore at her some more.

Indignantly, she explained how the house had been searched, and his passport confiscated.

'There wasn't anything I could do about it. It's not my fault. I guess they must have been worried you might try to leave the country. Looks like they were right about that,' she added bitterly.

'Shit,' he said. 'I'm fucked.'

'Ben,' she hesitated. 'Why don't you hand yourself in? If you're innocent, they'll have to let you go.'

'If?' he hissed. 'If? What's that supposed to mean? Of course I'm bloody innocent. And yes, they might let me go, but they've gone to so much trouble to fit me up, it's hardly likely, is it? And in any case, if this is all just one big mistake, how long do you think they'll keep me locked up before they discover they made another blunder? It's more likely they'll keep quiet about their cock-up and leave me to rot. I'm not going back in a cell, Chrissy. I'd rather die than be locked up again for something I didn't do.'

'Don't say that.'

Everything was so horrible, she began to cry. She couldn't help herself. A man came marching along the tunnel towards them and she lowered her head, sniffling back her tears. The man gave them a curious glance as he passed, but he didn't alter his pace.

'I don't know what to do, Ben,' she said. 'I don't know what to do.'

Instead of offering words of comfort, he sneered at her. '*You* don't know what to do?' he repeated scornfully. 'How the fuck do you think *I* feel? I tell you what you can do. You can go home and carry on with your life as though nothing's happened and everything's perfectly fine. Pretend you never married me. Better still, you can forget you even met me. Cut loose and make a proper life for yourself. I'm no good for you, Chrissy. I'm no good to anyone. '

With that, he turned and shuffled away.

'Ben,' she called after him softly. 'Ben?'

He did not turn or even falter in his shambling stride, but kept moving steadily away from her. With a lurch, she wondered if she would ever see him again. She nearly ran after him to grab hold of him with both hands and insist he accompany her to the police station, but something held her back. The police had let him go once, but now they were looking for him again. There had to be a reason for their renewed interest in him.

38

GERALDINE AND IAN WERE taking a break to discuss how they were going to proceed with questioning Andy.

'You know, I almost preferred it when we had no suspects at all,' she said. 'This is getting confusing, because we know both Andy and Ben worked with Jamie, so they both had the means and opportunity to kill her.'

'But it was Ben's glove that was stuck in her throat,' Ian replied.

'Andy could have stolen the glove.'

'Stolen a rubber glove from Ben and shoved it down Jamie's throat?'

'He might have picked it up by chance. The point is, Andy had a motive for getting rid of her. What reason did Ben have?' Geraldine asked.

'We don't know anything about the relationship between Ben and Jamie.'

'It's mere speculation to say there was any sort of relationship between them. We don't know if they even spoke to each other. But we know Andy could have had a reason for wanting to silence her. For all we know, she was threatening to tell his wife about her affair with him.'

'Which he could have denied,' Ian pointed out. 'No one else knew they were having sex. Even if Jamie had gone to his wife with the truth, Andy could have claimed she was a hysterical woman, bent on revenge after he had rejected her amorous advances. There was no one to produce any evidence to disprove him. We can't even be sure that Ben hadn't caught them at it and been blackmailing them. Andy might have wanted to get rid of his blackmailer, Ben, and shut Jamie up before she could blackmail him, or tell his wife about his dalliance. Jamie might have had proof of the affair. We don't know she didn't. She could quite easily have taken a photo and saved it somewhere safe. Andy had motive and opportunity because, by his own admission, he and Jamie often stayed at work after everyone else had gone home. As for means, there were any number of tools in the workshop that he could have used to knock her out.'

'But she wasn't "knocked out", she was suffocated with a glove shoved down her throat. That's a pretty aggressive assault and it sends a clear message that someone was trying to silence her.'

'Yes,' Ian agreed. 'I'd say the attack was pretty aggressive, seeing as it killed her. But if Andy killed her, and I'm not saying I think he did, I can see why he might have used Ben's glove, but then why has Ben done a runner? Surely that points to him being guilty? He must be in hiding somewhere or we would have come across him by now. Only someone intent on remaining hidden can possibly stay off the radar for so long. It's like he's literally vanished.'

'Are you saying we should consult a magician?' Geraldine laughed.

'No, of course not. This isn't a joke, Geraldine. And where does George Gardner fit into all of this? He was killed with Ben's scarf. That's two murders where the evidence points to Ben, and we've let him slip through our fingers,' Ian scowled. 'We have to find Ben. I can't believe you think there's any way he could be innocent, after the way he disappeared like that.'

Geraldine thought about what Ian had said, not so much in relation to the case, and Ben's disappearance, but in terms of what Ian was implying about her. She wondered what their relationship might have been like if they had not worked so closely together, talking about their cases at home as well as during their working day.

'What was it like being married to Bev?' she asked.

Ian's eyebrows shot up at the question. 'Why the hell are we talking about her?'

Geraldine shook her head. 'No, it's not that I want to talk about your ex-wife. I just wondered what it would be like, between us, if we weren't working together. I wondered what difference it might make to our relationship.'

'Well, we *are* working together,' he replied, 'so let's stick to the real world, shall we? You haven't forgotten that we have a potential murder suspect waiting for us, have you?' They set off down the corridor. As they neared the interview room, Ian paused in his stride. 'If you want to know, nothing would be any different between us, except that you wouldn't be with me so much. But that wouldn't stop me thinking about you all day every day,' he said in a low voice. 'And as for my ex-wife, she hasn't once crossed my mind since we separated, except when we were discussing our divorce.'

Geraldine smiled as she followed him into the interview room.

Ian went straight in. 'How well did you know George Gardner?'

Andy looked baffled. 'Who's he?'

Andy turned to his lawyer who was staring coldly at Ian, with a calculating look in his eyes. The stiffness in his expression indicated that he had recognised the name, which was hardly surprising given the amount of attention the case had received in the media. His client seemingly had not been following the news.

'George Gardner. He lived in York all his life, was married, and worked for the railway. An inoffensive man. A harmless man, who never hurt anyone.' Ian paused, his eyes fixed on the suspect.

Andy turned to his lawyer. 'Why are they talking about

this guy? What's going on? Are they saying he killed Jamie?' He turned back to Ian. 'If he's your suspect, you should be hounding him, not me. You know, you're wasting my working time. I've got jobs lined up, waiting; customers with deadlines, work promised, and you're dicking about questioning me about some guy I've never even heard of.'

'We think you know who he was,' Geraldine said softly.

She placed a photograph of the dead man on the table between them. Andy glanced at it and frowned.

'What happened to him?' he asked. When he looked up, his eyes were frightened. 'What happened?' he repeated, in a whisper.

'I think you know,' Ian replied. 'He's dead, and you were there when it happened.'

'What?' Andy gaped. 'What's going on? You can't pin this on me.' He nudged his lawyer. 'Do something. They can't just go throwing accusations around like that, can they? What the hell's going on?'

The lawyer gave a deliberate, lazy smile. 'Calm down, they're doing their best to rattle you, and it looks like they're succeeding. Of course they can't make any of this stick. If they had a shred of evidence for any of this, they would have arrested you by now. But they haven't. They're just fishing. You'll be out of here in no time, and this will all be over.'

He turned to Ian and his lethargic mien snapped into a kind of ferocity. Geraldine was impressed with his ability to change so completely at will. She had underestimated the old lawyer, who clearly had some tricks up his sleeve.

'Your treatment of my client is not merely outrageous, it is unlawful. Charge my client or he will walk out of here right now. And if you continue to harass him, he will file a suit against you personally, Inspector Peterson. My client admits he worked with Jamie Benson. He has never attempted to conceal that fact which, in any case, is easily proved. He further made no attempt to conceal the fact that he engaged in a sexual relations with Miss Benson for a short period of time, a relationship he ended, to protect his marriage. There was no need for him to reveal that relationship, but he did, in a spirit of co-operation. You have deliberately misrepresented that casual relationship as something more serious, in a pointless attempt to smear my client's name and reputation. On the back of that misrepresentation you have made the fanciful claim that my client murdered Miss Benson in order to keep their relationship quiet. You have no evidence to back up your supposition, and it takes very little thought to work out that your theory makes no sense. In fact any such action would have had the exact opposite effect, involving not only the police but, inevitably, unwanted publicity. Not only that, but you have taken a further fanciful leap to accuse my client of a second murder of a man he has never met. Surely even a man of your limited imagination can see how futile this interrogation is? My client is now going to leave the police station and return to work. He is prepared to overlook this unfortunate episode. But if you try to come after him again, unless you bring evidence that he is guilty of a crime, he will be lodging a complaint against you personally, Inspector Peterson.'

'You raised Jamie's salary,' Geraldine commented quietly. 'Was that to keep her quiet?' She leaned forward. 'Listen, Andy, we don't think you killed Jamie, but we do think if you co-operate with us, you can help us to nail whoever did. We're trying to find out more about her. We know you withdrew substantial amounts of money out of your account, and we believe you used it to pay for her silence about your affair. We can investigate your financial affairs and trace the payments if we have to, but it would save time all round if you just told us how much you paid her and why. We will find the information with or without your help, but your co-operation will help your case.'

Andy was looking increasingly uncomfortable. 'If I tell you what I know, will you let me go?'

'Unless we find evidence that implicates you in Jamie's murder, then yes, if you help us, we can make all this go away,' Ian said.

Andy looked at his lawyer who gave a brief nod.

'All I did was have an affair and give her a gift of money,' Andy said.

'Was it a gift or was she blackmailing you, threatening to tell your wife about the affair?' Ian asked.

Andy refused to answer, insisting it was personal. But they all understood what had happened.

'Jamie wasn't a very nice woman, was she?' Geraldine asked, forcing a sympathetic smile.

'She was a first-class bitch,' Andy replied sourly. 'She trapped me. God knows, I had reason enough to want her gone from my life, but I never killed her. That's not who I am. I gave her as much as I could afford, and told her if she threatened me again, I'd tell my wife myself. I would have done. It would have been a relief. But Jamie left me alone after that. She knew she'd got as much out of me as I was going to give her. I think she moved on to her next poor sucker.'

'Who was that?' Ian asked.

But Andy shook his head. 'I never asked her. I didn't want to know. To be honest, I was pleased to get her off my back. She set the whole thing up to trap me. It should be illegal.'

Geraldine refrained from pointing out that no one had coerced him into having extramarital relations, nor did she suggest that if he wanted to protect his marriage, he ought not to be screwing another woman.

39

'JUST BECAUSE HIS LAWYER starts getting heavy and threatening harassment claims doesn't make him any less of a suspect,' Eileen pointed out at the morning briefing the following day.

Everyone had read the transcript of the interview with Andy, who had left the police station grumbling furiously about having so much of his time wasted over something so stupid and pointless. He had seemed pumped up when he was released, and spoiling for a fight, but his lawyer had succeeded in persuading him that suing the police for wrongful arrest was not a sensible route to follow.

'You were never arrested,' Geraldine pointed out. 'You came here willingly to help us by answering a few questions, just for the purpose of elimination.'

She did not add that although Andy had not been arrested, he had not yet been eliminated from the enquiry into Jamie's death. Finding a connection between him and George was proving more difficult. A team of constables were working on it, but so far no one had come up with any way in which George and Andy could have met.

'They both lived and worked in York, for goodness sake,' Eileen said. 'There are any number of places they could have met. The absence of proof doesn't mean it never happened.'

'It makes proving it more difficult though,' Geraldine murmured.

Eileen glared at her to show that she had heard what Geraldine said.

'We've gone right back to their school days,' Ariadne said. 'They would have been in the same year at school, but there's nothing to show their paths ever crossed. They went to different schools, and were never neighbours. George didn't take his car to Andy's garage for its annual check-up and MOT, and they were never in hospital at the same time, as far as any records show. They didn't seem to have anything in common.'

'What about the wives?' Geraldine asked. 'Were they ever in contact?'

'Not as far as we've been able to ascertain,' Naomi said. 'They weren't the same age and didn't attend the same school. Neither of them has children and they don't seem to have mixed socially in any way we've been able to trace.'

Geraldine nodded. 'We could ask them,' she suggested.

Geraldine started with Michelle, as her bereavement had happened first. She found her at home, dressed in her usual flared skirt and blouse, looking perfectly relaxed, and nothing like the grieving widow Geraldine had expected to see.

'How are you coping?' she asked gently.

'Yes, we're fine. Thank you for asking.'

'We?'

Michelle smiled and invited her into the neat front room. A small ball of white fur lay curled up on one of the armchairs.

'George said I could have her,' Michelle said. 'That is,' she added quickly, 'George wouldn't have minded, not now he's no longer here. I always wanted a cat, but he never liked animals and in any case he was allergic to cats. So we could never have one, but he did say that if he was ever no longer around, I could get a cat.'

'He said that?'

It seemed a slightly strange conversation to have had with a spouse.

Michelle nodded. 'Well, not in so many words. What he actually said, when I suggested we get a cat, was "Over my dead body". We never talked about it again. There was no point. But now that he's dead, I thought it would be fine to go ahead. I've always wanted a white cat.'

She smiled affectionately at the tiny bundle of white fur which suddenly uncurled itself into a kitten and stood up on all fours on the seat of the chair.

'She's called Angel,' Michelle said.

Pleased to see that Michelle had found a distraction from her unexpected solitude, Geraldine murmured that the kitten was beautiful. It was true. People dealt with bereavement in many different ways, and consoling herself with a cat wasn't a bad way for Michelle to cope with her loss.

Geraldine held out a photograph of Christine. 'Do you know the woman in this picture?'

Michelle looked up from stroking the kitten and peered at the image. After a few seconds, she shook her head.

'No, I can't say that I do. Is she someone I should recognise?'

'What about the man?' Geraldine asked.

Michelle shook her head again. 'No, I don't think I've ever seen either of them before. Inspector?' she added timidly.

'Yes?'

'Have you caught the man who killed my husband?'

It was Geraldine's turn to shake her head.

Although Christine's husband was not dead as far as they knew, she didn't appear to be coping with her loss very well. She looked as though she had been crying when she opened the door, and she glared at Geraldine without stepping aside to allow her to enter the house.

'Well?' she asked. 'What do you want?'

There was something fearful in her expression, as though she was afraid Geraldine had come bearing bad news. At the same time she sounded despairing, as though things could not actually be any worse.

'What is it?' she asked again.

Geraldine asked if she could go in, and Christine finally moved aside grudgingly. Standing in the hall, Geraldine showed her a picture of Michelle.

'Do you recognise this woman?'

Christine's response startled her. 'Is that who he's run off with?'

She spoke so fiercely, Geraldine started back in surprise.

'Run off?' she repeated.

Christine shook her head, seeming to recall where she was. 'He can't have run off with anyone, not looking like that.'

Geraldine glanced at the photograph of Michelle. She was older than Christine, and nowhere near as good-looking, but men had been known to fall for outwardly unattractive women.

'This is your fault,' Christine hissed suddenly. 'You and your lot. You drove him to it. He's innocent–' Her voice cracked and she burst into tears.

'Would you like to–'

'No, no, I don't want anything from you. Just go away and leave me alone.'

'Do you recognise the woman in the photograph?' Geraldine demanded, holding up the picture again.

'No,' Christine replied promptly. 'I've never seen her before and I never want to see you again.'

'What about the man?' Geraldine asked, indicating the image of George who was standing beside his wife, now his widow. 'Please, look carefully. This could be important.'

Christine stared at the picture. 'Is that the man who killed Ben's colleague?' she asked. 'No, I've never seen him before but I hope you lock him up and throw away the key. He's the reason Ben's gone. Let me meet him, just once, so I can spit on him.'

'I'm afraid he's dead,' Geraldine said.

'Ben?'

'No, the man in this picture. He's dead.'

Christine frowned, shaking her head. 'What? Why are you

telling me? I didn't do anything. I don't know who he is. Please, go away and leave me alone.'

'Has Ben returned home yet?' Geraldine enquired, glancing at the stairs.

'No. I haven't seen him.'

Geraldine had a feeling Christine was lying. Although she had no reason to doubt her, she decided to challenge her. A direct demand often achieved surprising results.

'Where is he, Christine?'

But Christine shook her head. 'I wish I knew.'

Back at the police station, Geraldine joined Ariadne for a coffee.

'I don't know why,' she told her friend, 'I just thought she was lying when she said she hadn't seen him, but she was adamant she had no idea where he was.'

'Both are possible,' Ariadne pointed out. 'She could have met him somewhere, or he might have gone home, but now she doesn't know where he is.'

Geraldine nodded. 'Yes, it's possible. Anything's possible. That's the trouble. Until we can narrow down the possibilities, we're nowhere.'

40

HE HAD RETURNED TO the pub three times without seeing her. Once or twice the landlord had sought to engage him in conversation. He was a bluff man with a loud voice who wore his shirtsleeves rolled up to the elbows. The muscles in his thick forearms rippled under his skin as he polished glasses and wiped down the top of the bar. In a way it might be helpful for the landlord to view him as a new regular, a bloke who liked to sit in the corner and be left alone. Before long he would blend into the background and become almost invisible. Almost, but not quite. The landlord was sharp and likely to remember who had been drinking in his pub. On balance, he realised he was far too exposed for comfort in the pub, but he didn't know where else he could go to see Naomi again.

Now that he had succeeded in meeting her, he was frantic to see her again. It was like an itch. The desire had nothing to do with her, although she was attractive enough. He wanted to see her so that he could question her about the recent murder and the police investigation. More than anything else, he wanted to find out how much the police knew. His liberty might depend on his knowing and keeping one step ahead of them. If necessary, he would flee, in disguise, and disappear. But before he took any such drastic action, he needed to be sure it was necessary. Naomi might be able to tell him. But waiting for her in the pub was too risky.

He took to sitting in his car, watching the entrance to the police station car park. After a few days, his patience was rewarded when he spotted Naomi driving out of the police station, alone. Warily he started up his engine and followed her, always leaving at least one other car between them. She led him through the centre of York and along the Holgate Road, finally turning off into a side street where she parked her car and went into one of the properties. He sat for a long time watching the outside of the building and smiling to himself, because now he knew where she lived. He followed her around for a couple of days after that, but he had to be careful. Naomi was trusting, but being a police officer she was bound to be alert to anything unusual. Their next meeting had to appear coincidental.

After a few frustrating evenings, he finally had an opportunity to speak to her again. He had followed her into town on Sunday morning, and watched her visit the Apple shop along Spurriergate. There would be CCTV cameras everywhere, which was a pity, but he was only intending to have what would appear to be a perfectly innocent chance encounter with a woman he had recently had coffee with. Leaving the Apple store, she entered a women's clothing shop. Taking care not to get too close to her, he followed her inside. He felt awkward hovering between rails of women's clothes, but he didn't want to lose sight of her by waiting outside the shop. Thankfully she left there quite quickly after rifling through a few rails, and went into a shoe shop. This sold men's shoes as well as women's, so he felt quite comfortable going in behind her. She was still on her feet when he walked in, studying the shoes on display.

He toyed with the idea of pretending to accidentally knock into her but decided against it. Instead, he walked over to her.

'Hello. Naomi? It is Naomi, isn't it?' He knew perfectly well it was her.

She spun round. For a second she looked confused, but then she smiled before he had to jog her memory by mentioning their previous meeting.

'Sid,' she replied.

He regretted having come up with that name as soon as he had uttered it in the pub. It was the first thing that had popped into his mind when she introduced herself and asked his name. He should have been better prepared. Now he was stuck with her calling him 'Sid'. But it would have been too dangerous to have told her his real name. Nothing about Sid could lead anyone to his true identity. Sid he was, and Sid, for now, he must remain, whenever he saw Naomi.

'How have you been keeping?' he asked

She smiled again. 'I'm fine. Thanks. How are you?'

He nodded. 'Can't complain. Have you been here long? I mean, are you ready to take a break from shopping or have you just started?' He grinned sheepishly. 'What I'm trying to say is, would you like to join me for a coffee?'

He held his breath. She had come there to shop, and for all he knew she was in a hurry.

'That would be lovely,' she replied.

A few moments later, they were seated in the corner of a café, chatting like old friends. Their conversation was innocuous and impersonal but, if he was careful, with luck he might begin to learn something about the murder investigation.

'So, it must be exciting, working on big cases,' he ventured. 'I don't suppose you've ever been involved in a case that was in the news? One that I might actually have heard about?'

He hoped she would assume he was interested in her, rather than in any current case. He was obviously fishing for details about her work, but reassured himself that many people might be interested to hear about what she did, out of innocent curiosity.

'I work in serious crime,' she replied quietly.

'Serious crime?' he repeated. 'How serious is that?'

He hoped his slightly teasing tone would provoke a response, and he was right.

'Would you call murder serious?' she answered with a question of her own.

With a flutter of satisfaction, he realised she was keen to impress him. There was no doubt Naomi could turn out to be a useful ally, if he could hide the true reason for his interest in her.

'Murder?' he whispered, opening his eyes wide. 'What are you talking about?'

She shook her head. 'There's nothing more I can tell you.'

He lowered his gaze, aware that she had shut down. He had been too pushy.

'I understand,' he replied. 'That is, I think I do. Is your work top secret?'

He was teasing her again, but this time she was more circumspect. Perhaps she felt she had already told him too much, but her revelations had scarcely begun. Somehow he was going to find a way to make her talk, without her realising she was being indiscreet. He didn't yet know how he was going to gain her confidence, but he would find a way. Unless he had misread the signs, she was interested in him romantically. There was no other reason for her to be so willing to spend time with him. He decided to ask her out on a date. The occasional chat over a cup of coffee wasn't getting him anywhere. He needed to ply her with alcohol and encourage her to trust him. Taking a deep breath, he heard himself ask her out for dinner.

41

IT HAD BEEN THREATENING to rain all day. Taking shelter outside the stores in the centre of town would be too public, with people scurrying past with their shopping bags. Knowing the police were looking for him, Ben had to avoid attracting attention, so he was skulking in the narrow snickelways of the city, where no one could see him from the street. He hadn't shaved for days, had given his denim jacket to a tramp in exchange for an old raincoat, and had deliberately walked across the edge of a muddy puddle so that his trainers were now stained with dirt. It was worth walking around with damp feet for a day, for the security of knowing he looked just like a rough sleeper. Which was, in fact, exactly what he was. Except that he was no longer penniless. He had nearly five hundred pounds in his pocket. He just had to decide what to do with it.

As he gazed miserably at the rain, he suspected it had been a big mistake to overreact to the police interest in him. After all, he had been arrested before, and the police had released him then. Was he being more than a little crazy hiding from them now, when he knew they couldn't possibly convict him of any crime? The trouble was, in his panic he had all but proved his guilt. He had spent time in a prison cell before, and he was never going back there. Now, having acted in a way that was bound to confirm their suspicions of him, he had no other choice but to keep running. Besides, the prospect of leaving York, and possibly England, to start a new life somewhere else was almost irresistible. He was done with his lousy life, scratching around for a living with his record hanging over him. He was done with York and its grey skies and wet pavements. And now he was done with his marriage.

He was not confident his disguise would protect him if he risked catching a bus out of the city. There were cameras everywhere on public transport. At the same time, he was never going to be able to hitch a lift, looking as disreputable as he did. His escape needed careful thought, because he had to get away from York. On balance, he decided it would be best to lie low and do nothing for a week, by which time the police might have relaxed their search. They couldn't keep up a full-scale man hunt indefinitely with their limited resources. Before too long, with any luck, another crime would pop up that would divert attention from him, so that he could simply slip away and start a new life somewhere else. He fancied making his way to the south coast, as far away from York as possible. Or he might travel north and vanish somewhere in Scotland. He couldn't decide whether he would be safer in a remote place where his arrival was likely to be noticed, or in a densely populated area, where it would be easier to remain anonymous. The problem was that seeing more people increased the danger that someone would recognise him from his picture that was circulating in the media.

He cowered in a doorway in an alley, wishing he could lie down and rest. There were hostels for rough sleepers, but he couldn't risk going anywhere official. He might be able to get away with giving a false name, although even that was dubious, but he couldn't risk being caught on a camera. His description had probably already been sent out to all the guesthouses and hostels in York. He had a vague idea that the rough sleepers in York were a fairly tight-knit community. People came and went, but someone might notice a new face. He was fairly confident he wouldn't be recognised as long as he did nothing to draw attention to himself. Even his own wife hadn't recognised him. But if anyone looked closely at him, they might spot his resemblance to a man wanted by the police. A bright spark might clock that he had appeared on the street at the same time as a suspect had disappeared. His existence in York was fraught with danger, but attempting to travel away might be even more hazardous. He wished there was someone he could approach for advice, but he was cut off from all human aid.

Fortunately he had some money, thanks to his wife. Now he had to decide what to do with it. The police might not realise how much cash he had in his possession, but he couldn't be sure Christine hadn't spilled the beans. In any case, the police could see she had withdrawn money from the bank, and if they were able to discover that she had been given an advance at work, they would be able to work out how much money he had. That would help in their search for him, knowing he could pay cash for a bus or train ticket. In addition to that, he was nervous about going into a restaurant or shop to buy food. He was starving, with money in his pocket, but a vendor might suspect he had stolen his cash, and alert the police. He cursed himself for not having asked Christine to bring him some food. The stupid cow ought to have thought of it for herself.

He had not recognised her in her wig, but nor had she recognised him at first. To be honest, he barely recognised himself any more but hunger, lack of sleep and the constant terror of living on the street had wormed their way into his psyche, however hard he struggled to retain his customary decency. It had taken him less than a week to change from a cheerful kind of a guy into a bitter vagabond. He knew he had been cruel to his wife. Although he could not remember exactly what he had said to her, he could recall his anger. Even if all this blew over and the police reinstated him in his former life, insisting his old job be given back to him, and on top of all that apologised for causing him so much pain and terror, he could never return to his former self. Ever since the accident that had placed him in a cell for the first time, he had been unable to relax. Now, further traumatised by his experience as a fugitive, he was afraid his paranoia would never leave him.

A woman walked past and he called out to her, asking if he could hand her some money so she could buy him food. She dropped a coin at his feet and hurried away. He swore under his breath. He couldn't eat coins. Miserably, he turned into one of the narrow lanes that criss-crossed the city. A tramp lay slumped in a doorway at the back of a shop in the alley, clutching a ripped sleeping bag around his skinny body.

'Here,' Ben whispered, crouching down.

He wasn't sure what he was going to ask the man. Perhaps he would just have given him some money. Very slowly the other man opened one eye. He looked pissed. Ben changed his mind and was about to move on, when the tramp reached out and grabbed his wrist in an unexpectedly strong grip.

'What you after?' he lisped and Ben saw that all but one of his front teeth were missing. 'I could slay a beer.'

He leered hopefully up at Ben who snatched his arm away and hurried off down the alley, trying not to wonder how the tramp had lost his teeth. Poor hygiene or being punched in the face were the most likely explanations. Ben shivered. Whatever happened to him, he had no intention of ending up like that. Pausing to count his money before he stepped out into the street, he glanced up and cursed. A young lad was staring at him from across the street. He couldn't tell if the boy had seen his wad of cash, but he wasn't going to hang around to find out. Stuffing the money into the pocket of his coat, he turned on his heel and hurried back along the alley. Hearing footsteps behind him, he broke into a run. But he had forgotten about the old soak, who suddenly reared up, blocking his route.

'Out of my way, you tosser,' Ben shouted, waving his arms at the other man.

'A few bob for a beer,' the old man wheedled.

Something struck Ben between the shoulder blades. He staggered and fell forward, barging into the homeless man who fell to the ground in front of him. Ben's fall was broken in part by the other man, who crumpled beneath Ben's weight, and lay beneath him, groaning. Sharp pain sliced up Ben's arm and he suspected he had fractured a bone. Rough hands grabbed at him, turning him over and punching him in the face before he could recover from his shock. He tried to raise his hands to protect his face, but could only move one of his arms. Shivering with pain, he blacked out. When he came to, his assailant had gone, leaving Ben lying on top of the tramp. His arm hurt. The man underneath him was no longer groaning and he was making no attempt to push Ben away. Wriggling cautiously backwards, trying not to move his mangled arm, Ben raised himself on his uninjured elbow and squinted down at the man. He noticed a pool of blood forming beside the other man's head. Just before he passed out again, he realised the sleeve of his coat was drenched in blood.

42

'WELL, WOULD YOU BELIEVE it? Ben Foster has turned up,' Eileen announced, her eyes gleaming in a rare smile.

Ben's image and description had been circulated to every police station in the United Kingdom, as well as sent to all the ports, airports, stations and bus depots, and every taxi company in the country. In addition, requests for information had been broadcast on television and radio, and published in newspapers in the area, with warnings to the public not to approach the fugitive.

'It seems he was right here in York all the time. He's been beaten up, and has been admitted to A and E, along with one other man, as yet unidentified.'

'Was the other man his attacker?' Ian asked.

'That's unlikely, by all accounts. A team from a shelter for rough sleepers came across the two casualties in an alley. I want you to go straight there and see what SOCOs have come up with so far.'

Geraldine frowned. 'But you said Ben's been taken to hospital. Why don't we see him there?'

'Why is he in hospital?' Ariadne asked. 'What's the damage?'

'He was admitted with a fractured arm and broken ribs. It seems he was assaulted while he was dossing on the street.'

'So he was sleeping rough, and his wife was probably telling us the truth when she told us she didn't know where he was,' Geraldine said. 'Who was the other man?'

'The other man was a rough sleeper who was out cold when the shelter team found them.'

'Will he survive?'

'That's not clear. Ben was found lying semi-conscious on top of him and the man underneath was quite badly injured, it seems. He hit his head when they fell to the ground, and cracked his skull.'

'Oh Jesus,' Ariadne blurted out. 'Don't tell us Ben was trying to kill someone else?'

A couple of Geraldine's colleagues glanced at her to observe her reaction to the question, but she remained poker faced. If Ben killed again, after she had released him, no one could hold her in any way responsible for the murder. She hoped she had not made a gross error of judgement, but that was the worst accusation that could be levelled at her. She had not been negligent in carrying out her duties by releasing a man she was convinced was innocent. She had good reason for holding that opinion. The evidence at the time had definitely indicated he was innocent. All the same, she hoped desperately that Ben's name would be cleared, and her own reputation would be salvaged.

'We're not yet sure what happened,' Eileen replied. 'But neither of them is dead. It's clear that Ben was assaulted, and his injuries were deliberately inflicted. He was stabbed in the left side. The other man may have merely fallen and not been attacked at all. That's why I need you to go along there, Geraldine. Find out what SOCOs have been able to gather at the scene so far. Ben's been sedated and is asleep, but he should be able to answer questions tomorrow. It seems he hadn't slept for a few days while he was living on the street and is suffering from nervous exhaustion, as well as from the injuries he sustained in the course of the assault. In the meantime, here's the address of the location where he was found. Let's get there straightaway.'

Geraldine nodded, keen to set off. Even the least experienced constable knew the importance of viewing a crime scene as soon after the incident as possible, before evidence had time to deteriorate. This was not the first time a homeless man had been assaulted in York in a seemingly motiveless attack. The media made a fuss about it, often in ways that were politically fuelled and singularly unhelpful to the reputation of the police. As far as Geraldine and her colleagues were concerned, all victims were treated the same, whether they were homeless paupers or business magnates. But when it came to impartiality, death far surpassed the efforts of men. Once their clothes and jewellery had been removed, apart from subcutaneous fat and other effects of good living, there was little to distinguish the wealthy from the poor as they lay on a slab in the mortuary.

The alley where Ben had been mugged was closed off at both ends. Behind the yellow police tape, a few white-coated scene of crime officers were working busily. No one had yet stopped by to peer into the alley to see what was going on, but a small crowd would no doubt gather later if the rain held off. Geraldine pulled on her protective gear and made her way carefully along the alley. Inching forward, she gazed down at a dirty cobbled pathway running between two narrow pavements, the kerb on both sides black with grime. Near the scene of the assault, a discarded cigarette packet lay on cobbles stained dark red with blood. From the photographs taken before the two casualties were rushed to hospital, she knew the two men had been found lying nearby, eight limbs splayed out, like some monstrous spider.

'The blood marks the location where they were attacked and fell,' a scene of crime officer told her. 'Unfortunately there's no functioning CCTV along here, but we should be able to see who entered the alley, and when, from the cameras in the street. Luckily for us, outside one of the shops there's a badly aligned camera which is pointing this way.' He turned back to the cobbled ground. 'The victim underneath must have been knocked out instantaneously, because he didn't budge from the spot where he fell. The blood on the ground wasn't disturbed until we removed him.'

Geraldine nodded. Ben had been found, barely conscious, lying on top of another man, which might explain why the latter had been unable to stir. She studied an image of the two men on her phone. Although the old man's limbs were concealed in clothing, his emaciated face and bony hands suggested he had probably lacked the strength to push Ben away, even if he had been sufficiently conscious to attempt to wriggle out from under him. He looked unlikely to have inflicted much damage on a younger and healthier man, although that was speculation. She was in the alley to gather facts, not to theorise. She gazed around the melancholy scene, a miserable setting in which to lie bleeding. If they had not been found that night, the old man would almost certainly have bled to death.

'We think he was sleeping here in this snickelway,' the scene of crime officer said, with a sigh. 'I mean, he was obviously homeless and there's a sheltered doorway that looks as though it was being used by a rough sleeper.'

Geraldine nodded. A picture of the tramp showed that one of his trainers was tied on with string threaded through the eyelets, and he was wearing a grubby raincoat with a torn pocket and several stains, only one of which was blood from his recent injuries.

'Poor bugger,' the scene of crime officer added. 'At least we got him out of here before the rain. Not that it would have made much difference to him,' he added with a shrug, glancing up at the sky.

'Getting him out of here so quickly probably saved his life,' Geraldine said.

Neither of them asked what he had been saved for. Geraldine thought fleetingly of her own flat, with its well-appointed bathroom and comfortable bed, and felt a tremor of despair that life could be so unfair. Shaking the thought away, she turned and walked slowly out of the alley, shedding her pity along with her protective clothing. She could not afford to become emotional when there was work to do.

43

WITH A SHOW OF reluctance, a doctor allowed Geraldine into the ward to speak to Ben.

'Just for a few minutes,' the doctor warned her, gazing at Geraldine earnestly through black-rimmed glasses. 'He's still very weak, and he's not ready to be disturbed.'

'Was he badly injured in the attack?'

'No, but he was shaken, and he was already extremely weak before he was mugged.'

'In what way was he weak? Do you mean physically?'

'Yes, he was dehydrated and he didn't appear to have eaten for several days.' The doctor hesitated. 'He's a rough sleeper, isn't he? We understand his wife threw him out?' He paused again, peering inquisitively at Geraldine. 'Something doesn't quite add up, because he has a wife and a permanent address, but he has clearly been sleeping on the street and he hasn't been eating, yet there's no record of any mental health issues. It seems to be a domestic, but he flatly refuses to tell us what happened.'

Geraldine enquired about the other man who had been found lying in the alley.

The doctor screwed up his face. 'I'm afraid he's in a far worse way. In fact, we're not sure he's going to pull through. He's not recovered consciousness yet, and we suspect he's been accustomed to drinking far more than is good for him. His liver is shot to pieces, which doesn't help the prognosis. In a nutshell, he's in pretty bad shape. What happened to him?'

Geraldine prevaricated, saying she was not at liberty to

discuss either patient's current situation, before she swept past the doctor and entered the ward. Ben was lying behind a curtain. His eyes were closed and she had a chance to study him before he stirred and saw her. His face was bruised and swollen on his left side, although his nose and the right side of his face appeared to be undamaged. One of his arms was in plaster, and one of his legs was swathed in bandages. As she stood gazing at him, his eyelids flickered. One eye suddenly glared at her, but the other remained half closed, too puffy to open.

'Is there any part of you that hasn't been injured?' Geraldine enquired gently as she placed a plastic chair at the head end of the bed and sat down.

'I was attacked. For my money. The bastard. Nicked it all,' Ben spluttered. 'All of it.'

His mouth only opened on one side, thanks to an inflamed cheek which prevented him speaking normally, and his speech came out in short bursts. It was clearly an effort for him to talk.

'Money?' Geraldine repeated, raising her eyebrows. 'What money are you talking about? How much money did you have on you?'

If Ben wanted to discuss the mugging, Geraldine was happy to go along with that for now. He was still clearly woozy and, once he started talking, he might let a lot more slip than he intended. He nodded and then winced; the movement evidently caused him some pain, jogging his fractured arm and disturbing his sore face.

'Christine. Gave me five. Hundred quid,' he gasped. 'I wanted her. To bring me. Passport. She told me you lot. Had taken it.'

He scowled and winced again, cursing and muttering about being held prisoner.

'Well, it's just as well we do have your passport, or that might have been stolen too,' Geraldine replied.

'No, no. It's not. It's not just. As well. Listen.' He attempted to sit up and fell back with a low moan. 'Listen. Someone killed.

211

The receptionist. Who worked. At the garage. It could have been. The same person who did. For that bloke. George. I don't know. If it was. The same killer. Or not. I've no idea. What's going on. All I know is. Whoever killed them. Is still out there. And you're wasting your time. Hounding me. None of this. Makes sense. I never even met. Anyone called George. And I don't recognise. His face. Why the hell. Would I want. To kill him? I have no idea. Who he is. And why would I. Kill Jamie. At work? You know I've. Had trouble with. The police before. Which was not. Of my making. I'd done. Nothing wrong. Except drive. Too fast. But that was. Enough for your lot. Wasn't it? All you're interested in. Is getting people. Locked up. You don't. Give a shit. Whose life you. Destroy. With my record. Do you think. It was easy. To find work? I was desperate. To keep my job. At the garage. Desperate. The last thing. I wanted. Was any trouble. I had no reason. To kill. That girl. And every reason. To keep my nose. Clean. Shit, I'm not. A murderer. This is just. Plain crazy. You think I killed. Two people? Are you nuts?'

Geraldine studied him gravely. He had managed to accidentally knock down and kill a pedestrian while he was driving, and now he was suspected of killing two more people, one of whom he had definitely known. Avoiding challenging him directly about George or Jamie, she turned the conversation to his own recent injuries.

'Who was the other man in the alley?' she asked.

'I've no idea. He was a stranger. Who mugged me. That's all. I know.'

Geraldine shook her head impatiently. 'No, I mean the other man, the one you fell on top of in the alley.'

Ben sighed. 'I've no idea. Who he was. Just some old soak. He was on at me. To give him money. For booze. I told him. I was skint. I was just. Passing through the alley. Looking for a doorway. To sleep in. It looked like. It was going to rain. So I walked. Away from the old guy. And stopped. To check the cash. And some fucker. Across the street. Must have seen me. Next thing I knew. He was chasing me. Back down the alley. He whacked me. On the back. And I crashed into. The old guy. Knocked him. To the ground. Landed on top of him. It was lucky I suppose. Because he broke my fall. But it still. Smashed my arm. Multiple fractures. Jesus. It was agony.'

'It wasn't very lucky for the old man you fell on,' Geraldine said.

'But he's going to be. All right?'

Geraldine shrugged. 'He's still unconscious. He had a nasty knock on the head.'

'Jesus. What?' Ben looked genuinely shocked. 'Listen. I must have passed out. Because when I came to. The old guy I'd fallen on top of. Wasn't moving. My sleeve was soaked. In blood. And my money had gone. Jesus Christ. How much bad luck. Can one guy stomach? I'm telling you. For two pins. I'd end it all. Right here right now. I'm in pain. You're on my case. And wherever I go. There's trouble. Always trouble. First there was the woman. I knocked down. And by the time that was. All over. No one wanted. To hire me. If my wife hadn't. Stuck by me. God knows what. Would have happened. To me. And then. You guys were. On at me about. Some bloke called George. Whoever the hell he is. And because of that. I lost my job. The woman. At the garage. Where I was working. Has been murdered. And now. You're telling me. The old guy. I crashed into. Is dead as well.' He shook his head and tears slid down his pale cheeks. 'I never meant. Any of this to happen,' he wailed softly. 'I never wanted. To hurt anyone. I'm not an angry man – that is, I wasn't. Until now. But I tell you what. Right now. I'd just as soon. Punch a man. To death. As give him. The time of day.'

'Is that how you would do it?' Geraldine asked softly.

'What?'

'Punch a man to death? Is that what you'd do if you were going to kill someone? Hit him with your bare fists?'

'Oh Jesus,' Ben replied. 'Give me a break. Will you? It's just. A manner of speaking. Only words. I never killed anyone. And I never would. But you're not going to. Believe me. Are you? So what's the point. Asking me any more. Questions? And what's the point. In my answering you? You've made up. Your mind. And that's all there is. To it.'

'Wouldn't you rather suffocate someone? It would be neater and there would be no blood.'

Ben shuddered. 'Listen, Inspector. You might get off. On all this talk. Of killing. But it's not for me. I'm not. A violent man. Ask anyone. So you tell me. How is it. So many people. Have died. After coming in contact. With me? It's like there's some. Malevolent force.'

He closed his eyes and turned his head away from her.

'One more question. Did you lose any rubber gloves recently?'

'What? Rubber gloves? What are talking about? What would I be doing. With rubber gloves?' He frowned. 'I can't remember. I don't care. Please, just piss off. And leave me alone. As soon as they've. Patched me up. You can put me back. In a cell. You can do. What you like. With me. But I'm not saying. Another word to you. I'm done. It's over. Everything's over. I'll never get. Another job. Will I?'

'Can you describe the man who stole the money from you?'

Ben shook his head. 'He was an ugly brute. Youngish. He had dark hair. I think. Although he could have been. Wearing a hood. I barely saw him. And that was across. The road. Evil bastard.'

44

'HE WAS CERTAINLY FEELING very sorry for himself,' Geraldine told her colleagues when she returned from the hospital. 'The way he was talking, he might almost be suicidal. He seems to feel genuinely aggrieved at his bad luck in having so many people die around him.'

Since her colleagues all seemed to be of the opinion that Ben was guilty, she did not add that if he was actually innocent, as he was insisting, then he had certainly been unfortunate.

'Bad luck?' Ian raised a quizzical eyebrow. 'Is that what he calls it?'

Not for the first time, Geraldine wondered if she was misguided in feeling sorry for Ben. None of her colleagues seemed to agree with her view, and it was true that Ben could well be responsible for two deaths, possibly three, since the only known witness to the attack in the alleyway had died without recovering consciousness. Once the post mortem was completed, they would know more about the cause of the old rough sleeper's death. Still, there was no doubt that George and Jamie had been deliberately murdered. What was equally clear was that Ben could have killed them both. Only the word of a random eyewitness called Ben's guilt into question. Sallyanne Hodgskin remembered Roxy's name, but she might have overheard Ben summoning his dog on a different day. It was possible she had seen another man and his dog on the morning of George's murder, and in her memory had conflated the two occasions.

Christine had corroborated Ben's claim that she had given Ben five hundred pounds. Admittedly she had visited her husband in hospital and he could have told her what to say, so she could be lying, but her boss had confirmed that Christine had asked her for an advance on her salary. On top of that, Christine had withdrawn two hundred pounds from her bank account. So far, Ben's story checked out, assuming his wife's statement was true. The team from the homeless shelter, who had found Ben after the alleged mugging, had found no money on him. So it seemed Ben had been telling the truth when he said he had been mugged, because the money Christine had given him had vanished. But that had no bearing on whether or not he had killed George and Jamie.

Once again, Geraldine made her way to the mortuary where the latest body was being examined.

'He was in a weakened state,' Jonah said, shaking his head with a sombre expression on his face. 'He could have been knocked over with the proverbial feather. He was an alcoholic who hardly ate and slept rough.' He shook his head again. 'He was in a very bad way: liver pickled, lungs dried up, malnourished, guts rotted, you name it. His filthy exterior housed a decaying carcass. He was a disgusting specimen of a man.'

Shocked to hear Jonah speak so disparagingly of a dead human being, Geraldine was about to remonstrate when the pathologist resumed.

'How he managed to cling on to life at all is a mystery, a minor miracle. By rights he should have been dead a long time ago. He was a physical wreck of a man. It's impossible to say how old he was.' Jonah sighed. 'What a miserable life. What kind of civilised society allows people to live like that? It almost makes you want to start a revolution, until you realise that no other system would be any better. It's human nature that does it. We do it to ourselves. Collectively speaking, that is.'

Geraldine interrupted his mournful rambling. 'What can you tell me about his injuries?'

'He wouldn't have lasted another winter without proper care. He needed shelter, decent food, help with controlling his drinking, not to mention the lice, and every crevice of his body was affected by eczema. He must have been really uncomfortable. What a life. Why do we allow people to do that to themselves? To suffer like that? How can people live without any access to regular medical attention and dental care in this day and age, in a so-called civilised society? What are we doing, Geraldine?'

Ignoring Jonah's passionate outburst, Geraldine focused her attention on her task.

'I'm interested in how he died, not how he lived. What was the cause of death?' She paused. 'Was he suffocated?'

Jonah shook his head. 'He might have been. There was a weight on top of him, but it wasn't only covering his face, it was pressing down on his body too.'

Geraldine nodded. She had seen photographs of the scene.

'There were fibres from another coat all over the front of his own coat,' Jonah went on. 'But that wasn't what killed him.'

He had the body turned over to reveal an ugly contusion on the back of the dead man's head. Delicately, Jonah peeled back a flap of skin to expose the shattered skull beneath it.

'This is what did for him,' he said. 'He appears to have fallen backwards and hit his head on the ground. He tried to put his hands out in an effort to break his fall, and broke one elbow in the attempt. My guess is he was caught off guard when someone barged into him, and was too drunk to regain his balance. His insides were awash with alcohol – more alcohol than blood flowing through his veins – so it's not too difficult to understand why he fell so awkwardly. At any rate, he did, and he managed to crack his skull in the process. He wouldn't have known much about it once his head hit the ground, even if he had been sober enough to realise he was falling over. Goodness knows why he was attacked.'

'That's not exactly what happened. It was more of an accident, I think.'

Jonah frowned. 'I heard something about him being the victim of a violent mugging?'

'He was found in a snickelway, unconscious, along with our suspect, Ben Foster, who was also unconscious when they were discovered.'

Jonah let out a low whistle.

'It was Ben who was mugged,' Geraldine continued, 'not this poor old guy, who just happened to be in the wrong place at the wrong time and was caught up in the attack. Ben was running from a mugger and crashed into this guy, and they both fell over. That's what appears to have happened anyway.'

Jonah nodded. 'That fits,' he said.

They had no idea who the old man was, but the evidence provided by his unidentified corpse bore out Ben's story. Constables were sent to all the shelters for rough sleepers, and all the food banks, and all the churches that offered assistance to the homeless. At first none of the volunteer helpers or visitors recognised the picture of the dead man's pale face. Eventually a key worker at one of the shelters recognised the picture as one of the local rough sleepers who turned up at the shelter in extreme weather. The member of staff who worked at the shelter did not know the man's name. All he was able to tell the police was that he recognised him and thought he had been living on the streets of York for several years. Several other rough sleepers recognised the man's photo and confirmed he had been living on the street for as long as they could remember. One of them thought his name was Richard, but he wasn't sure. No one really seemed to know who he was.

'He kept to himself,' was the general impression the street community gave of him.

'Which is another way of saying no one cared enough to bother to find out who he was,' Geraldine said to Ian when she met him back at the police station.

Ian replied that it went with the territory for a rough sleeper, but Geraldine struggled to dismiss the old man's situation so easily. Thinking about her twin sister, she knew how it could so easily have been Helena lying fatally injured in the street, with no one able to identify her.

'How can something like that happen in a so-called caring society?' she asked, echoing Jonah's question. 'Does no one know who he is? Has no one missed him?'

Ian sighed and didn't answer.

45

THE NEWS THAT BEN had been mugged and was recovering in hospital came as a shock. Christine's first thought was that he might die. She sat down with a jolt, physically shaking, wondering how much more stress she could cope with. The nurse who spoke to her on the phone was reassuring when Christine recovered her composure sufficiently to enquire about her husband's condition.

'Just a few broken bones,' the nurse replied cheerfully.

To a nurse in a hospital, bones that could mend were of little consequence. Listening to the details of Ben's condition, Christine tried to feel relieved that he was not going to die.

'He has a broken arm and several cracked ribs, but we should have him bandaged up and ready to go home in a few days, assuming there are no complications. In the meantime, you can come and see him, Mrs Foster.'

Christine felt a flutter of discomfort. She had not considered going to the hospital to see him. Her husband had walked out on her without a word, only contacting her when he was desperate for money. And when she had given him as much as she had been able to lay her hands on, he had been hostile and dismissive, nothing like the husband she had lived with happily for years. Now he was going to need her to take care of him, and be sympathetic, and strong. But where had he been when she was frightened and alone? Not only had he failed to be there to support her, he was the one who had made her wretched in the first place. She was tempted to leave him to rot in hospital and not let him come home. The police were after him. They could have him. She didn't want him back. She broke down in tears of rage.

After a while, her anger turned to a dull grief at the realisation that her marriage was over. It had ended the moment he left her. If he could walk out on her like that, she could never trust him again. However much trouble he was in, a husband should be able to confide in his wife, and share his problems with her. Without that mutual trust, there was no relationship. Once she calmed down, she decided there was a chance they might salvage their marriage, but only if Ben was sufficiently contrite. He would have to confess that he had lost his head and acted in a panic when he left home. As she drove to the hospital, she resolved to abandon him unless he apologised, as he had abandoned her.

Ben stared miserably at her. He said very little and she could see he was in pain, but there was more to it than that. He seemed different, or perhaps she was the one who had changed. She felt unaccountably distant from him, as though they were strangers. She didn't even like him any more, and wondered how she had ever thought she was in love with him. It wasn't just that they were unable to embrace. His hand lay on top of the bed, not far from where she was sitting, but she felt no impulse to lean forward and take it, and he made no move to reach out to her. A wave of sadness hit her and she blinked back tears that threatened to blur her vision. Now more than ever she needed to think clearly. No one noticed, nor would anyone have remarked on her emotion. People cried in hospitals all the time. As for Ben, he wasn't even looking at her. She might as well not have been there.

'So, how are things with you?' he asked.

He was speaking in a low voice, as though it was a struggle to speak to her at all, and he made no effort to look at her. Even if it hurt him to move his head, he could have swivelled his eyes, but he did not seem to want to look at her. She frowned and for a moment did not answer.

'I'm sorry, but what do you expect me to say?' she blurted out at last. She glanced around and lowered her voice. 'First you were taken away, again, by the police and I had no idea when you would be coming back. Again. After what happened last time, we both know it could have taken months for them to clear your name. Yes, yes, I know, it wasn't your fault. You were the victim of circumstances. All you did was drive too fast. Everyone does it, I know. I've heard it all before, and I forgave all of that. There was nothing to forgive,' she added quickly, as he opened his mouth to remonstrate. 'I know, I know, none of it was your fault. It never is your fault, is it? The police carted you off, when you were innocent. You were the victim. I know. I know all that. But none of that explains why you just buggered off and left me last week. You didn't even tell me where you were going. Don't you trust me? I'm your wife.'

Ben shook his head. 'I had to get away,' he replied. 'Surely you can understand that?'

'But why couldn't you tell me where you were going?'

'Because I didn't know. I just had to get away from them before they locked me up again. Like you said, we both know it can take months before you get out, even after a wrongful arrest. And there's never any guarantee of getting away. Especially after it's happened before. What do you suppose a jury's going to make of it all?'

It was difficult to follow what he was saying, because he was speaking in odd jerks. She wondered if they had ever really understood one another. She supposed it was something to do with the injuries to his face, but the horrible thought struck her that perhaps his brain had been damaged in the attack, and he would never return to his former self. She was not sure she could cope with that. He had already changed, since his first arrest. Only gradually had he been recovering from the trauma of knowing he had killed someone while he was behind the wheel and driving too fast. Now this new trouble was bound to set him back again, even if he recovered physically from his injuries. With a sickening thud in her guts, she knew that she could not handle this new Ben. She would rather face the world alone. This time she was the one who had to leave.

'I'm sorry,' she said suddenly, standing up. 'I have to go.'

'Where to?' he asked.

She walked away without answering, hating herself for giving up on him, but hating him more. She was an innocent victim of their marriage and she had no pity left for anyone but herself.

46

'LOOK AT THE PICTURE again,' Ian insisted, sounding increasingly disgruntled.

Screwing up his one open eye, Ben scrutinised the image before looking away, wincing. Geraldine couldn't help feeling a frisson of pity for him. One side of his face was still puffy and bruised, the eye swollen and closed, and his face was pale and unshaven. He swivelled his eye back and scowled at the picture of the dead woman's face.

'You know who she is,' Ian demanded.

Ben grunted before admitting grudgingly that she looked familiar. Geraldine was pleased to note that at least he was talking more freely than he had managed the previous day. Although he still looked dreadful, the swelling on his cheek and lips had gone down quite a lot, enabling him to move his lips.

'She should look familiar,' Ian snapped, no longer making any attempt to conceal his impatience. 'You used to work with her. That's the woman you suffocated. Where did you do it this time, Ben? In a car? There's no point in holding out on us. We know it was you.'

As Ben opened his mouth to reply, a very young-looking nurse arrived to check on him. She smiled at Geraldine and Ian before tending to her patient, who protested when she moved his arm to take his blood pressure.

'I think you need to leave him to rest now,' she said tentatively, as though she was unused to issuing orders. 'The doctor will be releasing him later this afternoon, I expect, and you can continue your conversation then.'

'Call us when he's due to leave and we'll send a car to pick him up,' Ian replied, returning her smile.

'That's nice now,' the nurse said. Her smile turned into a broad grin as she turned to her patient. 'Isn't that nice, Ben?'

Ben closed his eye and grunted, but it was obvious he was in no position to refuse the offer. With no money, and broken bones making it difficult for him to move, he was hardly able to go on the run again.

'His ribs will heal within a couple of months. You can expect his chest to be painful for a while yet, but as long as he's careful – no sports, no heavy lifting–'

'Don't worry, we'll make sure he doesn't exert himself,' Ian said, grinning down at Ben.

Clearly the nurse was under the impression that Ian and Geraldine were relatives who were going to help take care of Ben once he had been discharged.

'And we'll have that plaster off in a matter of weeks,' the nurse added, smiling at Ben. 'Don't look so down in the dumps, you'll soon be out of here and in a few weeks, it will be as though this never happened.'

Ben muttered darkly about getting out of the frying pan into the fire, but the nurse was already moving on to her next patient and didn't hear him. Ian could scarcely conceal his amusement at her misunderstanding.

'Yes, we'll take very good care of you,' Ian assured Ben, who glared up at them.

It was another twenty-four hours before Ben was discharged from hospital and, true to his word, Ian sent a patrol car to pick him up. He wondered if the young nurse was around to see Ben being driven away from the hospital in a police car. It was late afternoon by the time Geraldine and Ian gathered in an interview room to face Ben and his smartly dressed lawyer across a table. Jerome was wearing a navy suit, his shimmering blue tie held in place by a gold tie pin, his hair slicked back as before.

'Tell us about the woman you killed,' Ian began.

He was immediately interrupted by the lawyer protesting at the police line of questioning.

'I believe you may be familiar with the notion of innocent until proven guilty?' he enquired, leaning back nonchalantly in his chair and speaking very fast. 'This kind of browbeating of an innocent suspect is completely out of order. If you attempt to force a confession under such duress, you must know perfectly well that it will not be admissible in court. My client's state of physical distress is not being considered. He is in a great deal of pain after being viciously mugged, both physically and mentally. He is traumatised and in no fit state to be harassed. I take it you are looking for the mugger, and not focusing all your attention on the victim of such a violent crime? My client would like to know what is being done to find the vicious thug who attacked him.'

Ian glared at the lawyer. 'No one is browbeating your client,' he hissed through clenched teeth. 'We are not attempting to force a confession under duress, nor is he being harassed. Far from it. I think you will find your client has been afforded every right to which he is entitled. But we need to ascertain why he attacked his latest victim. As for the attack on his own person, I assure you we have a team searching for the mugger as we speak, checking CCTV and examining the scene forensically. Everything possible is being done to apprehend his assailant. As you must be aware, the assault is being treated as a serious crime since the other victim died without regaining consciousness. Ben has already given a statement to the inspector investigating that particular assault. We are here to question him about another matter, namely the murder of Jamie Benson.'

'Well, it's nothing to do with me,' Ben blurted out. 'I never touched her.'

'You told us yesterday you thought she looked familiar,' Geraldine reminded him. 'But we all know you must recognise her. You worked in the same garage, with just five staff including the boss. There were two other mechanics, the boss, Jamie and you. There is no way you didn't know Jamie, but admitting you knew her won't change anything. The fact that you knew her won't automatically make us assume you killed her. She must have known a lot of people, none of whom were involved in killing her. But we have evidence that places you at the scene of the murder. We know you worked together. So tell us what happened, Ben. It will be easier for you if you co-operate with us.'

The suspect glanced at his lawyer who shook his head, and Ben refused to say anything else.

'No comment,' he muttered sullenly.

Eventually they had to accept that he was not going to share any information about a possible relationship he might have had with Jamie.

'Ben,' Geraldine said, 'can you think of anyone who might wish to harm you?'

His face twisted as he frowned with one eyebrow. 'No,' he replied. 'Only you.'

'And your wife,' Geraldine thought, but refrained from saying.

Ian terminated the interview and sent Ben back to his cell.

'I might as well stay here,' he growled. 'Seeing as my bitch of a wife has thrown me out.'

'Obviously he knows who Jamie is,' Ian said, when Ben had shuffled out of the room. 'They worked together.'

'It doesn't mean he's lying about killing her,' Geraldine protested. 'Or that he's lying about whether he knew George.'

'The question is, do we have enough evidence for a conviction?' Ian asked, as they left the interview room together. 'Surely the glove and the scarf are enough to nail him for George and Jamie. Even without a confession, we've got him.'

'Do you think Christine has really thrown him out?' Geraldine replied with a question of her own. 'I wonder what he did to upset her. I think I might pay her another visit.'

Ian gave her a curious glance. 'If Ben is a serial killer,' he said softly, 'you're going to have to deal with it. We all make errors of judgement about people. Don't judge yourself too harshly.'

Geraldine didn't trust herself to answer him.

47

IN DISCUSSING HER SUSPICIONS with Eileen, Geraldine repeated her suggestion that Ben might have been set up. On the face of it, the idea seemed crazy, but Eileen had to agree it was possible Ben's scarf and glove had been deliberately stolen and used by someone else to murder George and Jamie.

'That would explain why we haven't been able to find any connection between Ben and George,' Geraldine said. 'Perhaps Ben didn't kill him after all.'

'There isn't always any clear link between victims and their killers, of course,' Eileen pointed out. 'It could have been a random encounter with George. Doesn't it strike you as unlikely that someone would set out to frame Ben for murder, and go to so much trouble to fabricate evidence of his guilt? It seems to be a highly risky strategy. For a start, your phantom killer could have left evidence of his own presence at the scene, and Ben might have had a watertight alibi for the time of the murder. Why would anyone go to so much trouble for so precarious a chance of success?'

'I'm just saying it's possible,' Geraldine replied.

Geraldine realised she was starting to sound desperate, especially as she had begun to doubt her own conviction that Ben was innocent.

'But if someone was determined to cause Ben harm,' Eileen continued, 'surely they could have come up with a better idea than to use his scarf and glove to murder innocent victims? I understand what you're saying, Geraldine, but the idea seems rather too far-fetched for us to devote any manpower to pursuing it.'

'Yes, of course, on the face of it the most likely scenario is that Ben himself is the murderer. First there was a random encounter that ended with Ben using his own scarf to strangle a stranger, a scarf that he mistakenly left at the scene. After he was released on the strength of a statement from a completely independent eyewitness, he immediately went out and killed a woman he worked with, this time leaving his glove not only at the scene, but in the victim's mouth, as if he wanted to make sure it was found. It just strikes me as a bit clumsy, which leads me to suspect that someone was trying to point the finger at Ben. Such obvious clues were left at both murder scenes, and I just don't see why Ben would do that. Maybe he might have panicked once, and left his scarf behind, but surely he would have been more careful on a second occasion, which suggests someone is setting him up. Because what I don't understand is why he would have used his own glove for the second murder.'

'He probably didn't intend to leave it behind but when it came to it, he couldn't pull it out. The rubber glove was stuck in her gullet. She must have swallowed while it was being pushed in her mouth.' Eileen shuddered. 'I know we ought to be hardened to all this, but–' She shrugged. 'Every once in a while you hear something that just turns your stomach. Still,' she went on more briskly, 'we've seen worse and I dare say we will again. Now, let's get back to work, shall we?'

'But don't you think we ought to explore the possibility that someone wants to get Ben out of the way?'

'Out of the way?' Eileen raised her eyebrows. 'Anything's possible, Geraldine, but in the meantime, we'll keep Ben safely in custody,' she said firmly.

Geraldine wanted to protest that it simply did not make sense for Ben to have even considered using his own glove in the first place, especially as he had been told that the police had traced him from his scarf being left at the scene of George's murder, but it was evident that Eileen had dismissed her. In any case, she had done her best to make her point. But she was beginning to wonder if Ben's wife might be at the centre of the mystery. Someone clearly wanted Ben locked up and his wife, or someone involved with her, was the most likely suspect. Determined to prove whether Ben was in fact guilty or not, she left the police station and drove to his house.

'What do you want?' Christine asked when she finally responded to Geraldine's knocking.

Christine looked as though she had been crying, but her voice and expression were devoid of all emotion. Geraldine suspected she was sedated, and pressed on gently. Everyone had their breaking point, and Christine had suffered years of stress, having fallen in love with a man whose bad luck had blighted her own life as well as his.

'I came to ask you about Ben.'

Geraldine braced herself to react, but Christine made no move to close the door.

'Ben's not here,' she said.

Her eyes did not show so much as a flicker of interest when she said his name, and her voice remained flat.

'I know that,' Geraldine replied. 'He's back with us for now, where we can keep an eye on him.'

Christine gave a hollow laugh, but her eyes remained cold. 'So he's been arrested again,' she said.

'We know you saw Ben and gave him money.'

'He hasn't got that money any more. He was mugged.'

'Yes, we know about that as well. We spoke to him in hospital.'

'Well, if you've got any questions for him, you can ask him yourself,' Christine said, still not showing any emotion.

Carefully, Geraldine manoeuvred her way into the hall. Christine made no attempt to stop her entering the house and followed her to the narrow living room without protest. The first time Geraldine had visited the house, the room had been neat and comfortable. Now the floor was littered with dirty plates, overflowing ashtrays and empty cigarette packets, and it stank of stale cigarettes. The wedding photographs had disappeared from the mantelpiece, and there were no pictures of Ben anywhere in the room. A few splinters of glass glittered in the fireplace, suggesting that Christine had smashed the photographs of her husband.

Geraldine sat down on one of the settees and leaned towards Christine who had taken a seat on the other. 'Christine, we're looking into the possibility that Ben was framed.'

Christine shrugged. 'So what?'

'Do you think it's possible?'

'Do I think what's possible?'

'Do you think Ben could have been framed?'

'I don't know and I don't care. I don't know what you want from me but I haven't got anything to tell you. He's gone, and he's not coming back. I never want to see him again.'

Tears rolled down Christine's cheeks as she spoke, but her expression and her voice remained deadpan. When Ben had told them that his wife had thrown him out, Geraldine had been unsure whether or not to believe him, but his story was beginning to look sadly credible.

'Do you have any idea what's been going on?' Geraldine asked.

'What do you want me to say?'

'You can tell me if you can think of anyone who might have held a grudge against Ben.'

Christine shook her head.

'Did he have any enemies?'

Christine shrugged. 'How should I know?'

'Please, Christine, we need you to help us to help Ben.'

'Why would I want to help him?'

Geraldine let out a silent sigh. 'Do you know of anyone who hated Ben?'

'Hated him?'

'Did anyone wish him harm, or dislike him?'

'Only me.'

Geraldine hesitated, wondering if Christine had just confessed to killing George and Jamie, but somehow she didn't really believe that. All the same, she felt she was missing something.

'Christine, is there anything you would like to tell me?' she asked gently.

'I was a good wife,' Christine blurted out. 'I was a good wife. I don't deserve this. I don't deserve this.'

'Christine,' Geraldine spoke softly. 'We're trying to help bring Ben home to you so that you can get on with your lives, together. You want that, don't you?'

Christine began to sob loudly. 'We don't have a life together any more. I don't want to see him again. Never, never, never!'

48

AFTER THE POLICEWOMAN HAD gone, Christine burst out crying. Her whole life was in ruins, and it was all Ben's fault. She bitterly regretted having married him. More than that, she wished they had never met. It was hard to believe she had ever thought she loved him, although that wasn't strictly true because she had loved him, genuinely and completely. She had loved him with a passion she would never feel again. Knowing he had destroyed her capacity to love wholeheartedly, she wept for herself and her wretched future that stretched out in front of her, bleak and lonely. She would never trust another man again, as long as she lived. She had loved Ben enough to defy everyone she knew in marrying him, but it turned out that her family had been right all along.

Before his first arrest, they had been happy. Since then, he had changed. She had stood by him all through the court case, and for a long time she had hoped he would eventually recover. But shortly before he recently lost his job he had begun acting strangely. For the first time in their troubled marriage his love making had become oddly dispassionate. They had been like animals coupling in the dark. When she had questioned him about his coldness towards her, he had become hostile, not at all like the charmer she had fallen for. He had become tetchy when she pressed him, accusing her of not trusting him.

'If you've lost your job, just tell me,' she had urged him. 'I won't mind, really I won't. Things happen. I know it's not your fault you're having trouble with the police again.'

But he had glared angrily at her and told her he was going out.

'There's someone else, isn't there?' she had shouted, provoked to fury by his refusal to talk to her.

'Oh Jesus, not this endless suspicion again,' he had replied, although this was the first time she had accused him of being unfaithful.

His response had been so excessive that, since then, trusting him had cost her an effort. She was sorry she had been stupid enough to confide in Francesca. As soon as she told her sister, Christine had regretted her indiscretion, knowing that Francesca told their mother everything. Christine had made her sister promise never to breathe a word of her secret suspicions to their parents. Christine was confident Francesca had kept her word, because their mother never mentioned Ben's infidelity. Once their mother knew about Ben's behaviour, Christine would never hear the end of it. There was a painful irony in her mother's complaints about Ben's lack of faith, when Christine was afraid he had been unfaithful to her.

Christine dried her eyes and reapplied her make-up. Her eyes looked slightly red and inflamed, as though she was suffering an allergic reaction to something, but she felt a new resolution. She was done with Ben. A woman didn't need proof to know when her husband was lying to her. 'Once a cheater, always a cheater,' her sister had warned her, and Christine had known all along that she was right. Ben had been hiding something from her. It could only be another woman. Even if he reformed and became the most devout Christian in all England, she didn't think she would ever be able to trust him again. And without trust, there could be no relationship. It was that simple. They had both tried to keep the marriage going, but she had known for a long time that it was no use. She had been kidding herself to think she could ever trust him again. He had always been wild. Ironically, that was what had attracted her to him in the first place.

Despite her resolution to tell them nothing of what had

happened, it did not take her family long to discover the reason for Ben's absence. Predictably, her mother was the first to remark on it.

'It's a pity Ben's not able to join us. Again.' The expression on her face was strangely complacent. 'Clearly he has found something better to do with his time than spend it here with us. Well, if he can't be bothered to turn up to a family dinner, that's his loss.'

'He never really fitted in here,' Christine's father murmured, gazing anxiously at his wife.

Christine smiled uncomfortably and watched her mother bringing in bowls of soup, one at a time.

'Let me give you a hand, Mum,' Francesca exclaimed, standing up.

Christine rose to her feet as well, intending to help, but her foot caught on her chair and she tripped. As she reached out to stop herself from falling, she knocked into her mother's arm, and the bowl of soup her mother was carrying flew from her grasp, landing on the table with a loud crack. Hot soup splashed up in the air and spread out from the smashed bowl, soaking into the paper napkins and covering the nearby cutlery with glistening oily liquid.

'You clumsy idiot!' her mother snapped. 'Can't you watch what you're doing? You've brought nothing but trouble to this family.'

All at once, everything seemed to close in on Christine and she could no longer control herself. Tears slid from her eyes, and she let out a wail. Once she began, she couldn't stop, and she slumped down in her chair, sobbing.

'It's only soup,' Francesca said.

'Pull yourself together,' their mother said as she fussed around, mopping up the mess. 'It only spilled on the table. There's no need to carry on like that.'

'It's not as if you spilled the milk,' Christine's brother-in-law said, grinning stupidly. 'You know, crying over spilled milk,' he added by way of explanation.

No one took any notice of him.

'It's Ben, isn't it?' Francesca demanded. 'Christine, where is he? What's going on?'

Her mother continued wiping the table, her lips pressed together in silent disapproval. At last she finished and sat down, heedless of the soup she had not yet finished serving.

'Now perhaps you'll tell us what's going on with that husband of yours,' she said, fidgeting with the tablecloth and not looking at Christine.

'We're your family,' Francesca added earnestly. 'You know we're here for you if things have gone wrong.'

Christine nodded. 'He's – he's been arrested again,' she stammered, no longer caring what her family thought of him. 'He's in custody.'

'Oh dear, oh dear,' her father said, sounding genuinely concerned. 'So we were right all along, Hilary.' He turned to Christine. 'What's he done this time?'

Christine shook her head.

'Well, better it should come to this now, while you're still young enough to start again with someone else,' her mother exclaimed, with an air of triumph. 'You're better off without that lowlife, and I don't care who knows it. You deserve better and now you're going to get it. Not that I'm not sorry he turned out so badly,' she added.

'So he's gone?' Francesca asked. 'You're finally leaving him? This time, surely there's no going back. Not again.'

'Not again,' Christine echoed wretchedly.

'You must come and live here with us,' her mother said. 'At least until after the divorce.'

'What about Roxy?' Christine asked miserably.

'Never mind about the dog,' her mother replied. 'Someone will take him off your hands. He's Ben's dog, isn't he? And Ben is gone from your life for good. You must see, Christine, that although getting rid of Ben will be painful for a while, in the long run this is all for the good. A man like that has no place in our family. We're all better off without him.'

49

IAN RETURNED FROM THE kitchen, where he had been clattering around clearing up after the curry he had served. Geraldine had offered to stack the dishwasher and scrub the pans, which seemed to her only fair after Ian had done the cooking, but he insisted on cleaning up after himself.

'What are you up to?' he enquired, seeing Geraldine put down her iPad when he entered the living room. 'You're not working again, are you? Come on, we've had an excellent dinner – at least, I hope it was good – and it's time to relax.'

Geraldine murmured her enthusiasm for his curry.

'So come on, put that away. Here, let me pour you another beer.'

Seeing him pick up the bottle opener in preparation for going to the kitchen to fetch a bottle from the fridge, Geraldine shook her head impatiently.

'I'm looking at this from a different angle,' she replied.

'This?' he repeated, putting the bottle opener back on the table and sitting down on an armchair at right angles to the sofa where she was seated. 'You're not talking about the beer, are you?' he asked, gazing intensely at her and sighing.

'What? No, I'm talking about the case. Do you remember what we're working on, by any chance? Two murders. Does that ring any bells?'

Ian grinned tolerantly at her. 'Okay, my little workhorse. What angle have you come up with? I'm all ears.' He leaned back in his chair and put his head on one side.

She shook her head again, smiling. 'I only said I was working. I never said I'd tell you what I'm doing.'

'Come on, you tease.'

She put her iPad down, and explained that she had been thinking about who might possibly have wanted to frame Ben.

'You're not still banging on about him being set up, are you? The evidence against him is pretty strong.'

'That's the problem. It's too obvious,' she replied.

Ian laughed. 'How can the facts be too obvious? You're never satisfied, are you?'

'Not until I'm one hundred per cent convinced we've got to the truth,' she replied severely.

'Well, go on then, what's the big idea?'

'I've been going over and over Ben's history,' she replied. 'And it occurred to me that we ought to look into the woman he knocked down and killed.'

'We've already checked that out, and we know everything there is to know about it.'

'We don't know everything,' she protested.

Ian continued, ignoring her interruption. 'The accident happened more than four years ago. Ben stood trial and was found not guilty. He was released three years ago, and now there have been two murders, both of which appear to have been committed by him. That's what the evidence points to, regardless of any theories to the contrary.'

'Yes, yes, I know all that. But I still thought it might be worth taking a look. Anyway, the victim was called Laura Barton.' She paused. 'Look, here's a picture of her.'

She turned her screen around to show an image of a young blonde woman smiling into the camera.

'She was attractive,' Ian commented. 'But I'm not sure where you're going with this.'

'Ben was prosecuted for dangerous driving, but the jury

found him not guilty as he was only going less than ten miles an hour over the limit.'

'Hardly a boy racer.'

'Yes, he was just unlucky, as was the victim. If she hadn't been carrying a glass bottle, she would have survived with a few nasty injuries that would have healed.'

'This is a tragic story,' Ian said, 'but I'm still not sure what point you're making.'

She closed her iPad and turned to face him. 'My point is that Laura had a husband, Matthew Barton.'

Ian nodded slowly. He was beginning to see where her line of enquiry was heading.

'I know Ben got off,' Geraldine continued, 'but did her husband agree with the jury? Isn't it possible he blamed Ben for his wife's death, and has been harbouring a grudge all this time?'

'Which means it's possible he set these murders up to look as though Ben was guilty,' Ian said softly. 'Do you really think Matthew Barton could have framed Ben?'

Geraldine shrugged. 'I have no idea. All I'm saying is that it's possible. It makes sense. Matthew Barton moved, but he still lives in York.'

With a sigh, Ian agreed it would be worth tracking down the witness who had corroborated Ben's story, in an attempt to establish exactly what had happened.

'The whole thing sounds fanciful,' he concluded, 'but I'd back your crazy instincts against any amount of evidence.'

The following morning, Geraldine set to work trying to track down the woman who had witnessed the fatal car accident. All she had was a name and an address. Angela Clark lived on the road where the accident had occurred. Geraldine pulled up in a nearby parking space and walked quickly to the right house, wishing she had put on a warmer jacket. When she had left home earlier that morning, the sky had been clear and the air had felt warm, a faint reminder that summer was on its way. Now, beneath an overcast sky, a chill wind had picked up and was agitating the branches of the sparse trees into a frenzy. Overnight the weather had changed, so that it felt less like spring and more like the end of autumn.

Geraldine rang the bell, which chimed loudly. After that, she waited. A moment later, she heard someone stir on the other side of the door, which opened to reveal a wizened old man.

'Yes?' he enquired with a hesitant smile. 'How may I be of assistance, young lady?'

His back was bowed and he squinted up at her over rimless half-moon glasses. He was wearing a dark red dressing gown over blue striped pyjama trousers and fabric tartan slippers. Geraldine wondered if he was going to be able to answer any questions sensibly.

'Can I help you?' he repeated, in a thin high-pitched voice.

A young man appeared behind him, calling out impatiently. 'Granddad, how many times have we told you not to open the front door to anyone? You don't know who might be out there.'

'It's this nice young lady,' the old man replied in his reedy voice. 'I don't know what she wants,' he added. 'Should I leave and give you some privacy?' He sniggered.

'What are you after?' the young man enquired, fixing a faintly hostile gaze on Geraldine. 'What do you want?'

'I'm sorry to disturb you. I'm looking for Angela Clark,' she replied, holding up her identity card.

The young man looked puzzled for an instant, then his expression cleared and he nodded. 'Oh yes, Angela Clark,' he said. 'She moved out a year ago. We bought the house from her, didn't we, Granddad?'

The old man nodded, and smiled, mumbling to himself. He did not appear to understand what his grandson was talking about. Geraldine cursed her oversight under her breath. She could have checked her information before driving there. Apologising for disturbing the new householders, she asked whether they knew where the previous householder had gone, but the young man regretted he was unable to help her. Geraldine wondered whether the accident had been a factor in Angela Clark's decision to move away. She could understand that might have been upsetting. Every time the woman went out, or returned home, she would be reminded of the bloody corpse she had seen lying in the road outside her house.

50

THE FOLLOWING MORNING, GERALDINE asked a constable to find Angela Clark's address, only to discover that she was too late.

'What do you mean, too late?' she asked the constable she had tasked with tracking down the witness. 'Don't tell me she's left the country? Can you find out where she's gone?'

'Hardly.' Her colleague showed her an image of a death certificate. 'I had this sent to me, just to make sure,' she explained. 'It's her all right. I traced her last address and everything matches. We're six months too late.'

'So much for questioning Angela Clark,' Geraldine said, with a faint scowl. She had an uneasy feeling in the pit of her stomach. 'Was there anything suspicious about her death?'

Her colleague hesitated. 'Nothing that I came across. But I didn't scout around.'

'How did she die?'

'It just says death by misadventure on the death certificate. I could look into it further if you want me to. There is a next of kin I came across, a brother, Lester Clark, living in Scarborough.'

Geraldine thanked her and made a note of Lester Clark's details. Then she went to talk to Eileen. The detective chief inspector was not keen to send Geraldine off to Scarborough to speak to Angela's brother, and suggested they send a local constable round to talk to him instead.

'Although I'm not sure what you expect to find out,' Eileen added.

Geraldine agreed that it was probably a waste of time, and

244

they left it that she would return to Eileen if she had anything further to say about this line of enquiry. Geraldine walked out of Eileen's office, wondering if the senior officer realised she had determined to make the trip to Scarborough that evening, in her own time. She would probably end up regretting making the journey, but there was a slim chance Lester Clark might add a fragment of information to the picture Geraldine was building concerning Laura Barton's death. She did not tell Ian where she was going, as she was fairly sure he would dismiss her line of enquiry as pointless. If it was a dead end, no one else needed to know she had taken herself off to Scarborough on a wild goose chase. The man she wanted to question had assured her he would be at home when she called, but her journey would probably still turn out to be a complete waste of time. She set off anyway. It would do her no harm to take a drive and clear her head.

As it turned out, not only was Lester Clark at home, but he seemed happy to talk to Geraldine about his dead sister.

'Angela?' he repeated. 'You want to know about Angela? Yes, of course I'd be willing to tell you whatever it is you want to know, but I'm not sure there's anything much to tell. But goodness, where are my manners? Do please come in.'

Geraldine thanked him and followed him into a small kitchen where he bustled about putting the kettle on.

'My partner's out,' he explained, 'so we won't be disturbed. Not that there's anything secret to tell you about Angela. On the contrary, she was – well, she was ordinary. I don't mean that in a bad way.' He smiled sadly. 'If Michael comes back, he can join us, can't he?'

'Of course,' Geraldine replied.

She had not expected her visit to be treated as a social event, but was pleased when Lester brewed a pot of fresh coffee and set out some cake. It was past seven by the time she arrived in Scarborough, and she hadn't eaten since lunchtime.

'Now,' Lester said when they were settled with coffee and cake on the small table between them. 'How can I help you, Inspector? What is it you want to know?'

Before Geraldine could answer, they heard footsteps and a narrow head appeared around the door.

'Ah, Michael,' Lester greeted him with a smile. 'We have a visitor, a police inspector who's come here to ask me about my sister.'

Michael made an appropriate excuse and left Geraldine and Lester to continue their meeting.

'He's an angel, but he's not much of a one for company,' Lester explained fondly. 'He's quite shy around strangers.'

Geraldine asked him about his sister, and Lester grew sombre as he told her that Angela had died six months earlier.

'She'd only just moved house,' he added. 'It was – well, it was a terrible tragedy, poor Angela. I miss her terribly.'

'What happened to her?'

'Like I said, she's dead.'

'Yes, but can you tell me how it happened?'

Lester sighed. 'She fell in the river and well, that was the end of her, I'm afraid. They pulled her out, of course, but not until the next morning, and by then it was too late to do anything for her. She wasn't a strong swimmer and the general view was that the shock of the cold water was too much for her.'

'Do you know what she was doing down by the river?'

'Oh, there was nothing unusual about that. She liked to walk along there. She was always careful about her health. Ironic, isn't it? She went for walks to keep healthy, and in the end that's what killed her.'

'So it came as no surprise to you when you heard she'd fallen in?'

'Well, actually, to be honest, I was quite surprised. Angela was always so careful. I used to tease her for being risk averse. She never went anywhere, and never did anything, and she was nervous about entering into a relationship with anyone. She used to like walking by the river. She said it made her feel calm. So when we heard she'd fallen in, well, yes, I was surprised, but of course accidents happen, don't they? Apparently she tripped over a tree root or a weed. They said it's very overgrown along there, near where she fell.' He sighed. 'There was nothing anyone could do.'

'So you never thought it was anything other than a tragic accident?'

Lester's eyebrows shot up. 'I'm not sure what you mean by that. Are you saying Angela's death wasn't an accident?'

'No,' Geraldine hastened to reassure him, although that was exactly what she had been implying. 'I'm just exploring the possibility. Did you never wonder about it?'

Lester shook his head. 'I mean, there was no reason to suspect anything untoward had happened. Angela wasn't the sort of person anything unusual would ever happen to. She just wasn't like that. It was a lovely funeral,' he added thoughtfully. 'I was very fond of my sister, Inspector. I wanted to do her proud, and I really think we did. She would–' He broke off and sighed. 'Well, she's gone and I miss her dreadfully. Michael's been a rock through it all. I don't know what I would have done without him. But as far as poor Angela's death is concerned, I'm not sure what more there is to say.'

Geraldine nodded. There was nothing else to say, but Lester had given her a lot to think about.

51

GERALDINE AND IAN SPENT most of Saturday morning re-organising the flat. Ian had been living with Geraldine for a couple of months, and he had finally agreed to sell his apartment and make the move permanent. Putting his own home on the market necessitated his depositing several carloads of his belongings at Geraldine's. Although her flat provided ample room for a single person, and was in theory spacious enough to accommodate two people, Ian had a lot of belongings. He was keen for them to buy a house together, but Geraldine was reluctant to move. She wondered if Ian was bringing so many of his possessions with him in an attempt to persuade her they needed to move somewhere bigger.

'I love this place,' she murmured.

'I love the woman who lives here,' Ian replied.

They had discussed their living arrangements at length. With the equity from both of their flats, Ian argued they would be able to afford a very decent house, with a good sized garden. The problem was that Geraldine didn't want to leave her flat, which was located right in the centre of the city, overlooking the river. She could not imagine being as happy anywhere else as she was there. It was late morning and Ian was taking a break from unpacking his belongings. Sitting on her balcony, gazing out over the water, Geraldine sighed.

'It's so lovely here,' she said. 'Having coffee on the balcony, watching the river. It's beautiful.'

But Ian insisted they ought to find somewhere larger. The

flat had two bedrooms, and Geraldine had given up the second bedroom so Ian could have his own study, but he was not happy with the arrangement.

'I feel as though I've cannibalised your space,' he told her.

She laughed. 'Well, you haven't. I offered it to you because I don't really need my own space as much as you do.'

'Bullshit.'

'All right, let's agree it's a compromise I'm prepared to make to have you living here with me.'

'But it's a compromise you don't have to make if we move somewhere bigger, and we can afford it. Besides, this is always going to feel like your flat, and I want us to have a place together. Listen, I'll sell up and then we'll talk about it again.'

Geraldine sighed. She knew Ian was probably right and that they would end up moving. That was the downside of being in a relationship. However much she loved Ian, and however happy he made her, she was no longer independent. Her decisions about how she lived her life had to accommodate his wishes as well as her own. She wondered if it was too high a price to pay for living with him. If he kept his own flat, they could still live together, but they could have separate homes to go to if they needed space.

'You don't have to take over my second bedroom,' she pointed out tentatively.

'But then I'd have nowhere to keep all my stuff.'

'You don't have to sell your own flat,' she went on, watching him warily.

'Don't you want me here?'

'Of course I do,' she replied quickly. 'That's not what I meant at all. I just meant you could keep your things where they are and still live here with me.'

'But without my own desk and music system and everything else that makes a place my own home?'

Geraldine shook her head. She could see she was being unreasonable.

'No,' she agreed, 'I can see that wouldn't work, not in the long term.'

'Shall I put my flat on the market then, or are you having second thoughts about all this?'

'No, no, I'm not having second thoughts. Go ahead. Sell your flat, and then, like you said, we can take it from there.'

Ian nodded. 'Yes, one step at a time. Change is always hard.'

She smiled, grateful for his understanding. 'You're right. Just because something is hard doesn't mean we shouldn't attempt it.'

'I hope it's not too hard, living with me,' he replied, smiling. 'Now, isn't it your turn to make the coffee?'

Late that afternoon, Geraldine slipped out to speak to the widower of the woman Ben had knocked down. He lived in North Parade, not far from her own flat.

'Where are you off to?' Ian asked, when she told him she was popping out.

She hesitated, reluctant to admit that she was still working in the evening. She knew Ian would be irritated that she was choosing to work when they could be spending the evening together. At the same time, reason combined with instinct to warn her not to go and see Matthew Barton without telling anyone where she was going.

'I'm just going to have a word with Laura's widower.'

'Laura?'

'Yes, Laura Barton, the woman Ben knocked down and killed.'

Ian smiled. 'Still investigating clues to Ben's innocence?' he chided her gently. 'I don't see how the man who was married to Laura is going to help you.'

'Well, you're probably right and this will turn out to be a complete dead end, but I just thought it would be worth a try. I won't be long. He lives in York.'

As it happened, the visit took less time than she had expected, because when she knocked on the door of Matthew Barton's house in North Parade, there was no answer, even though she had a feeling someone was inside the house. There was nothing more she could do there so she went home, determined to return and speak to Matthew another day. It was frustrating, but at least Ian was pleased to see her.

'How did you get on?' he asked.

'I didn't. He wasn't there.'

'Never mind. You can probably catch him at home tomorrow. Now, what shall we do? Do you fancy going out for a meal?'

Geraldine smiled. It was nice to feel like a normal couple, discussing what to do on a Saturday evening.

'Sure,' she replied. 'You choose where to go. Just give me half an hour to get ready.'

She almost felt as though she wasn't caught up in a murder investigation. Almost, but not quite.

52

ON SATURDAY EVENING, HE picked Naomi up from outside her front door as they had arranged, and drove her to a pub out of town that served excellent food. She was clearly dressed for a date in a low-cut top that glittered as she moved, and tight-fitting jeans. Had he been interested in finding a girlfriend, he would have been pleased. As it was, he was gratified to discover that she was interested in him. She was certainly attractive, but he had something more important on his mind than romance or sex. Despite his dedicated surveillance, over a week had passed since he had seen the killer, and he was frantic to discover what had happened to him. If the killer had left home, never to reappear, everything would be over. Naomi was his best chance of discovering the truth. He had to make her talk.

It took him a couple of hours to persuade her to relax, but she finally finished her steak, drained one glass of decent red wine too many, and began to drop her guard. Her speech grew slightly slurred as she confided to him the details of her previous relationship.

'Would you believe it turned out the rat was married all along? So much for my expertise in spotting when people are lying.' She giggled. 'You're not married, are you?' she asked, suddenly serious. 'You're not wearing a wedding ring,' she added. 'See, I'm still a detective.' She laughed again, slightly hysterically.

Hoping she was not too pissed to be useful, he shook his head solemnly. 'No, I'm not married,' he assured her.

He sighed. There were so many things about Naomi that

bugged him, but he couldn't stop seeing her, not until he had pumped her for information. Without warning, she reached across the table and put her hand on his.

'You're very beautiful,' he lied, without moving his hand away.

Watching the flickering of her eyelids, coloured with a dusting of blue to match her eyes, he felt her fingers tighten around his own. He gazed at her, struggling to conceal his triumph at having gained her trust.

'Let's talk about you,' he said, refilling her glass and nodding at the waiter for another bottle. 'Tell me about your week.'

'Do we have to talk about work?' she replied, pouting.

'Of course not,' he said.

He was determined not to force the issue and cause her to clam up. Not only would a subtle approach help him to wheedle more out of her, he couldn't afford to alert her to the real reason for his interest in her.

He smiled. 'That's the last thing we want to talk about. What else have you been up to since I saw you?'

She shook her head morosely. 'Nothing else. Honestly, Sid, when we're on a case there's no time for anything else.'

'Are you working on a case right now? This doesn't feel like work,' he said, raising his glass, and she laughed.

'Actually, we've had a good week at work. A bloody good week.' She glanced around before adding in an exaggerated whisper, 'You mustn't tell anyone.'

'I promise not to blab. Whatever you tell me stays between us. You know you can trust me to be discreet.'

Actually, she didn't know him at all.

She leaned forward and then drew back, as though she had changed her mind. 'No,' she murmured. 'I'd like to tell you more, but I just can't. You understand, don't you?'

'Is it a big secret?' he asked, doing his best to sound contemptuous, as though she was behaving like a child. 'Do you work for MI5?'

'All I can tell you is that we have a suspect,' she replied with a hint of impatience, but still with the wherewithal to speak very quietly. 'It's a man we've been after for weeks.'

He raised his eyebrows. 'I thought someone had already been arrested recently for the murder in York?' he whispered back. 'Is this another one?'

'No, it's the same suspect. He was arrested, but we let him go. And now we've nicked him again. I really can't say any more than that.'

In spite of her reticence, he thought he understood the gist of what she was telling him, and could scarcely contain his elation. Swiftly he refilled her glass.

'What?' he replied. 'So the man you arrested before and let go has been arrested again?'

She nodded. 'Honestly, we should never have let him go. It wasn't my fault. It was nothing to do with me, thank goodness. It was a DI who released him.'

She burped and giggled, and he thought what a ridiculous trollop she was. Her make-up was smudged where she had rubbed one eye, and her lipstick was all but wiped away from eating. If she hadn't been so drunk she would probably have gone to the ladies room to tidy her face by now. He didn't doubt he could take her home with him and spend the night with her. The way she kept leering at him, he suspected she was expecting him to make his move. Nothing could have been further from his intentions. He almost felt sorry for her. But he was too jubilant to care about anything other than the news she had just given him. With a rush of gratitude, he smiled at her and complimented her on her outfit.

'You only just noticed?' she slurred, grinning. 'What you after then?'

He smiled. 'I think it's time I dropped you home,' he replied, waving at a waiter for the bill. 'I've had a lovely evening,' he added with genuine enthusiasm.

It was true, the evening had been very satisfactory. He hadn't even minded having to spend so long in her company, because she had given him exactly what he wanted. She was clearly keen to move the relationship on, but he excused himself, on the pretext that she was drunk and he didn't want to take advantage of her.

'What if I want to take advantage of you?' she giggled.

He shook his head, but only managed to persuade her to leave the car by inviting her to his house for supper during the week. She seemed content with that, and clambered out of the car. A man genuinely interested in her would have escorted her to her door. Instead, he remained behind the wheel and watched her lurch unevenly up her path and fumble with her key. At last she opened the door and he was glad he had not driven off straight away, because she saw that he had waited when she turned and blew him a kiss.

He drove off without responding. But she would remember that he had waited and seen her safely home and what she would regard as his respectful restraint would only serve to increase her trust in him. He could not defer physical relations indefinitely, but he would deal with that another time. For now it was enough to know the police had their suspect locked up in a cell. Smiling, he drove home.

53

On Sunday morning, Ian said he would finish his unpacking as Geraldine began clearing up the breakfast things.

'I'm off then,' he said, without moving from his seat.

'Oh for goodness sake, it's only a few boxes,' Geraldine replied, laughing at his reluctance to deal with it. 'You'll be done in an hour.'

'Hardly,' he replied. 'It's not just a case of unpacking things. With such limited space, I have to decide what to keep and what to throw out. These decisions can't be made lightly, you know. A bit of help wouldn't go amiss.'

Unwilling to enter into a discussion about moving to a larger home together, Geraldine was pleased when Ariadne texted her to ask if she would like to meet for lunch. Since they saw one another almost every day at work, and only occasionally met up socially at the weekends, Geraldine guessed her friend wanted to talk to her about something outside of work. She could imagine what that was.

'You don't mind if I go out?' she asked Ian.

On his knees in the second bedroom, surrounded by open boxes and piles of clothes and books and gadgets, Ian raised his head to look up at her with a pained expression.

'So you're abandoning me to my unpacking?' he complained. 'Cruel, cruel woman. You're off out to chase after another man, leaving me drowning in stuff.'

'Well, it's not as if there's anything I can do, is there? Everything here is yours, not mine. You can chuck the whole lot away if you like.'

'You are joking.'

'Seriously, Ian, you don't need my help.'

'You could bring me cups of tea and express your sympathy for my plight,' he replied. 'But if you insist on chasing the widower of a woman who was knocked down by our suspect a few years ago then bugger off, and leave me to struggle here all on my own. I dare say I'll survive.'

Geraldine grinned. 'That's good to know. Right then, I'm off. Oh, and by the way, this isn't work. I'm meeting Ariadne for lunch.'

'Well, why didn't you say so?' he replied, sitting back on his heels. 'I'm delighted to hear it. Just leave me slaving away here, while you go out and have a good time.'

Geraldine laughed. 'Don't worry, I will. See you later.'

Ian grunted and leaned forward again over an unopened box. 'What the hell is in here?' he muttered to himself. He looked up in mock alarm. 'I've absolutely no idea what this is.'

'I'll leave you to it then.'

As it turned out, Geraldine thought it was not a bad idea to go out and let Ian carry on with his unpacking uninterrupted. She set out early to give herself time to take a detour to Matthew Barton's house but once again he was not in. It was probably just as well because she barely had time to drive to the Turkish restaurant near Museum Street where she had arranged to meet Ariadne, who was already seated when Geraldine arrived. After exchanging greetings, they studied the menu and placed their order.

'Good,' Ariadne said, smiling, as she handed her menu to the waiter. 'Now we can have a good old natter.'

Geraldine thought she had a fairly good idea what Ariadne might want to talk about, and she was right. It wasn't long before Ariadne launched into a detailed account of the preparations for her wedding. Her curly dark hair bobbed around as she spoke, gesticulating energetically.

'Can't you just pop along to the registry office, tie the

knot, and have done with it?' Geraldine asked.

'Am I boring you?'

'No, no, not at all,' Geraldine hastened to assure her friend, realising she had sounded unintentionally curt.

Ariadne gave a good-natured grunt. 'Of course I am. Bloody hell, Geraldine, I'm boring myself, and it's my wedding we're talking about.'

Geraldine sighed. She wondered if weddings were always so complicated to arrange. Her thoughts wandered to Laura, and how many members of her family she had invited to her ceremony. Perhaps she had organised a grand affair, only to be knocked down and killed after three years of marriage. She wondered if Laura had met up with a friend to discuss the complications of her wedding party, or if she and Matthew had simply gone to the registry office, or the church, with two witnesses they had invited along off the street.

'Well?' Ariadne asked. 'What do you think?'

Geraldine hesitated, reluctant to admit that she had been too distracted to take in what Ariadne had been saying.

'Whatever you think,' she murmured. 'It's your wedding, and you ought to do whatever you feel is best. It's your big day and no one else's.'

Ariadne burst out laughing. 'You haven't been listening to a word I said, have you?'

'What?'

'I just asked if you want to get a bottle of wine.'

As it was lunchtime, and they were both driving, they settled on a large glass of wine each, and Geraldine settled down to listen to Ariadne more carefully.

'I'm not the best person to consult about weddings,' she added.

'Oh, I don't want to consult you,' Ariadne assured her. 'There are already more than enough people giving me the benefit of their advice, in other words telling me what I ought to do. I just want to vent. My grandmother's getting involved now, and although she and my mother don't see eye to eye about anything, my mother always does whatever my grandmother tells her to do. So now I'm having to agree to the wedding my grandmother wants, and she doesn't even live in England. We hardly ever see her, she doesn't know me at all, but suddenly she's issuing instructions that have to be obeyed or the whole family will be thrown into turmoil. You know what, I think I might just follow your advice and drag Nico off to the registry office. Will you be a witness?'

Geraldine shook her head. 'Oh no, you're not getting me involved in this.'

She did not add that she was in enough trouble as it was, for listening to another witness, Sallyanne Hodgskin. She wasn't about to become a witness herself, encouraging Ariadne to defy her family in the process.

'I don't want to sound unsympathetic, but you have to sort out your family problems yourself.'

'We all have our problems,' she thought to herself. 'Now,' she went on aloud, 'let's talk about what you're looking forward to at your wedding. You're going to have a party, aren't you?'

Ariadne grinned. 'A party with my friends after the family event is over.'

'And you'll be Mrs Moralis.'

They chinked glasses and laughed, although it wasn't really funny.

Driving home, Geraldine thought about Ariadne's issues with her family, and decided to call on Christine's family. The last words Christine had said to Geraldine were about her husband. 'We don't have a life together any more. I don't want to see him again. Never, never, never!' On reflection, that sounded like someone who might want to see her husband put away. Christine's mother might know about any problems in her marriage. It might be interesting to talk to her.

54

THE FOLLOWING MORNING, GERALDINE called on Christine's parents on her way to work and found them both at home. Hilary seemed reluctant to invite her in, protesting sourly that she and Derek were having breakfast.

'Can't decent law-abiding citizens be allowed to sit over breakfast in peace?' she grumbled, as she led the way to the dining room. 'I suppose this is about that godless man who led our poor Christine astray?' she added as Geraldine sat down.

There was a pot of tea and a plate of toast on the table, but Hilary didn't offer her visitor anything.

'I won't keep you long. I just wondered if you were aware of any problems in Christine's marriage,' Geraldine enquired.

'Oh, that's over,' Hilary replied without any hesitation. 'She's left him. And she won't be going back. We've already found a lawyer to arrange a divorce for her.'

'On what grounds?' Geraldine asked.

'Irreconcilable differences, abandonment, you name it,' Hilary replied firmly. 'Our daughter made a mistake, and now it's time to put things right for her.'

She spoke sorrowfully, but Geraldine suspected she was pleased her daughter's marriage had failed. Hilary's next words only served to confirm Geraldine's impression.

'It might seem rather sudden,' she said, 'but Derek and I have known for a long time that her marriage wouldn't last, right from the day Christine came home and told us they'd had a civil ceremony in a registry office. We knew then that it wasn't a marriage in the sight of God. How could we welcome such a man into our family? It went against our consciences to congratulate her and pretend to be pleased.'

After that, Christine's parents refused to discuss Ben any further, insisting he was no longer part of their daughter's life, and they wanted to get on with their breakfast before the tea was cold. None the wiser, Geraldine left. She needed to reach the police station in time for their next interview with Ben. They were not surprised when he proved uncooperative. His lawyer seemed even less bothered about the arrest than before, and gazed around the interview room with a bored expression. Dressed in a navy suit, and sporting a tie pin adorned with a row of tiny silver studs, he looked like a man vain of his own abilities and good looks. Geraldine thought he saw her notice his tie pin, and she bristled at his complacent air.

'You must admit, Inspector, this is becoming tiresome,' he said. 'You drag my client to a cell and then find you have to release him almost immediately, in the absence of any evidence with which to charge him. A week or so later, unable to find the real murderer, you drag my innocent client back here in order to convince your senior officers that you're pursuing a credible lead. That's nonsense, of course. Perhaps you're trying to convince yourselves that you're doing something worthwhile, but we all know where this is going to end up. Once again, you'll be releasing my client because you have no grounds for detaining an innocent man. All you have to work on is supposition. In the absence of any real lead, instead of doing your job and discovering who killed George Gardner, you mistakenly seem to believe it's easier to haul my client in and question him again. What is the point of that? His answers aren't going to change. You seem to be overlooking the fact that there's a killer at large, and you're allowing yourselves to be distracted from trying to track him down. Inspector, I suggest you abandon these futile attempts to force a confession out of my client, and focus on your job of finding the killer.'

He turned and nodded at Ben who was staring at him, as though Jerome was speaking in a foreign language.

'Ben, we know you killed George Gardner,' Ian began.

Ben shook his head. 'I don't even know who he is. At least, I'd never heard of him until you started talking about him. I didn't kill him, whoever he is.'

'And you already have a statement from an independent witness to corroborate what my client has told you.'

'A witness who is not as sure as she was that her testimony is accurate,' Geraldine said.

'Of course not. With the passage of time, none of our memories remain clear a few days after the event. But she made her statement, and is prepared to repeat it in court. So I suggest we drop this nonsense and all go home.' Jerome smiled pleasantly at them.

'Drop this nonsense?' Ian repeated, in as scornful a tone as he could muster. 'We're talking about a man's death.'

'A death that was not caused by my client,' Jerome was quick to respond.

'We have evidence that places him at the scene,' Ian said.

'Circumstantial evidence,' the lawyer replied dismissively. 'We've been over and over this. Yes, my client's scarf was used in the unlawful killing of George Gardner. That much is clear and my client has never disputed it. My client has never denied having owned such a scarf. But he has not seen it for a long time, and he did not use it to suffocate anyone.'

They were going round in circles, and it was clear that Ben was not going to back down. With a quick glance at Geraldine, Ian moved on.

'Where were you on Wednesday evening, two weeks ago?' he asked.

Ben frowned and, for the first time, Geraldine thought he

looked uncomfortable. But he merely shook his head and mumbled that he had been at home all evening.

'Can anyone confirm that?'

'Yes, of course. Ask my wife.'

Geraldine changed tack. 'Tell us about you and Jamie Benson,' she said gently. 'It's all right, Ben. It's not a crime to have an affair with a colleague. You were both adults. We're just trying to build a clear picture of her behaviour, and we're hoping you can help us.'

Ben scowled but didn't answer so Geraldine pressed him.

'Is there any reason why you don't want to tell us about your affair with her?'

Ben muttered that he had not had an affair with anyone. 'I'm married,' he snapped.

Geraldine smiled sympathetically. 'We know you had an affair with her. Come on, Ben, we're not accusing you of anything. It's just that while we have you here, we're asking you to tell us everything you can about her. What was she like? You knew her, didn't you?'

'I knew who she was,' he replied, staring at the table and refusing to look up. 'That's all. She worked in the office. I barely spoke two words to her.'

'That's very hard to believe, seeing as you were giving her money,' Geraldine pointed out quietly. 'I wonder what the two words could have been that led you to give her two thousand pounds?'

'What? That's a lie. It was only four hundred–'

Geraldine smiled. It was such a simple trick, she was amazed Ben had fallen for it. Ian stared at her, evidently wondering how she had known about money changing hands.

Realising his mistake, Ben shook his head. 'No, no, it wasn't Jamie. I never gave her anything. You're making me confused. I gave my wife four hundred pounds. My wife. Ask her. She'll tell you. It was my wife.'

But they all knew he had made a damning admission. Jerome cut in quickly, insisting he needed to speak to his client in private.

'Again?' Ian enquired drily, but he and Geraldine agreed to give them a moment.

'How did you know he was giving Jamie money?' Ian asked when they were in the corridor.

'I didn't,' Geraldine replied, smiling. 'It was a guess. An informed guess. I asked Naomi to check Ben's bank account for unusual cash withdrawals. She couldn't establish for certain what Ben had done with the money, but I took a guess.'

'Well, your hunch paid off,' Ian replied.

'He was careful to stick to cash, and leave no record, but we already know Jamie was blackmailing Andy and threatening to tell his wife about their affair. So when we suspected Jamie was having an affair with Ben, I took a wild guess that she moved on from blackmailing Andy to seducing Ben and blackmailing him.' She shook her head. 'Jamie wasn't interested in the unmarried mechanics she worked with, but she had sex with Andy and Ben, the two married men who worked at the garage. They were both prepared to pay for her silence to protect their marriages, but they couldn't keep their dicks in their trousers. How does that make any kind of sense?'

'Well, your ruse paid off,' Ian said with a touch of admiration in his voice, ignoring her question. 'I don't know how you do it, Geraldine.'

She shrugged. 'Eileen will be pleased we've found a motive, but it doesn't make him any more likely to have killed Jamie than Andy, and we still have no proof Ben killed George,' she said.

'Well, like you I'm going to take a wild guess and say that Ben killed them both,' Ian replied. 'Now we just have to find out why.'

55

GERALDINE WAS RIGHT ABOUT Eileen. The detective chief inspector was visibly gratified to learn that the murdered woman had been blackmailing not only her boss, but also her co-worker, who was already the main suspect in the investigation into her murder. She assembled the team and gazed around the room with an expression approaching a smile, which was rare when an investigation was still ongoing.

'We have the case against Ben more or less tied up, at least as far as Jamie's murder is concerned,' Eileen said. 'But that still leaves the question of the first murder.' Her expression grew severe. 'We haven't yet worked out how George fits into all of this. What's the link between him and Ben? Why was George targeted in this way? Or was he a completely random victim who happened to be in the wrong place at the wrong time?'

'And why did Ben use his own clothes to suffocate both victims?' Geraldine added, almost to herself.

Geraldine was growing increasingly frustrated at her own failure to see how the clues surrounding the two murders could fit together. She suspected Christine's mother hated Ben enough to want to destroy his marriage, but it was a stretch to believe she could have committed two murders to remove him from her daughter's life. If it offended her conscience to lie to Christine about her feelings concerning her daughter's marriage, it was quite unbelievable that she could have committed two murders to achieve her goal. Yet Geraldine knew from experience that the most unlikely people could resort to unexpectedly evil acts, given the right circumstances. Christine herself might have had few scruples about killing, but that too made little sense in this case. Women divorced their husbands all the time without feeling the need to have them incarcerated for murder. It wasn't even as though Christine was going to be isolated after her marriage failed. She could simply have left Ben, with the full support of her family. Yet there was nothing to link Ben with either George or Michelle, and no evidence of money passing between Rodney and Ben. She seemed to be going round in circles. Given that Ben was not stupid, the only explanation that made any sense to Geraldine was that he had been framed. In the meantime, in the absence of any other likely suspect, she was struggling to persuade anyone else to agree with her hunch that Ben was not guilty.

'Had George somehow discovered what was going on?' Eileen went on, ignoring Geraldine's muttered interruption. 'Was he also threatening to tell Ben's wife about the affair? We must do whatever it takes to dig up the connection between George and Ben, or perhaps between George and Christine, or Michelle and Christine.'

So far no amount of investigation had uncovered any apparent connection between George and Ben, although the two men had both lived in York so could have come across one another almost anywhere. According to Ben, their paths had never crossed, and the police had found no evidence at all to suggest that might not be true. Reviewing everything they had learned, Geraldine was no longer completely convinced that Ben was innocent, but they had yet to establish a connection between the two men. All they had to establish Ben's innocence was the statement of an eye witness, who could have been mistaken. Geraldine decided to pay a visit to Sallyanne, the woman who had claimed to see Ben by the river with his dog at the time of George's death.

Sallyanne Hodgskin lived in a terraced cottage near Rowntree Park. Geraldine drew up outside Sallyanne's York stone house and knocked on her neatly painted black front door. Sallyanne came to the door almost at once, and led the way into a tidy dining room with wood block floor and pine furniture. A small grey and white kitchen was visible through an arch, and the sun shone in through a glass door that led out to the back garden. It was a pleasant house, clean and orderly. Sallyanne invited Geraldine to sit at the table.

'To what do I owe the pleasure of this visit, Inspector?' she enquired, with a nervous smile.

Geraldine sat down. 'I want to ask you about the man you reported seeing in the park.'

Sallyanne nodded. 'It was such a long time ago,' she replied.

'Three weeks ago.'

'It might not seem like a long time to you but, to be perfectly honest, I'm really not sure I can remember exactly what I saw that morning. I know I was in a hurry to get home. I signed a statement when it was relatively fresh in my memory, but now, I just don't know how I can add to what I've already told you.'

Geraldine hesitated. The last thing she wanted to do was put pressure on the woman who had come forward, but she needed to establish whether her statement was credible. If it transpired that Geraldine had been wrong to release Ben on Sallyanne's word, she would have to live with the knowledge that Ben had claimed a second victim straight after she had released him. But whatever the truth was, she had to know. Sallyanne offered her tea, and was clearly being as helpful as she could, but she could add nothing to her previous statement.

'What name did you hear the man call out to his dog?' Geraldine prompted her.

Sallyanne shook her head. 'I'm so sorry, I can't recall... Did I remember that when I came to the police station?'

Geraldine nodded. It was pointless trying to wheedle any further information out of the witness.

'Was it Rusty?' she hazarded.

Sallyanne frowned. 'I don't know. It could have been. It was something like that. What did I say in my statement?'

Geraldine wondered how Sallyanne was going to fare if she was cross-examined in court by a hostile prosecutor.

'If that's what I said in my statement, I'll stand by it,' Sallyanne said, perhaps guessing what Geraldine was thinking. 'Whatever I said in my statement was my honest belief at the time. I'm not going to deny a word of what I signed. It's just that I can't remember everything clearly after all this time.'

A court case was going to take a lot longer to process, Geraldine thought glumly. By the time Ben stood trial, the police's main witness would be effectively useless.

'I stand by my statement,' she repeated firmly. 'When I made it, I could still remember what I saw.'

Of course the defence would show Sallyanne a copy of her statement before the trial, so that she could repeat it in court. It was almost like hearsay, only Sallyanne would be repeating her own words, not something she had heard from someone else. Geraldine sighed. There was nothing else she could do but thank the witness for her co-operation and leave. It had been another wasted journey. With a sigh, she drove to Christine's house. It was mid-evening and she found her at home.

'What is it this time?' Christine asked, glaring sullenly and making no move to invite Geraldine inside.

'I have one question for you,' Geraldine replied, judging it best to keep her visit as brief as possible.

'Well?'

'Did you know a man named George Gardner?'

Christine frowned. 'I don't know anyone called George. Why? What's he gone and done? And what's it got to do with me?'

'I think he may have known your husband,' Geraldine said tentatively. 'Did you ever hear him mention anyone called George?'

'No, never. But if Ben knew this George character, why don't you ask him? You've got him locked up, haven't you?'

'The trouble is, we're not sure if Ben's being completely honest with us,' Geraldine said, lowering her voice confidentially.

'I'd be surprised if that lying toad *was* honest with you,' Christine retorted. 'He isn't with anyone else. Now shove off and leave me the hell alone. I've had enough of your lot sniffing around, poking your noses where they're not wanted. Go on, beat it.'

Another door shut on what had not been an entirely wasted journey. There had been no flicker of recognition in Christine's face when Geraldine had mentioned George's name. She was inclined to believe that Christine had not known him.

56

ON TUESDAY MORNING, ARIADNE handed Geraldine a printed wedding invitation.

'We're doing the whole shebang,' she said. 'Big church ceremony, party in a swish venue, the works. There's going to be a band, and a three-course dinner, and don't ask me what else because I don't know. I've handed the organisation over to my mother and I'll turn up like a guest at my own wedding.'

'Oh, Ariadne, I'm sorry,' Geraldine began.

'No, don't be. There's no need. It's fine. It's actually better this way. All I really want is to be married to Nico. How we get there isn't the point. If my mother wants to knock herself out booking singers and photographers and caterers and florists and whatever else goes into making one of these events happen, that's up to her. This way, I don't need to spend a year of my life fussing over menus and flowers and napkins.' She smiled. 'But I am keeping control of my dress. That was the one thing I insisted on. It should take all of an afternoon to find, and maybe another afternoon for a fitting, and I'm done. And I've agreed the colour scheme, blue and silver.'

'But don't you want to choose your own music? And the menu?'

Ariadne shook her head. 'That's all going to be traditional Greek. My mother's inviting hordes of family over, and Nico's family are all Greek Orthodox, so it'll be fine.' She stifled a sigh. 'To be honest, it's not exactly how I imagined it would be when I was little, but then I always wanted to marry a prince and Nico's an accountant. Hardly royalty.'

They exchanged a few quips about marrying into royalty, and how well that usually turned out.

'You're better off with Nico,' Geraldine said. 'But who's paying for this extravaganza?'

Ariadne shrugged. 'We're all chipping in,' she said. 'My grandparents are over the moon that I'm finally getting hitched. It matters to them. Before you came to York I used to live with a boyfriend.' She gave a wry grimace. 'It so very nearly worked out, but it didn't, and my family all blamed the failure of the relationship on the fact that we never got married in church. It's just the way they think. So now that I'm finally marrying a Greek boy, in a church wedding, they're all really pleased. So pleased, they're all prepared to help out with the cost of the wedding, which is frankly a ludicrous expense. But if they want their big party enough to pay towards it, I don't want to spoil their celebration. I'd be just as happy to go to a registry office with Nico and pay fifty quid, and he says he feels the same. Yet here we are, preparing to walk down the aisle in front of hundreds of people.'

Geraldine laughed. 'You might as well be marrying royalty.'

Geraldine spent the day reading up about the accident where Ben had knocked down and killed a pedestrian. That evening, she drove to Matthew's house again, fighting against the sense that she was being ridiculous in clinging to the hope that she could prove Ben's innocence. She no longer believed in it herself. Nevertheless, she was determined to pursue her investigation to the end. This time, the door was opened by a tall, slightly stooping figure.

'Yes?' he enquired, gazing at Geraldine over the top of rimless glasses with a quizzical expression. 'How can I help you?'

Geraldine held up her identity card. Well spoken, with a gentle air about him, the man did not recoil or scowl as members of the public did with increasing frequency on learning who she was. Instead he stared blankly at the card in her outstretched hand, without moving. There was something faintly reassuring about his uninterested response to her visit, although she had studied the map carefully and worked out that it would be possible to cycle from Claremont Terrace around the back of York City Church. From there it would be a short ride across the car park to Portland Street, and along the footpath to Bootham and out into North Parade where Matthew lived. She had not even shared the details of her findings with Ian, for fear he would criticise her obsession with proving that someone other than Ben could have killed George.

Geraldine smiled reassuringly at him. 'We're looking into the death of George Gardner,' she said.

'Who?' the man enquired. 'George Garner?'

It was possible he had misheard her, but it was equally possible he was attempting to mislead her. She hesitated before asking to go in, but he nodded at once and took her straight into a small front room. The furniture was somehow efficient rather than comfortable, reminiscent of a doctor's waiting room with brown padded upright chairs set around a low coffee table, with a small television on a corner cupboard.

'May I wish you belated condolences on the loss of your wife?' Geraldine said gently. 'I know it was a long time ago.'

Matthew seemed to stiffen. 'It feels like yesterday to me,' he replied.

It sounded like a reprimand.

Geraldine nodded. 'Yes, of course. I'm sorry.'

'Not at all,' he replied. 'It was good of you to remember her at all. Your colleagues were happy to write off the case as soon as possible.'

Geraldine felt a frisson of interest in his bitter response to her comment. 'No crime was committed,' she ventured.

'A man was driving without care and as a result of his inattentiveness my wife is dead,' he said bluntly.

'It was an accident,' she replied quietly, watching him closely. 'The driver stood trial.'

Matthew scowled, apparently aggrieved about the result of the trial.

'It can be very hard to pick yourself up and move on after such a tragedy,' she said.

It wasn't difficult to sound sympathetic. She did feel genuinely sorry for him. But at the same time, she had to remain alert, aware that she had only gone there to discover if there was any link between Matthew and the two recent murder victims. There was no reason to suspect Matthew was involved, but a vague idea had begun to form in the back of her mind and she was determined to pursue it. In a murder investigation, no stone could be left unturned.

Matthew sighed. 'It has been very difficult,' he admitted. 'I thought moving house would help, a fresh start and all that.' He shook his head. 'But you didn't come here to talk about my wife,' he went on, suddenly brushing her enquiry aside. 'And as you said, it was a long time ago. How can I help you, Inspector?'

It could have been her imagination, but he sounded impatient. He wouldn't be the first person to feel uncomfortable entertaining a police officer at home. She quizzed him gently about George and Jamie, but he said he knew nothing about either of them. Presumably he had not followed their cases in the media. There was nothing more for Geraldine to do but thank him and take her leave. She had reached another dead end.

57

HE SPENT SOME TIME preparing dinner that evening. First there was the shopping, making sure he had the right ingredients. It was a long time since he had experimented in the kitchen. Living alone had given him no reason to make any effort. He did not enjoy cooking for himself, any more than he enjoyed eating alone. Having rashly offered to make dinner for Naomi, he already regretted having made the invitation. He ought to have simply taken her out for a meal again, but he wanted to do something to establish a more relaxed relationship in an environment where she might feel less constrained to be discreet. Chopping vegetables was easy enough, but making a cheese sauce proved problematic. Frustrated, he hurried to the supermarket and bought a ready-made béchamel sauce for his home-made lasagna. She would never know the difference and would accept without question that he had spent time cooking for her.

Naomi arrived promptly. He hated that. It was a long time since he had thought about the niceties of socialising. He had grown accustomed to his own company, and Naomi's arrival felt like an intrusion, even though he had invited her over. They exchanged trivial pleasantries as he led her into the dining room where he poured her a large glass of wine. He was not keen to sit in the living room with her for an aperitif before dinner, although he wondered if that had been a mistake. He was more comfortable with the table between them, but she seemed faintly surprised to be sitting in the dining room straightaway, without any preliminaries. But she sipped her wine and complimented him on it. He didn't say that she bloody well ought to enjoy it, as the bottle was expensive. Instead, he smiled and said he was glad she liked it.

'You obviously have good taste,' he said, and she smiled.

She had looked good in jeans, but this evening she had chosen to wear a short skirt. Models with impossibly long slim thighs could look elegant in such an outfit, but it made her look squat. She was not unattractive, but her attempt to look fetching had backfired miserably.

When he stood up to fetch the starter, Naomi offered to help, but he insisted she remain at the table, and was back a moment later with their prawn cocktails, which he had managed to produce from scratch. It was his first attempt, but he had checked a recipe online, and it was ridiculously easy, just a mixture of ketchup and mayonnaise dolloped on a spoonful of prawns lying on what the restaurants would call a bed of lettuce. Naomi complimented him on his creation and he cringed at being so patronised. But he smiled and lamely repeated what he had said about the wine.

'I wasn't sure if you liked prawns,' he added, hoping his smile masked his true feelings.

Clearly she was determined to be pleased with everything he said and did, and her blatant attempt to ingratiate herself with him was almost unbearable. He smiled and smiled. Smiled as he cleared the plates, smiled as he brought in the lasagna, smiled as he poured the wine. Smiled until his face ached. And after all that effort, she said she didn't want to talk about work. Behind his smile, he cursed silently.

'Don't you want to tell me about the man you arrested and released and then arrested again?' he prompted her, trying to sound nonchalant. 'It sounds quite incredible.'

'Not really.' She shrugged. 'It happens all the time.'

'Tell me about it,' he urged. 'I'm intrigued.'

She looked at him, faintly uneasy, and he knew he had pushed too hard.

'My job's so dull,' he explained, a trifle too quickly. 'And I want to hear everything about your day,' he added, with a flash of inspiration. 'I want to know everything about you.'

He could see her relax.

'Yes, I want to know all about you,' he continued, pressing his advantage. 'What you do, what you think, what you like, what gives you pleasure.' He let his voice tail off suggestively.

Unless he had misread her behaviour, she was interested in a physical relationship. He was right. She looked down, slightly flustered, and he thought she blushed.

'Tell me about yourself,' he said softly, reaching across the table to take her hand in his.

Her skin felt smooth and warm and for a second his breath caught in his throat. Unconsciously he tightened his grasp on Naomi's hand and she smiled at him. Clenching his teeth, he smiled back.

'I want to know everything,' he insisted. 'Tell me everything there is to know about your day. Start with today.'

She laughed and shook her head. 'It's really boring,' she replied. 'People think being a detective is glamorous and exciting, all car chases and violent confrontations with ferocious criminals, but honestly, it's nothing like that. It's mostly desk work and researching boring information online. Even that makes it sound more interesting than it is. There's nothing more I can say about it. Tell me about what you do. I bet it's more interesting. It is to me, anyway,' she added coyly.

He was nearing the end of his patience. 'I'll get dessert and we can talk some more,' he said.

In the kitchen, his hands shook as he infused her custard with the strangely named drug he had procured at considerable expense, and at some personal risk. The dealer he had encountered had assured him the pale milky liquid would relax whoever ingested it, and make them lose any sense of caution.

'And it'll make her talk freely?' He had been insistent on this point before he handed over the cash.

'Sure, man. Whatever you want to know, she'll spill the beans. Works like a dream.'

'I just want to know if she's having an affair,' he had explained, speaking in a deliberately hoarse voice from behind the scarf that was covering his mouth and nose.

'Whatever, man,' the dealer had replied, glancing along the empty alley and holding out his hand. 'Just give me the dosh.'

Nervously, he had placed a wad of notes in the greasy glove. He half-expected the dealer to scarper with his money, but was too afraid to remonstrate about handing over the money before receiving the gear. He just wanted to get out of there alive. But true to his word, the dealer had handed him a small package. As he stammered his thanks, the dealer snapped at him to beat it. He didn't need to be told twice.

Out of sight back in the kitchen, he retrieved the package from its hiding place and opened it for the first time, while Naomi waited for her dessert. He wondered if he had been ripped off after all. The little bottle looked as though it contained a small quantity of milk. Resisting the urge to sniff it or taste it, he removed the shop-bought raspberry trifle from its packaging. Dishing out two generous portions, he poured the milky liquid into her bowl, and stirred it vigorously into the custard. It was a mess, but he smoothed it down as well as he could. Then he poured a little milk into his own custard and stirred it until it looked similarly runny and botched.

'I made it myself. I'm afraid the custard hasn't quite set,' he apologised as he put the dish in front of her. 'I hope you don't mind it so runny. And I'm sorry it doesn't look very neat. It kind of fell apart when I was dishing it up.'

'It looks delicious,' she replied, spooning the doctored trifle into her mouth.

He hoped it wouldn't kill her, at least not until he had found out what he wanted to know. The drug worked faster than he had expected. Within minutes her eyes glazed over, the pupils oddly dilated, and she slumped awkwardly on her chair, apparently struggling to sit upright. Carefully he lifted her up by her armpits and half dragged, half led her into the sitting room where he deposited her on a settee. He had covered it with a plastic sheet, on top of which he had spread a blanket. She lolled sideways and began to giggle uncontrollably. He realised he would have to act quickly before she became incoherent or lost consciousness. He had a feeling he had given her too much of the alleged truth serum. Just for a moment he wondered what the hell he was doing, but it was too late to back out now.

'Tell me about Ben Foster,' he said, looking into her eyes and speaking firmly and clearly.

'Ben Foster,' she repeated, giggling as though the name was amusing.

'Yes, very good, Ben Foster,' he said. 'Tell me about Ben Foster. Tell me everything you know about him.'

'Arrested. Second arrest in shortest time,' she mumbled.

'Why was he arrested? Tell me.'

He had to restrain himself from grabbing her by the shoulders and shaking her, although she was probably too far gone to notice if he did.

'It was him,' she explained groggily. 'We had him and let him go. But we found him again. He was mugged. Mugged. Mugged. Mugged. Another one. Mugged. Not our case. No, no, we don't invest... Mugging. No.'

'Who did he mug?'

'No, no, no,' she shook her head vehemently, her blonde hair splaying out against the back of the sofa. 'Ben was mugged. He was mugged. Ben. Ben,' she said, her voice so slurred he could scarcely understand what she was saying. 'Ben and mugger.'

He thought he caught the gist of what she was saying.

'Was Ben mugged?' he asked, wanting to be clear.

She nodded. 'And,' she went on, her eyes beginning to close, 'the wife threw Ben out.'

'Is Ben Foster a murderer?' he asked urgently, afraid she was going to pass out before he had found out what he needed to know.

She nodded, giggling faintly, but her eyes were shut.

'Naomi, tell me,' he insisted desperately. 'Has Ben Foster been arrested for murder?'

'Yes, oh yes,' she replied. 'Yes. Yes. We got him. We got Ben Foster.' She grinned. 'Case closed.'

'How many victims did he kill?'

'Two,' she replied promptly. 'George and…' Her eyes closed.

'George and who?'

'Yes. George and… George and… Jamie.' She let out a gentle sigh and fell sideways.

He tried to question her further, but she was asleep, or unconscious, and unable to hear him or to speak. It didn't matter. He had found out what he wanted to know. He gazed at her for a moment, wondering whether to leave her there until she woke up. The trouble was, he had no way of knowing how much she would remember of their conversation when she came to. Perhaps he had been rash in drugging her like that. If she remembered what had happened, she might have herself tested, and he didn't know how long traces of the drug would remain in her bloodstream. She had been of some help, but now that he knew Ben was in custody, she had become a useless liability. He ran upstairs and lay a plastic sheet over his spare bed before carrying her upstairs. Wrapped in the blanket she had been sitting on, he lay her down on the bed. She had become a nuisance, but she wouldn't be a problem in the long term. He just had to make sure she never left the house alive.

58

GERALDINE DIDN'T BELIEVE BEN would have been foolish enough to use his own clothes to murder two people, and then leave them behind at the scene to incriminate him. He simply did not strike her as that stupid. At the same time, there was no reason to suspect the recent murders were related to Ben's accident four years ago. The most likely explanation had to be that Christine had kept hold of some old clothes of his that he had thrown out so long ago that he had forgotten about them. That evening she tried to discuss her ideas with Ian who wasn't very receptive.

'We've been through this, Geraldine. It's quite possible he simply forgot to take the scarf with him, in the heat and emotion of the moment, after he strangled George. As for Jamie, well, we've established he probably wasn't able to pull the rubber glove from her once she had half-swallowed it, so he had no choice but to leave it there.'

'So you don't think Ben was being set up?'

'Honestly? No. It sounds far too complicated. Face it, Geraldine, it was never really going to fly as a theory, was it?' Ian said, as he poured her a glass of wine. 'I mean, granted we have to pursue every possible avenue, but it was always a bit far-fetched. If Ben's wife wanted to kill him, surely she would have attacked him in some way, pushed him down the stairs or poisoned him or something like that. There must be any number of ways a woman can murder her husband, or vice versa. We know that better than most people.'

'So you're saying if Ben was framed, it must have been someone who couldn't get at him easily?'

'No,' he replied with exaggerated patience, 'I'm saying I don't think Ben was framed. It just seems crazy that anyone would kill two innocent people just to try and see someone else arrested for murder.'

'When did we last encounter a killer who wasn't in some way crazy?' Geraldine asked quietly. 'No, don't worry,' she went on, seeing Ian's expression, 'I'm not going to pursue this any further. Not unless we come up with some new evidence that might support my theory.'

All the same, something was bothering Geraldine and after supper, while Ian was clearing up in the kitchen, she glanced through her notes on Ben, closing her iPad with a guilty start when Ian returned to the living room.

'What's that?' he asked.

She shrugged. 'Just reading,' she replied, truthfully enough.

'You don't have to stop on my account,' he said, stooping down to plant a kiss on the top of her head as he passed her armchair.

But she put her iPad away and they watched a film, seated side-by-side on the sofa, with Ian's arm around her shoulders, warm and comforting. If something about the case hadn't been niggling at her, she would have felt perfectly content. As it was, they spent a companionable evening together, and went for a walk after the film. Neither of them brought up the subject of moving, and they both agreed it had been a lovely evening.

Unable to sleep, Geraldine climbed quietly out of bed in the middle of the night. Leaving Ian snoring gently, she went into the living room where she spent the night on her iPad, rereading her notes on the case. She went over all of Ben's statements carefully without coming across anything that might help to prove his innocence. Finally, she glanced through the notes she had made immediately after meeting the man whose wife Ben had accidentally killed. One line in the seemingly innocuous report caught her attention. Matthew Barton had mentioned in passing that he had moved house after his wife was killed. At the time, it had struck Geraldine as perfectly understandable that he would want to leave a home where everything inevitably reminded him of his dead wife. All the same, she checked through whatever records she could find and eventually discovered where he had been living when he was married. She stared for a moment, unable to take in what she was reading. Matthew and his wife, Laura, had lived in Montague Street, next door to the Gardners.

Ian was stirring. Before he had opened his eyes, she told him what she had discovered.

'So?' he replied sleepily.

'Don't you see? This is the connection we've been looking for, between Matthew and George.'

Ian shook his head and yawned. 'You might have been looking for it. Well, okay, perhaps it is a strange coincidence, but I still don't see what this has to do with the case. Why would Matthew want to kill his former next-door neighbour?'

'He killed him with Ben's scarf,' Geraldine replied. 'Don't you see? If Matthew wanted to set up Ben to punish him for Laura's death, what better way than by framing him for murder? And now we know Matthew must have known George; it makes sense he could have used him to set Ben up. George wasn't the kind of man to put up much of a fight. It all makes sense.'

Ian frowned. 'It doesn't actually make any sense at all. Still, now you've found a connection of sorts, why don't you take the theory to Eileen and see what she thinks? But not before I've scrambled some eggs for breakfast. I have a feeling you're going to be running around all day, chasing your latest hypothesis, and you could do with a substantial breakfast before you start your day.'

Eileen was even less impressed with Geraldine's idea than Ian had been.

'So what?' she said, dismissing Geraldine's enthusiastic retelling of her discovery with a weary shake of her head. 'Every murder victim lived next door to someone. There's nothing to suggest Matthew was involved in George's murder, and nothing to connect him to Ben.'

'But Ben is connected to both of them.'

'He's hardly connected to Matthew,' Eileen said.

'Of course he is,' Geraldine replied, too frustrated to remain respectful. 'Ben knocked down Matthew's wife and killed her.'

'In an accident over which there was a court case. But why would Matthew want George dead?' Eileen asked.

'I think it's possible he was just collateral damage in Matthew's quest for vengeance for his wife's death. I think he might have killed George purely in order to frame Ben,' Geraldine said. 'No other reason.'

'That's ridiculous,' Eileen replied, although she did not sound very sure of herself. 'Quest for vengeance? What is this? A Renaissance tragedy? Or an honour killing? Surely Matthew would have killed Ben, if this was about revenge for his wife's death, or attacked him in some way? He would hardly have killed a perfectly innocent neighbour, just to incriminate Ben. It's too unlikely, and in any case it would have been too risky a strategy. Ben might have had a watertight alibi.'

'I'm not for one moment suggesting this is a sane idea,' Geraldine said.

'Well,' Eileen said, 'you can look into it if you think it's worth it, but I can't give you any resources, or allow you time when you should be working on the case. Other than that, Geraldine, you have a free hand, as you know. Just don't do anything illegal,' she added, with a warning scowl.

They both knew that Geraldine had broken the law in the

past, in order to save the life of her sister who had been a heroin addict at the time.

'That was different,' Geraldine muttered. 'She's my sister.'

Eileen shook her head and didn't answer. There was really nothing more to say.

59

NAOMI OPENED HER EYES. Her head was pounding and she needed the toilet. She lay on her back for a long time, feeling sleepy and wondering what had happened. Although she didn't recognise where she was, she was too drowsy to feel scared. The room had an unfamiliar smell, a mixture of pine needles and mould. She turned her head to look around without trying to get up. Gradually the shape of a window became visible. Faint light came in through a slit in the curtains, illuminating a narrow slice of the room. She screwed up her eyes and stared at a thin sliver of carpet but couldn't recall ever having seen the pattern before. With a sigh she started to sit up, but something held her back. It took her a moment to realise that her hands and feet were tethered to the bed, giving everything a curious quality of unreality. Even that discovery didn't frighten her. It was all too strange to take seriously. Yet her head hurt, and something rubbed painfully against her wrists and ankles when she moved. As her head began to feel less muzzy, the strange situation started to take on an air of reality. Fear lapped around her like ripples in an unseen lake. She was floating on the surface but at any moment she was afraid of being submerged, swept away by a terror she couldn't control.

She was lying on a bed. She couldn't see a door, although there must be one for her to have entered in the first place. By craning her neck she was finally able to see it, on the wall behind her head. It looked like an ordinary internal door and she didn't think it was locked, but it made no difference because she couldn't get up to find out. She had no idea who was on the other side.

Someone must be there, because she must have been carried to this place, and laid on this bed in this silent room, where her hands and feet had been tied together, before she had been left alone in the darkness. She had no memory of having got there by herself. That was the most terrifying part of her situation, that she couldn't remember how she had come to be tied up on this bed. She didn't think she had been assaulted in any way. Certainly nothing hurt, expect her aching head and her wrists and ankles. Her hands were tied on either side of her. By turning her head she was able to see the rough rope that bound them, making her skin sting. Trying to free them she only succeeded in rubbing her skin raw. It was better to lie still and wait.

What was she waiting for?

'Where am I?' she called out.

Her voice sounded strange, as though it came from a long way off. No one answered. Slowly she began to gather her thoughts into some kind of logical order, despite her bewilderment. For a start, she had to resist the temptation to panic, nor could she afford to give way to despair. She was a police constable, which meant that it would not be long before her absence was noticed and acted on. She just had to patient until she heard sirens outside, and voices shouting at her captor to open the door. If he or she had left the building, the door would be knocked down. She closed her eyes and hoped it would not take too long. She was already lying in a wet patch of her own piss. Sooner or later she might defecate and that would be humiliating in front of her rescuers who might even be her colleagues from the police station. The rational side of her mind pointed out that the risk of such embarrassment was hardly an issue compared to the danger she was in, but it bothered her all the same.

She had no idea how long she had been lying there, no idea what the time was. The last thing she could remember was going to Sid's house for dinner. After that, everything was a blur. Raising her hands she could see that she wasn't wearing her watch and she had no idea where her phone was. It was curiously disturbing, not knowing what the time was, as though she had been cast adrift on a vast ocean, with no land in sight. She tried calling out, but her throat was dry and shouting was painful. All the same, she cried out for help. No one came.

Somewhere far away a doorbell rang. She howled frenziedly for help and almost immediately heard footsteps pounding on the floor outside the room where she was being held captive. Then someone was in the room and she barely had time to glimpse pale eyes glaring wildly at her before one hand was slapped over her mouth and another over her eyes.

'Shut up,' a voice hissed by her ear. 'Shut up.'

Her screaming muffled, she tried to force her lips open so she could bite him, but he moved his hand away and an instant later she felt a length of fabric thrust across her tongue. Pulling her head roughly forward, he secured her gag in place while she struggled to breathe. The gag tasted foul, salty and rancid like stale sweat. She could only see part of Sid's face while he was busy tying the gag behind her head, but he looked crazy. In the morass of confusion in her brain her fear was momentarily overwhelmed by a wave of despair at his betrayal. He left the room as rapidly as he had entered, without glancing round at her and a moment later she heard footsteps receding. She had never felt more alone, or more helpless.

Forcing herself not to cry, she worked at freeing herself from the gag. It was excruciating knowing there was someone in the house, and being unable to cry out for help. Downstairs, she heard the doorbell again and then, far off, voices. Someone had come into the house, someone who might be able to help her if they only knew she was there. Desperately she tried to cry out, and produced a faint muffled squeal. Only someone in the same room as her could possibly have heard it. Frustrated, she felt tears of rage spill from her eyes and course down her cheeks.

60

This time when Matthew opened the door, he made no attempt to conceal his irritation on seeing her. Geraldine wasn't surprised to find that he was irked at what he no doubt perceived as harassment. Many members of the public were less than pleased to see a police officer on their doorstep, especially one who had only recently visited them. All the same, she remained open to the possibility that he might have something to hide. Last time he had only let her into the front room and there had been no opportunity for her to view the rest of the house. On this occasion she was determined to find an excuse to have a look around but, unlike the previous day, he didn't invite her in but kept her standing on the doorstep. There was something different about him that she couldn't put her finger on.

'May I come in?' Hoping her question would suggest she found something unusual in his keeping her outside, she added, 'Or is there a reason why you don't want me in your house?'

She laughed as though she was making a joke, but he didn't smile. She took a step forwards, in an attempt to force the issue. He would have to let her in or deliberately bar her way. Scowling, he moved aside and she entered the house. Instead of following him into the living room straightaway, she lingered in the narrow hallway, listening. Something didn't feel right, although she couldn't have said what. On her previous visit he had been very accommodating, and had not seemed at all bothered on learning she was a police officer, but now he couldn't conceal his nerves, fidgeting constantly with his watch strap, and watching her closely. A bead of sweat trickled down his forehead and he dashed it away impatiently. As he did so, she noticed that he was wearing a woman's watch. Had he been wearing it the previous day, she thought she would have noticed. As her gaze slid past it, he slipped his hand behind his back in a surreptitiously casual movement that didn't fool her for an instant. He hadn't wanted her to see the watch. It could have been perfectly innocent, his wife's watch perhaps, but that wouldn't explain why he wanted to conceal it.

'Come in,' he muttered, ushering her into the room where they had been sitting the day before.

'Matthew, I'm not sure the man who was responsible for your wife's death really received a just sentence,' she hazarded when they were both seated.

'He wasn't sentenced at all.'

His response was so bitter, Geraldine almost felt sorry for him. But for the first time she also felt a flicker of fear at what he might be capable of doing. She nodded and continued to play along, keen to earn his trust so he would speak freely.

'Yes, he got off,' she went on, and lowered her voice conspiratorially. 'Some of us don't think justice was served that day in court.'

He started at her words.

'I wanted you to know that we are doing everything we can to rectify the situation,' she added.

Suddenly he lunged forward and his fingers closed on something lying on the table between them. She scarcely had time to see what he was doing before he slipped his hand in his pocket, but she could see he was on edge. Curiously excited, he fidgeted with the arm of his chair, and seemed unable to meet her gaze.

'Do you know Christine?' she asked, wondering whether Matthew and Christine had somehow plotted together against Ben.

'Who?' He seemed genuinely puzzled. 'Christine who?'

She shook her head. 'It doesn't matter. But you might be interested to hear that Ben Foster, who ran over your wife, has been arrested for another crime.'

She paused, observing his reaction. His pale eyes glittered and his face took on a vicious expression, but he didn't seem surprised.

'He should have been found guilty of murder,' he muttered. 'He should have been put away.'

His hands were trembling slightly.

'No one likes to see justice fail,' she agreed, choosing her words with care.

Eileen had given her carte blanche to pursue her hunch, but that permission had not extended to lying in an attempt to entrap Matthew. She gazed at him from beneath lowered eyelids, studying his face. She was convinced he was hiding something, although she had no idea what it might be.

'Have you spoken to a man called Jerome Carver?' she asked.

Matthew scowled. 'No, but I know the name. He was involved in getting Ben Foster off, wasn't he? They caught him, and then the bloody idiots let him go. It's unbelievable. I'm glad something is finally being done about it. It's taken long enough. If he hadn't been mugged, he'd still be free.'

'Who told you Ben was mugged?' she asked.

Matthew shrugged. 'I read it somewhere,' he replied vaguely.

Geraldine wracked her brains trying to remember if anyone had mentioned Ben's mugger to the press. She was fairly sure no one would have mentioned it outside the police station in connection with the murder investigation. As an ongoing enquiry, it was being treated separately from the murder case. It was really just chance that this particular victim of a mugger had been a suspect in a murder enquiry. She wondered how Matthew had made the connection.

'Anyway,' he went on more briskly, 'I appreciate you keeping me updated like this. Let's hope he's given a life sentence this time. A life for a life,' he added with a smile.

61

GERALDINE WAS PUZZLED ABOUT the source of Matthew's information. Apart from Christine and Jerome Carver, the only people who knew about Ben's mugging were the police officers on the investigating team. Matthew said he didn't know Christine or Jerome, and Geraldine was inclined to believe him. As she drove home, she decided not to tell Ian where she had been. He would only accuse her of being obsessed with proving that Ben was innocent and that she had been right to release him. Ian had a point. She was becoming preoccupied with Matthew and his grudge against Ben. She wondered whether Ian was right, and she should put her suspicions out of her mind. As soon as she reached home, Ian told her he had booked a table at their favourite restaurant, and she tried to forget about Ben and the woman he had accidentally run over and killed.

The next morning a small group of officers gathered around Ariadne's desk, murmuring in low voices. From their grave expressions, Geraldine could see that something was amiss.

'What's up?' she enquired as she walked past. 'What's going on?'

Ariadne glanced at a couple of constables who had been talking to her and replied that Naomi had not turned up for work that morning, and she wasn't answering her phone.

'Where is she?' Geraldine asked.

No one knew.

'Don't say anything to the DCI yet,' a red-haired constable said, scowling at Ariadne. 'She'll go ballistic if she finds out.'

'Let's leave it for an hour and then if she's still absent and uncontactable, someone needs to go to her home and find out if she's okay,' Geraldine said.

'I called her, but there's no answer,' another constable said.

'It's not like her,' someone else said.

An hour later, when Naomi had still neither appeared nor contacted the police station, Geraldine discovered that the red-haired constable shared a flat with Naomi. Geraldine had only spoken to Molly a few times, but she seemed sensible.

'When did you last see Naomi?' Geraldine asked.

'She came home from work yesterday, same as usual,' Molly said, 'but then she went out again and I don't think she came home last night, unless she came in very late and went out before I got up.'

A small group of women officers gathered around Geraldine's desk, as Molly told her that Naomi had a new boyfriend. A horrible suspicion struck Geraldine. It was almost too far-fetched to believe.

'How new is this new boyfriend?' she enquired.

Molly shrugged. 'She first mentioned him about a week ago. I think she'd only just met him but she was instantly smitten. If you want my opinion, it all seemed a damn sight too good to be true.'

'What's his name?' Geraldine asked.

'I don't know. She didn't mention it.'

'Are you sure?' Geraldine pressed her.

She was aware that everyone in the group was staring at her and she took a deep breath.

'Why are you so interested in him?' Ariadne asked.

'It's nothing,' Geraldine muttered. 'I'm sure there's a perfectly reasonable explanation and she'll turn up sooner or later. Let me know when you hear from her, won't you?'

But Naomi didn't come to work that day and nor did she answer her phone. Eileen appeared irritated rather than concerned, and

Geraldine seemed to be the only person at the police station who was actually worried about Naomi. But she was the only person who was wondering whether Naomi had shared information with a killer who might have a serious grudge against their suspect in a double murder enquiry. All she had was an uneasy feeling about Matthew, but it troubled her enough to make her pursue her suspicion. She slipped out of the police station on her own at the end of the day, but Ian caught up with her in the car park.

'I've just got an errand to run,' she said.

Ian took her by the arm. 'You're up to something.'

Standing in the car park, she expounded her theory to him and he laughed.

'That's why I didn't tell you,' she said crossly. 'It's a perfectly logical supposition and I don't like to be made fun of. You don't have to agree with me, and you certainly don't have to come with me, but I'm going to talk to Matthew again. He definitely knew more about our investigation than he should do. Where is he getting his information from? If I'm barking up the wrong tree, there's no harm done, but while there's a chance I could be on to something, I'm not going to let this drop.'

Ian gazed at her. 'Do you really think Naomi's been blabbing about the investigation?' he asked. 'Come on, Geraldine, Naomi's not that stupid. She's an experienced constable, and she'll soon be up for promotion. She's hardly likely to be indiscreet about an ongoing investigation.'

Geraldine sighed. 'It's not a question of stupidity,' she replied, although it actually was. 'Single women can be extremely vulnerable when they're lonely. Matthew's not unattractive, and who knows how he might have got round her if she's fallen for him?'

'She's a trained constable. No one's going to get round her.'

'She's also a woman, and a flawed human being who might mess up.'

'Anyone can fall for the wrong person,' he agreed, heaving a sigh. 'I should know. But you can't be suggesting he deliberately chatted her up in order to pump her about the investigation?'

Geraldine nodded. 'That's exactly what I'm suggesting. Listen, Matthew knew Ben was mugged. How did he know that? Someone must have told him and it could have been Naomi. Granted it's unlikely, but you have to admit it's possible.'

'So let me get this straight. You think Matthew might turn out to be a dangerous killer who has a colleague of ours trapped in his house, and you were planning to go there alone and challenge him? Come on then, let's go and check out this harebrained idea of yours, but we're going together, with backup, and you're going to promise me you'll never even think of doing something so bloody stupid again. Promise me. Jesus, Geraldine, it's just as well I'm here to keep an eye on you.'

'I'm not a child. There's no need to talk to me like that.'

'I wouldn't have to if you stopped taking unnecessary risks. What are you trying to prove?'

Still arguing, they climbed into Geraldine's car and set off. Despite her annoyance, she was relieved that Ian was going with her. She intended to tell him as much when he stopped being so disagreeably patronising. They drove to Matthew's house in silence. Geraldine was faintly surprised when he opened the door almost straightaway and greeted them with a relaxed smile.

'Really, Inspector?' he said with an air that was almost teasing. 'Can't you leave a man in peace for one day?'

'We'd like to come in,' Geraldine replied.

He smiled, and she was uncomfortably aware that of the two of them, she was the one feeling uneasy. She hid her feelings, but she couldn't help feeling baffled by Matthew's evident insouciance.

'This is becoming a habit,' he smiled as he led them into the front room.

Geraldine noticed he was no longer wearing a watch. Alert to any possible inconsistency, she saw a set of keys on the table, house keys and car keys on a sturdy ring. They reminded her of something she had seen in a bowl on the table on her previous visit. Just before Matthew had snatched it away and hidden it from view, she had seen a single key on a thin ring.

As they had agreed in the car, Ian began to question Matthew, while Geraldine asked to use the bathroom. It was a slightly unorthodox request, and she fully expected their involuntary host to refuse her request, but he merely nodded and directed her to go upstairs.

'I'm sure you'll find it,' he added, almost taunting her, as though he expected her to snoop around. Hiding her surprise, she went, leaving Ian to go over Matthew's account of his wife's death yet again.

'I recognise the name Ben Foster,' Matthew was saying as she left the room. 'Wasn't he the driver who knocked down and killed my poor wife?'

62

GOING QUIETLY UP THE carpeted stairs, Geraldine was confident Ian would keep Matthew talking. Not only that, he would contrive to warn her if Matthew was coming up after her. She was surprised that Matthew had seemed perfectly happy for her to leave the room. More than that, he had invited her to go upstairs, as though he knew she suspected him of some villainy and genuinely had nothing to hide and was willing to prove it. There was no doubt that everything about his behaviour suggested she was misguided in her suspicion of him. Yet she had overheard him lying to Ian, pretending to be unsure of Ben's name when he knew the name all right. He had recognised the name only the previous day. And he had been very eager to hide a key from her on her last visit. He was definitely up to something and she was determined to find out what.

She found the toilet at the top of the stairs. Walking by, she quickly checked in the two bedrooms. Both were empty. She looked around as quickly as she could, aware that she did not have much time. One of the bedrooms looked unoccupied. She decided to focus on the other and searched the drawer beside the bed. Hidden beneath a packet of tissues she found a woman's watch. She was almost certain it was the one Matthew had been wearing the previous day. She took a photo of it before hurrying back downstairs. She would have liked to look around for longer, but was aware that she had no justification for being there at all. Even so, she had a feeling she might have found what she was looking for.

Back at the police station, she checked every image of Naomi she could find. With a sickening lurch she found one where Naomi was wearing a watch that looked very similar, if not identical, to the one in Matthew's drawer. Next she researched images from the accident where Matthew's wife had died. In one of the pictures, she saw that Laura was wearing a watch that looked very different to the one Geraldine had seen in Matthew's house. She went to speak to Eileen straightaway.

'It's possible Matthew's wife had another watch similar to the one Naomi wore,' Eileen said. She sounded weary.

'But Matthew lied,' Geraldine insisted. 'He knows perfectly well who Ben is.'

Eileen nodded. 'Yes, there is that,' she agreed. 'And in the meantime, Naomi is still missing. We need to check the DNA on the watch in Matthew's house without delay.'

'We need to search the house,' Geraldine said. 'But we can't afford to arouse Matthew's suspicions. Someone who can dispose of a body won't have any problems getting rid of a watch.'

Eileen nodded again, but she looked worried. 'Could you have been mistaken?' she asked.

Remembering how Matthew had lied, Geraldine shook her head.

'I'm not mistaken,' she said firmly.

Of course she could be making another blunder, but at least this time no one was likely to die as a result. The worst that could happen was that she would make a fool of herself. And if she was right, she might well save Naomi's life. Understanding what was at stake, Eileen wasted no time, and that evening Geraldine and Ian returned to Matthew's house. This time they were accompanied by a search team, and Geraldine was clutching an emergency search warrant. Matthew looked startled to see them again.

'We have a warrant to search the premises,' Geraldine said, without wasting a moment.

If Naomi was being held captive somewhere in the house or grounds, every moment might count.

'What?' Matthew responded, his eyes wide with alarm.

He had lost any vestige of nonchalance and his face seemed to grow pale as Geraldine watched him.

'We're here to search the premises,' she repeated. 'Step aside, please.'

'No, I'm sorry, that's not going to happen,' he replied, recovering some of his composure. 'You're not coming in. Not again. This is harassment. This is the third day in a row you've been here, hounding me. Go away and leave me alone or I'm calling your senior officer.'

'She sent us.'

'I'm getting on to the local press and my MP.'

Ignoring Matthew's protests, Ian invited him to go quietly to a waiting police car.

'What? Why? No. There's no way I'm going with you. No way. This is harassment. I want a lawyer. I demand to see a lawyer.'

He went to close the door, but Ian seized him by the arm and led him away, still protesting.

'Yes, yes,' Geraldine heard Ian say. 'You can have your lawyer and anything else you're entitled to when we get to the police station. Now let's go quietly, shall we, and leave the search team to do their job. The sooner they get started, the sooner all this will be over.'

There must have been more along those lines from Ian, and more objections from Matthew, but they had moved out of earshot. She turned her attention to what was happening in the house.

A few hours later, Geraldine and Ian were facing Matthew across a table in an interview room. A duty brief was at his side. Under normal circumstances they would have waited until the morning to conduct the interview, but Naomi had still not appeared. Meanwhile the watch from Matthew's bedside table had been sent away for forensic examination, along with a soiled sheet that had been found in the bin outside Matthew's house.

'What the hell's going on?' he demanded. 'What am I doing here? You have no right to keep me locked in a cell. I've done nothing wrong.'

'That remains to be seen, doesn't it?' Ian said mildly. He leaned forward. 'Where is Naomi?'

'Who?'

'If she dies, you will never see the outside of a prison again,' Geraldine said. 'Murdering a police officer.' She shook her head. 'Even the best lawyer won't be able to do a thing for you. Not a thing.'

Matthew glanced at the brief seated impassively beside him, and shook his head.

'No,' he said, as if in answer to a question. 'I never meant it to be like this. Not like this.'

'How did you think it was going to end?' Geraldine asked. She leaned forward. 'Talk to us, Matthew. Tell us where she is.'

Matthew shook his head again, and refused to speak.

'You're not helping yourself,' Geraldine persisted. 'You know we'll find her. For your own sake you just have to hope we find her alive. Tell us where she is, Matthew, before it's too late for you as well as for her.'

Matthew smiled lazily and leaned back in his chair. 'If I tell you, what's in it for me?' he asked.

Geraldine bit back a vicious retort and returned his smile. 'You know we want our colleague back safely,' she replied. 'If you tell us where she is, we'll be very grateful to you, and will treat you leniently. We'll certainly do our best to make sure you get what you want.'

'So you'll let me go?' he asked.

She barely hesitated. 'That's certainly a possibility.'

'A possibility is not enough,' he snapped. 'I need a cast-iron assurance that you'll let me go. In fact, let me go now, and then maybe I'll tell you where she is. But as long as you've got me holed up here, you can whistle for any help from me. And without it, you'll never find her.' He stared at Geraldine. 'We both know that while you're wasting time here, she could be dying. So you don't really have any choice do you? Because you won't find her.' He grinned as he slipped his hand into his pocket in a movement that was almost unconscious. 'You have no idea where I've hidden her, but it's somewhere you'll never find her.'

In that moment, Geraldine thought she knew exactly where he was keeping Naomi.

63

'WE NEED TO CHECK all his keys,' Geraldine told Eileen, with such a sense of urgency that the DCI didn't remonstrate. 'I think he's got Naomi locked in an empty building, possibly a warehouse or a garage. Do we know where his car is?'

A set of keys found in Matthew's pocket had been brought to Geraldine, along with a single key on a ring. She passed that one on to a team of constables with instructions to find out as much as possible about it, since Matthew had been at pains to hide it from her. Keys to his house and car were identified, but several remained unaccounted for, including the single key on a ring by itself. At the same time as they were investigating Matthew's keys, Geraldine had tasked other colleagues with studying his bank records and credit card purchases. She had also contacted local key cutters in case he had paid to have any keys cut. In the meantime, they had been unable to trace the whereabouts of his car. They knew his registration number and the whole area had been searched without result. Geraldine wondered if he had left it in a garage and, if so, whether Naomi was with it. There were several banks of such garages in and around York. This was possibly a wild goose chase, but they had no other leads. Ian was still putting pressure on Matthew to reveal where he had taken Naomi, but so far without success.

Aware that time could be running out for Naomi, if she was still alive, Geraldine had replicas cut of Matthew's three unaccounted for keys, and sent teams out to check every warehouse, storage facility, and garage in the area. Every available officer was sent out with a set of keys, while another team was tasked with viewing CCTV of the streets, searching for any sighting of Matthew's car. It was a mammoth task that could take weeks. But time was running out for Naomi. Taking Molly and another female constable with her, Geraldine went to a row of garages close to Matthew's house. Parking in the alleyway that led to the garages, they started at one end, trying Matthew's unidentified keys in every door. Aware that freshly cut keys were not guaranteed to work, Geraldine pressed on desperately. None of the keys worked, and there was no response when they hammered on the door. They drove on to the next set of garages on their list, and met with the same result.

'This is hopeless,' Molly said. 'We're never going to find her.'

'We will,' Geraldine replied. 'We just have to keep going and we'll find her.'

They were almost ready to return to their car and move on from the next row of garages, when the key slid unimpeded into the last door in the row. Geraldine held her breath as she tested whether the key would turn. It did. Slowly she opened the garage door. A dirty black car was inside, its wheels and sides splashed with dried-on mud. She shone her torch inside and on the back seat made out the shape of a figure, a woman with fair hair.

While their colleague summoned urgent medical assistance, Geraldine and Molly tried the car doors, which were locked. Geraldine carefully smashed a front window, and released the handbrake, so they could push the car out into the forecourt where they had more space to manoeuvre. Unlocking the back doors, they checked the inert figure. As they established that they had found Naomi alive but unconscious, they heard a siren approaching, and a few moments later an ambulance arrived, filling the forecourt. Molly had tears in her eyes, and Geraldine felt like crying as Naomi was lifted out of the car and on to a stretcher. Leaving Molly to accompany Naomi in the ambulance, Geraldine drove behind it, concerned to learn about

Naomi's condition as soon as possible. By the time Geraldine was able to see Naomi, settled in a hospital bed, she was awake and half sitting up, connected to a drip.

'I'm just dehydrated,' she assured Geraldine. 'No real harm done, except to my pride, which has taken a battering.' She paused and lay back on her pillows, as though worn out with the effort of sitting up. 'I can't believe I was so stupid. How could I have been such an idiot?' she asked Geraldine, with tears in her eyes. 'I trusted him. Why wasn't I more careful?'

Geraldine shook her head. 'We all have to guard against our emotions leading us astray. We're only human. But without feelings, we wouldn't be very good at the job, would we? I mean, we have to care, or what's it all for? Listen, don't beat yourself up over this. We all make mistakes. And look on the bright side. At least we've got our killer now, and thanks to you there's no way he's getting off.'

There was little point in Matthew attempting to conceal what he had done now that Naomi had been discovered, tied up and drugged, locked in his garage. He listened impassively as Geraldine told him that Naomi had been taken to hospital, shocked and dehydrated, but alive. Listening to his statement, Geraldine felt a chill down her spine at his callous treatment of her colleague.

'I had to know what was happening to Ben,' Matthew explained, as though what he had done to Naomi was perfectly reasonable. 'She was able to tell me, you see. It was like being a fly on the wall of the police investigation.' He smiled. 'You have to admit, it was clever.'

'It was cruel and immoral, as well as illegal,' Geraldine replied coldly. 'And stupid,' she added.

'Hardly stupid,' he replied, stung, as she had intended. 'It was pure genius, but I don't expect you to appreciate that.'

'It was stupid because now you're not only going down for two murders, but for the attempted murder of a police officer.'

'But she's not dead, is she?' he replied with a cunning smile. 'And you can't prove I did anything to her. I barely touched her. I didn't know she was in the car when I left it in the garage. I thought it was empty. I thought she'd gone home.'

'What I don't understand is why you used Ben's scarf to kill George,' Geraldine said, in an attempt to draw Matthew into a confession. 'That has to be the clumsiest murder weapon I've ever come across.'

'But it worked,' Matthew replied. 'You arrested Ben, didn't you?'

'So you wanted him arrested for George's murder?'

Matthew nodded. 'You're dense, aren't you? If that witness hadn't come forward to muddy the water, he would never have been released.'

'But why did you want to kill George?'

'I didn't. But someone had to be killed, didn't they? And he was as good a victim as anyone. Someone had to die so Ben could be punished.'

'Why not just kill Ben?' Ian asked.

Matthew shook his head, his eyes blazing with a crazy excitement. 'Killing was too good for him. He killed my wife. He had to be punished. He had to be locked in a cell for the rest of his life and suffer for what he did. What kind of a punishment is death for a man who killed an innocent woman? He has to suffer for the rest of his life, like I suffer. He killed my wife.'

'But you killed an innocent man,' Geraldine protested.

'It was necessary. Don't you see? Ben was a cold-blooded murderer. He had to be punished.'

'No, what Ben did to your wife was an accident. You're the cold-blooded murderer.'

'It was revenge.'

'Against an innocent man.'

'Against my wife's killer. That's why I had to kill George.'

'And what about Jamie?'

Matthew shook his head. 'I don't know what you're talking about. I don't know anyone called Jamie.'

'We know you killed her, with a rubber glove.'

'I never killed anyone with a rubber glove. That's the most insane thing I've ever heard.'

'Coming from you, that's saying something,' Geraldine muttered.

The duty brief stirred at Matthew's side. 'If you did assault anyone else, now's the time to confess it,' he said. 'A senseless attack on a stranger calls into question the sanity of my client,' he added, glancing at Ian who frowned. 'As does his wild assault on your colleague.'

'I'm telling you, I never touched anyone with a rubber glove,' Matthew insisted. 'And it's a lie to say anything I did was senseless. I had a plan. It should have worked.'

Whatever they said, he insisted that he had never touched anyone called Jamie, had never killed a woman, and had not used a glove to attack anyone.

'Like anyone's going to believe him,' Geraldine said when she and Ian were discussing the interview with Eileen. 'But why would he lie about it?'

'He probably can't help lying,' Eileen replied, although she agreed it seemed odd. 'Anyway, we've got him, and that's what matters. We can release Ben.'

64

'SO YOU WERE RIGHT all along,' the custody sergeant said cheerfully when Geraldine went to release Ben for a second time.

He smiled at her, a stout unimaginative sergeant who had reached the zenith of his ambition and found his niche within the police force. In another life he could have been the landlord of a country pub, or perhaps a hotel porter, greeting guests and putting them at their ease with his comfortable presence.

'I must say I won't be sorry to see the back of him,' he added. 'He's done nothing but whinge since he was brought in.'

'It can't be pleasant, being shut up in a cell,' Geraldine replied.

The sergeant shrugged. 'I suppose,' he conceded amiably, as though he had actually never given the matter any consideration before.

With a nod, Geraldine accompanied him to Ben's cell where they found him lying on his bunk with his eyes closed. The custody sergeant made his way back to his desk, and Geraldine called out to Ben who opened his eyes slowly.

'What?' he demanded, without moving.

On the point of telling Ben he was free to go home, Geraldine hesitated.

'There's been a development,' she said instead.

'What?'

He didn't even sit up.

'I said, we have some news for you. We have some new information.'

'What do you mean?'

'We found the man who killed George Gardner. It was the husband of the woman you knocked over and killed. He's been harbouring a grudge against you all this time, and worked out a plan to frame you in revenge for his wife's death which you caused.'

Ben pulled himself up into a sitting position and frowned. 'But that's insane. His wife's death was an accident.'

'Yes, we know that. And then he went on to kill your colleague at work, Jamie,' she added, trying to sound casual. 'Although we can't quite work out why he killed her. He didn't even know her. If we could only work out his motive in killing her, we'd have this all tied up. As it is, we'll have to keep investigating what went on.'

Ben shrugged. 'Isn't it obvious? He killed her to frame me, of course.'

Geraldine shook her head as though she didn't quite follow his reasoning.

'He must have known she was blackmailing me so she was the obvious victim to implicate me.'

Geraldine nodded. 'Well, that's great, because it ties everything up for us. I just need you to explain it to us formally, and then you can go home.'

She smiled, hoping he would not see through her subterfuge. Ten minutes later, Ben repeated what he had told her, only this time he was facing her in an interview room and a tape was playing.

'So you're saying Matthew killed Jamie because he knew we would uncover that you had a motive for wanting her dead?'

'Yes, exactly,' Ben agreed. 'Can I go now?'

'There's just one more thing,' Geraldine said. 'How can we be sure you didn't put Matthew up to it? You were the one who had a motive for killing Jamie, weren't you? '

He shook his head, suddenly anxious at the unexpected turn the conversation was taking.

'Should I have my lawyer here?' he asked.

'Why? It's a simple question. If you tell us you never spoke to Matthew, we'll have no reason not to believe you.'

Ben sighed. 'I never told him to kill Jamie. It was nothing to do with me. I never even spoke to anyone called Matthew. I wouldn't know him if I saw him in the street. He's just a name to me, a guy whose wife stepped out in front of my car.'

'What I don't understand is this. You never spoke to Matthew, and he didn't know Jamie, so how would Matthew have known Jamie was blackmailing you?'

Ben muttered that he wanted his lawyer present if they were going to question him any further. In the meantime, he wanted to go.

'Although where I'm going to go is anyone's guess,' he added crossly. 'My wife's thrown me out, thanks to you.' He raised his voice suddenly. 'You've ruined my life with your endless suspicion. Arresting me, letting me go, arresting me again, and all for no reason. You people, you ruin lives. You know that? I don't know how you sleep at night. Where am I supposed to go now?'

Geraldine sighed. 'Don't you know? You're going back to a cell and this time no one's going to come along and release you, because you killed Jamie, didn't you?'

'What?'

'You were clever, Ben. But you killed Jamie, didn't you? No one else had any reason to want her dead.'

'No, no, you're wrong, Matthew knew I'd been released and he wanted me arrested again. He did it. He's a killer, not me.'

'But when you were released, Matthew didn't know about it until after you'd killed Jamie. So it couldn't have been him.

He wouldn't have killed Jamie when he thought you were still behind bars, would he? You suspected he'd framed you for George's death, but instead of telling us what you were thinking you decided to take matters into your own hands. So as soon as you were released, you killed Jamie and left an obvious clue that it was you, assuming we would immediately suspect he'd framed you again, in his anger at discovering you had been released. Only he didn't know about your release yet.'

Geraldine wasn't quite sure that was true. Naomi might have told Matthew as soon as Ben was released. But Ben didn't know about Naomi.

'You should have waited another day before killing her,' she said.

Ben's expression darkened suddenly. 'I had to get rid of Jamie to shut her up,' he snapped. 'She was threatening to tell my wife about our affair. When George was killed with my scarf and you realised I'd been framed, that gave me the idea to set up Jamie's death so it looked as though she'd been killed by the same person who was trying to frame me. So I did it, yes, and I left an obvious clue to point to myself. I knew you'd work out who had framed me for George's death and you were bound to think the same person had killed Jamie in another attempt to see me go down for murder. It should have worked. I never set out to kill Jamie. You have to believe me. I tried everything to persuade her to leave me alone, but she wouldn't. She kept on at me for money. And then when I was accused of killing George and let off, it was clear even to you that someone had tried to frame me for George's death. It was too good an opportunity to pass up. I thought if I killed Jamie, and left a clue that it was me, then you would reach the obvious conclusion. So yes, I killed Jamie, but I had nothing to do with George's death. I had no reason to kill him. I didn't even know him. And Jamie had what was coming to her. She was blackmailing me. Only now my wife's left me so silencing

Jamie was pointless anyway. I killed her for nothing.'

He dropped his head in his hands and began to sob.

'So he tried to frame the man who had framed him,' Geraldine concluded, when she told Eileen about Ben's confession.

'What a pair,' Eileen replied.

65

'CHEER UP,' IAN SAID.

His brow slightly furrowed, he watched Geraldine zip up her skittish and impractical frock, which had a fitted bodice above a skirt that swirled around her legs every time she moved. She had never worn anything quite like it before, and she loved it.

'If there's something on your mind, I'd rather you told me and didn't keep it to yourself,' he added, his frown deepening.

She sat down to put on her make up, and the folds of her skirt settled over her legs.

'Come on, what's up?' he persisted. 'I can tell there's something wrong.'

'Ben says we ruined his life,' Geraldine replied, without looking round. 'Do you think he's right?'

Glancing at him in the mirror, she saw him smiling.

'Not at all.' He sounded relieved. 'If you want my opinion, that's complete and utter balderdash and you know it. Once Matthew was arrested, whenever Ben was released he would have killed Jamie for blackmailing him. That had nothing to do with us, and it certainly wasn't anything to do with you. Listen, if we hadn't arrested Ben in the first place, he would still have killed Jamie, and sooner or later we were going to release him because he didn't kill George, so Jamie's death was inevitable, really. To some extent she brought it on herself,' he added thoughtfully.

'You don't believe that,' she said. 'You can't.'

'Well, only that in as much as a victim can ever be held at all responsible for being murdered, you could say she provoked him.

She wasn't exactly innocent, anyway. We know she seduced and blackmailed at least two men, and there were probably more. She was playing with fire and sooner or later she was going to get burned.'

'I was the one who released Ben,' she pointed out in a low voice.

'Geraldine, you only did what anyone else would have done in your place. Now stop beating yourself up about it. We have a wedding to attend and you owe it to your friend to at least try to look happy for her.'

Geraldine nodded, but it felt strange to be going to a wedding with Ian. She wondered if it had ever occurred to him that she might find it hard to accept he had once loved another woman enough to want to spend the rest of his life at her side.

'Are you jealous?' he had once asked her.

He had gone on to assure her that he had never really loved his ex-wife. It had been a teenage infatuation that had continued for too long, and had never developed into anything resembling real love. She had taken him at his word that his feelings for her were different. But the thought of his former marriage still bothered her when she thought about it.

The wedding proved to be a lively affair, with a bevy of women clucking around the bride, raucous in their joy. The general mood of exhilaration was infectious, and Geraldine felt herself beaming as she witnessed the celebrations. When the ceremony was over, Naomi followed Geraldine into the ladies room.

'I never thanked you for saving my life–' she began, but Geraldine interrupted her.

'I was just doing my job,' she said. 'You would have done the same for me.'

'But that would never happen,' Naomi replied, flushing with embarrassment. 'You'd never do anything so stupid. I can't believe I fell for his lies.'

Geraldine took Naomi by both arms and stared at her. 'Naomi, the man drugged you. It wasn't your fault. And never let me hear you criticising yourself for being human. That's what makes a good detective, which is what you are.'

'No, I'm a complete idiot and useless at my job–'

'Listen to me,' Geraldine interrupted again, 'you have no idea how stupid I've been in the past over men who turned out to be contemptible rats.' She smiled. 'So let's not hear any more self-recrimination from you, and for goodness sake don't lose your grip. You're going to be needed again. Given the chance I'd choose you to be on my team any day. Now come on, let's go and have a drink.'

Brushing Naomi's protestations aside, she went back to find Ian. A few moments later she was pleased to see Naomi giggling with Molly.

'Ariadne looks lovely,' she murmured to Ian.

'Sorry,' he replied in an undertone, 'I can't get as excited as you women about frilly white dresses. Don't forget, I've been married.'

'I haven't forgotten,' she replied, wishing he hadn't reminded her.

'I don't think I could go through that again,' he added.

'I didn't ask you to.'

She turned away from him to hide her dismay, but the joy of the day was tainted for her. He had loved his ex-wife enough to vow to spend his life with her, but he didn't feel the same level of commitment now.

'So you wouldn't like to walk up the aisle as a blushing bride?' he whispered as they watched Ariadne strutting past on her father's arm.

She frowned, wondering if he was recalling his own wedding day. His beautiful ex-wife would have been an exquisite young bride.

'Of course not,' she whispered back fiercely. 'Don't be ridiculous.'

'I was teasing,' he replied, taken aback by her vehemence. 'We could get married any time you want, but I never thought you would feel comfortable in a frilly white dress.'

She laughed, relieved that he hadn't been thinking about his ex-wife at all.

'I never hankered after frills,' she agreed, turning to him with a smile.

'I prefer you without any clothes at all,' he murmured in her ear.

They kissed, gently and almost chastely. There would be time for passion later. Right now there was a wedding to celebrate, and a party to enjoy.

Acknowledgements

I would like to thank Dr Leonard Russell for his medical advice.

My sincere thanks also go to the team at No Exit Press: Ellie Lavender for her invaluable help in production, Elsa Mathern for her brilliant covers, Lisa Gooding and Hollie McDevitt for their fantastic marketing and PR, Jayne Lewis for her meticulous copy editing, Steven Mair for his eagle-eyed proofreading, and Andy Webb and Jim Crawley for their tireless work at Turnaround, and above all to Ion Mills and Claire Watts. I am extremely fortunate to be working with them, and really happy that there are more books to come in the series.

Geraldine and I have been together for a long time, in the company of my editor, who has been with us from the very beginning. We couldn't have reached Book 17 in the series without you, Keshini!

My thanks go to all the wonderful bloggers who have supported Geraldine Steel, Anne Cater, Varietats Blog, Over the Rainbow Book Blog, The Book Wormery, Honest Mam Reader's Book Blog, The Book Lover's Boudoir, The Twist and Turn Book Blog, Books by Bindu, The Word is Out, Bookish Jottings, and Beyond the Books, and to everyone who has taken the time to review my books. Your support means more to me than I can say.

Above all, I am grateful to my readers. Thank you for your interest in following Geraldine's career. To those of you who write to me to ask when the next book is out, I am busy writing

Book 18 in the series right now, and there are more to come after that. So I hope you continue to enjoy reading about Geraldine Steel.

Finally, my thanks go to Michael, who is my rock.

A LETTER FROM LEIGH

Dear Reader,

I hope you enjoyed reading this book in my Geraldine Steel series. Readers are the key to the writing process, so I'm thrilled that you've joined me on my writing journey.

You might not want to meet some of my characters on a dark night – I know I wouldn't! – but hopefully you want to read about Geraldine's other investigations. Her work is always her priority because she cares deeply about justice, but she also has her own life. Many readers care about what happens to her. I hope you join them, and become a fan of Geraldine Steel, and her colleague Ian Peterson.

If you follow me on Facebook or Twitter, you'll know that I love to hear from readers. I always respond to comments from fans, and hope you will follow me on **@LeighRussell** and **fb.me/leigh.russell.50** or drop me an email via my website **leighrussell.co.uk**.

To get exclusive news, competitions, offers, early sneak-peaks for upcoming titles and more, sign-up to my free monthly newsletter: **leighrussell.co.uk/news**. You can also find out more about me and the Geraldine Steel series on the No Exit Press website: **noexit.co.uk/ leighrussellbooks**.

Finally, if you enjoyed this story, I'd be really grateful if you would post a brief review on Amazon or Goodreads. A few sentences to say you enjoyed the book would be wonderful. And of course it would be brilliant if you would consider recommending my books to anyone who is a fan of crime fiction.

I hope to meet you at a literary festival or a book signing soon!

Thank you again for choosing to read my book.

With very best wishes,

Leigh Russell

noexit.co.uk/leighrussell

BECOME A
NO EXIT PRESS
MEMBER

BECOME A NO EXIT PRESS MEMBER and you will be joining a club of like-minded literary crime fiction lovers – and supporting an independent publisher and their authors!

AS A MEMBER YOU WILL RECEIVE

- Six books of your choice from No Exit's future publications at a discount off the retail price
- Free UK carriage
- A free eBook copy of each title
- Early pre-publication dispatch of the new books
- First access to No Exit Press Limited Editions
- Exclusive special offers only for our members
- A discount code that can be used on all backlist titles
- The choice of a free book when you first sign up

Gift Membership available too – the perfect present!

FOR MORE INFORMATION AND TO SIGN UP VISIT
noexit.co.uk/members